"Keep Partin' Those Cool Carvings"

Gregory E. Kip Cooper

Goat Locker Strikes!

By

Steven G Shandrow

And

Greg E Riplinger

www.bookstandpublishing.com

Published by
Bookstand Publishing
Morgan Hill, CA   95037
3722_3

ISBN 978-1-61863-354-5

Printed in the United States of America

Cover design and artwork by Nick Pugh

iv

Harken my lad, and I shall speak,

To you of ships and sea;

Of sailors bold, of courage told,

In tales of eternity.

Our Navy is of proud old stock,

Brave men it took to found;

Jones, Decatur, Nimitz, and Halsey

With glories they were crowned.

'Damn the torpedoes, full speed ahead,'

'I have not yet begun to fight,'

These were the battle cries that incited

Those men, to fight back with all their might.

Our heritage speaks of glories at sea,

It speaks of battles and men;

Men who are driven by the fire of faith,

Men who would fight till the end.

The Imperial Navy of the Rising Sun,

Threatened to abolish peace;

'Twas the valor of men in the U.S. Navy

That brought the threat to a cease.

As years went by, our Navy changed;

At peace she was quite set.

Not much was done, but still prepared

   In case of sudden threat.

Then came the call, 'To arms once more

   There was still a job to do.'

The Navy sailed to take their place

   In a conflict that was old but new.

Old I say to you my boy,

   For tyranny is not of late.

New because the warfare used,

   Was totally new, by fate.

And here we are unchallenged my son,

   Determined to stand for a cause that's right

We'll ne'er give up and as Jones once said,

   'I have not yet begun to fight.'

Of ships and sea, my boy I'll say,

   We have a right to be.

Proud of our ships, proud of our seas,

   And proud of our liberty.

Don't ever forget the legacy my lad,

   That our fathers left you and me;

Don't ever forget the courage and might

Of our glorious U.S. Navy.

PC3 L.A. Colon

An old Shipmate of the Authors.

Pegasus class PHM

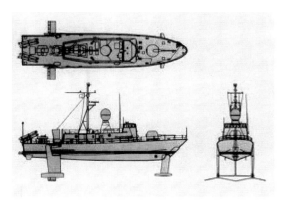

Acknowledgements

Steven G Shandrow

I would like to thank the Goat Locker website for their help. Special thanks goes out to Mr. Jim Coile, whose expertise in driving a PHM was invaluable. Special thanks goes out to my very dear friend Mr. Norm Miller whose weapons and technical expertise is widely used in this book. Next, a big thanks goes out to my co-author. I could not have completed this without his help. Lastly, my family whose invaluable help in editing and encouragement is appreciated.

Greg E Riplinger

Special thanks to my late friend "Arf", and all others I've met throughout the years who have contributed to my adventure, experience, and insight.

Chapter 1
Prologue

0831: I was on the fantail watching us get underway. Boats Clark had lines singled up and a security guard on the pier was ready to cast them off from the bollards. Masters finished his preps and just announced, "Cast off all mooring lines!" over the General Announcing System.

The last line was aboard and our stern slowly swung away from the pier. An agitated security guard hurried down the pier, wildly waving his arms, yelling to get our attention.

Masters, standing at the port bridge window, got on the bullhorn and yelled down to Boats. "We are going to moor back up to the pier." He maneuvered us back alongside.

Boats scrambled on deck, uttering unflattering platitudes to no one particular but still in control. "José! Quit skylarking' and help with this fuckin' Chinese-Fire-Drill. Get that messenger secured to the mooring line and heave that monkey-fist on the pier so that guy standin' by the bollard can pull it over!"

Once secured to the pier, Boats lowered the brow. The security guard, speaking rapid-fire Spanish, proceeded aboard before the brow was even secured.

"What's so urgent?" I asked when he stepped aboard.

"Señor Masters por favor." He managed to say. He was out of breath and flustered.

I don't speak Spanish but I knew what he wanted. José was standing by the aft line. I motioned for him to come over and translate. Masters was already on his way down from the bridge. In a few seconds, Masters was standing conversing with the security guard.

The conversation was short and to the point even though its content was Greek to me . . .

Masters turned to me and said "Looks like we are going to have company. Our radar picked up several small craft from the mainland heading this way. Our coastal watch seems to think this flotilla belongs to Don Carlos. They are moving too fast for fisherman or charter boats. He said there has been an increase in

1

radio chatter since we arrived. I think this might be a good time to either shit-and-git or stay and fight. If it were up to me Kensey, I would get the hell out of here and swing north, run for a few miles, head east and hit them on the flank... only going to take one or two hits from the 76mm to discourage them."

I mulled everything over and said, "What if they are not armed? Do we have any proof they are druggies? Could they possibly be Mexican Coastal Authorities?"

"Not a chance. Mexico doesn't have an effective coast guard and certainly not down here. If they were official, our coast watchers would have recognized the boats. It won't take much to find out if they are armed. Let's make a high-speed pass and see if they shoot at us. If they do you and Preacher can take them out. Jorge and Manuel need training and Preacher loves to shoot." He said with a laugh.

I came to a quick decision, "Masters we need to deal with this situation but we need to know if they are armed and hostile *before* we blow them out of the water. At any rate, we need to decide before we rendezvous with *Scrap Dealer*. We can't have armed boats harassing us during the loading operation. No need for stealth. They know we are here. We should see them on radar when you round the northern end of the Island. We'll plot a CPA, (Closest Point of Approach), of about 300 yards and see what they do. I'll take care of CIC. You and Boats can handle the bridge; José can translate for Preacher. Let's get underway as fast as possible. If they are hostile we'll introduce them to Davy Jones."

"Thanks! General quarters and get this ship underway. All in a day's work I guess!" He said and quickly returned to the bridge.

"Now hear this! Now hear this! The following is a test of the general alarm from the bridge." Erupted from the General Announcing System followed by, "*Bong! Bong! Bong*! All hands man your Battle Stations! All hands man your battle Stations."

That got everyone's attention . . .

"Life was so much easier two weeks ago . . . How the fuck did I get here?" flashed through my mind.

Two weeks ago, I was a retired Master Chief and retired Boeing engineer sipping a cold beer listening to the Beatles on an old jukebox belt out "It's a Hard Day's Night." I was wishing

2

for a little excitement. . .

The Beginning

I love Seattle. It is a small city with that big city feel. It reminds me of Frisco but without the character. I am no stranger to cities around the world both big and small but Seattle grew and expanded a lot since I visited aboard my first ship the *USS Chicago CG-11*. Seattle was my initial port visit and I was a wild-eyed kid, barely out of boot camp in San Diego, chomping at the bit to sample life. I found the waterfront bars and festivities of Sea Fair coupled with ever-willing college coeds magical. I still find Seattle somewhat magical but for different reasons.

I stay because I can hunt deer, elk, or black bear within a short drive. Last week a bear wandered into a local neighborhood and scared the crap out of everyone. In the autumn when I feel a little restless, I scoot over Stevens Pass, drive a few more hours and then do some serious moose hunting in Idaho or Montana. I spend a good deal of time fishing the Puget Sound for the ever-elusive salmon and occasionally zip over to the Hood Canal for Dungeness crab, one of my favorites, and oysters.

About a hundred miles west is Roosevelt Beach on the Pacific Ocean and some of the best razor clam digging on the Coast. When I want to get away for a few days of clamming, I check into the old Navy Communications Station at Pacific Beach, now a hotel, and passable restaurant. I can still picture the old facilities from the several times I helped with their IBM systems. I wonder if any of the Twidgets I got to know there are still around. I doubt it. The weather probably drove them all elsewhere…

The incessant rain takes some getting used to but I can tolerate it. The great outdoors is right on my doorstep and that is something I can live with. To say I am busy is an understatement yet a little something is still missing: the heart pumping excitement of shipboard combat. Nothing gets the heart rate up like the boom of the big guns or the *Pong-Whoosh* as a missile leaves the launcher or a careening ship as she maneuvers to outfox incoming ordnance. Organized confusion precisely describes

3

scrambling to your battle station. It barely takes three agonizing minutes to go from a dead sleep to General Quarters station but takes three days for the adrenalin to stop pumping. I miss that … Interdicting drug runners in and around the Keys was just as exciting and my ass was hanging-ten on most operations but I miss those days even more. Big ships . . . little ships . . . I can't make up my mind; I like them both. Regardless, a little "at sea" excitement would put me at ease. I wish my female acquaintances understood.

Most women don't seem to understand the relationship between a Chief and the sea and the ships he sails on… I was married once but it didn't work out. Those were the early days, I was young and times were tough. Later I couldn't find the time for family life. Following a quick painless divorce, I shied away from serious relationships and stayed single.

Lorie, my ex-wife, was not cut out for the rigors of Navy life. Months and years of managing everything including children if they eventually came along did not appeal to her. One day she up and left for parts unknown. I haven't heard so much as a peep from her since. Luckily, there were no children to muddy the waters. Lorie left and I stayed with my ships. Being at sea is something I like so it didn't bother me to spend the next twenty years on numerous ships. I served on carriers, cruisers, destroyers, hydrofoils, and fast frigates. One ship in particular, the *USS Ingraham*, home ported in Everett, Washington convinced me to settle in the Pacific Northwest. This small town is a quaint suburb a bit north of Seattle. I was there for several years and thoroughly enjoyed the rare days when I could sneak off for some outdoor recreation. I always knew I would return. I never had enough time to hunt and fish then and I fully intended to remedy that. With that in mind, when it came time to retire from the Navy, I settled in Seattle.

Once I left the navy, Boeing was my patron. I managed the installations of various radar and electronic control systems and troubleshot all sorts of high-tech equipment. Radar was my specialty. Boeing sent me all over the world but my home was permanently in Seattle and there was even less time for recreation. Twenty-four years of that was enough. I packed it in and retired. I

4

was finished with constant travel and not being home to enjoy the days and nights that Seattle offers. That was then…

Today I find myself at a small, quiet bar and grill on the waterfront. The weathered, fading sign swinging over the door says "*Safe Haven.*" Most of us call it "The Haven." The owner and bartender, Frank, runs it like an old-fashioned waterfront pub. The inside emulates the main deck of a Clipper Ship. An interesting sign points the way to the 'poop deck' and another prominently displays Uncle Sam with a fid in his hand saying "bend over!" The walls are decorated with pictures and artifacts from windjammers and steamships. The outside of the building is clad in weather-beaten planks. Some planks are said to be from the decks of the *HMS Discovery* and the armory of Fort Nisqually. A lithograph of Lt. Puget and an oil painting of Captain George Vancouver hang over the mahogany bar. A union jack takes up one corner. A hand painted plaque says it flew over Fort Victoria during the 'Pig War'. One wall is lined with display cases containing hundreds of Zippo lighters adorned with unit insignias from every branch of service and every commercial vessel you can imagine.

One corner of the bar, polished by thousands of elbows, houses Frank's '*I Love Me*' display. All of his medals, Bronze Star and Purple Heart included, unit photos, retirement shadow box, and souvenirs chronicle his twenty plus years in the Marines. I find it interesting that he did a tour of duty on the *USS Chicago* just after I left the ship. We usually call him '*Gunny*' but he doesn't talk much about his service. He is trustworthy to a fault and would do most anything to help you out in a pinch. He makes The Haven my home away from home . . .

I am not a heavy drinker. I do enjoy beer and especially San Miguel. Frank insists he is going to ban me from coming in. I take up space but don't spend much money. The waitresses and beer maids don't complain because I always tip well and never cause problems. The ancient jukebox in the corner contains only 50s and 60s music. That's about all I listen to after most music became noise in the 70s. Frank stocks large quantities of San Miguel beer lovingly dubbed "San Magoo" by Westpac sailors who drank a few too many and experienced trouble with their vision. The beer

5

alone would keep me coming back but the other regulars are The Haven's real draw. Most that spend time here are retired from the sea in one way or another. Navy, merchant marine, and fishermen make up the lot. At any given time an Acey-Ducey game or "intelligent backgammon" as it's sometimes called is in progress and on most evenings a double deck pinochle game can be found. The back corner table is reserved for a perpetual poker game. Ten dollars gets you a seat. The beer stops at 0200 but the game never does. None of us has much money but we all have a boatload of stories and experience. We are closer to a family than a gathering of mere acquaintances.

Chapter 2
The Meeting

It was a Saturday afternoon. I woke early, went fishing off Dash Point and limited out on "Spring Chinooks" before ten. I had two beauties in the smoker and decided to see if I could scrounge up an Acey-Ducey game at The Haven. Frank and I had the bar to ourselves and I sat nursing a San Magoo. The *'1946 Wurlitzer 1015'* was pumping out a Beatles tune and the TV was on, sound muted, and tuned to *CNN*. I was watching but not really paying much attention. One particular headline scrolling across the bottom of the screen caught my eye. It splashed across the screen in big bold yellow letters and proclaimed that a private, sixty-five foot, seagoing yacht was hijacked off the coast of northern Somalia.

I yelled, "Hey Gunny! Get your head out of the jar and turn up the volume."

"Fuck you Squid!" Immediately came back from Gunny but he turned up the TV's sound. I listened to the rest of the report. There was no mention about the fate of the passengers or yacht. I wondered who was on that boat and why they chose to sail in such dangerous waters. I soon forgot about the incident and decided to test my luck with the peas. Beating Frank out of a San Magoo always made my day.

With a fresh brew in hand I sat down and contemplated finishing it quickly and checking on the smoker and my salmon. I felt a slight draft as the front door opened. A slender man with an air of familiarity entered and glanced around the bar. He was in his late 50s, tall, and impeccably groomed. He wore a dark blue, expensive looking suit with a striped tie. His demeanor was that of someone who knew exactly what he was doing. He appeared out of place, but oddly enough, seemed to belong here. He took one long sweeping look around the bar taking in everything, and then walked straight toward me. I followed him closely with my eyes. He looked a lot like a civilian I worked with in Key West. I couldn't immediately place him, but seeing him triggered a tingle of excitement that ran up and down my spine.

He strolled directly to my table, glanced around, and then said, "Hello Chief, good to see you are still alive." My first hunch was right. Recognition hit me like a broadside!

"Good to be alive" I replied somewhat guarded. Why Jim, a highly placed DEA mover and shaker, from my days aboard *USS Hercules* was here disturbed me.... Twenty years of wear and tear changes ones appearance, but not ones character or importance.

"I'm still with DEA," he added quickly.

He was the chief DEA advisor attached to the PHM squadron home ported in the Keys. Our crews dubbed him *'Gman'*. He rode with us on some of the more *"dicey"* drug interdiction missions.

I half stood, leaned over the table, grabbed his extended hand and exclaimed "Jim, you old dog how have you been?"

Before I could get another word in edgewise, he said, "Did you hear about the latest bit of nastiness off the coast of Somalia?"

"Yeah I heard." I answered then continued, "It was all over *CNN*. Pirates boarded and captured a private yacht, the *'Alto y Poderoso,'* or in English *"High and Mighty*," according to Wolf Blitzer, they sailed her to a small coastal village and are demanding big bucks in exchange for boat and crew. Why are you interested in this particular incident?" *"... and what does it have to do with me?"* I couldn't help but think.

"We can talk about it but we need a bit of privacy." Jim said.

We moved to a quiet corner of The Haven away from the bar, TV, and jukebox.

"In a nut shell," He began in his quiet, businesslike manner, "There is a concern with who and what is on that yacht. The Government has its hands tied and can't get involved. We needed to think outside the box to resolve this delicate situation. During a high-level meeting in DC, I suggested contracting a retired chief named Kensey living in Seattle who has skills this situation needs, and here I am... Before we continue this conversation, I need your word that this is strictly between the two of us. Are you interested in a little change of scenery?"

"Not really, but my curiosity has the better of me." After a slight, pause I nodded my consent and said, "Please continue; if I agree fine, if I don't I'll buy you a single-malt and then we go our separate ways." A torrent of thoughts raced through my mind:

8

"Why did you seek 'me 'out…" *"What do I have that you want…"* *"What gives…"*

"You were considerably more than *'just'* a Chief Fire Controlman on PHMs. We did some good work in the Keys and this mission requires a similar operation and experienced men. Men who can think fast, take charge, and use their initiative to salvage a bad situation. We need men who will not fall apart when the going gets tough. Shit happens! Like The *"Custer Debacle…"*

"Not funny!" I interrupted!

"…comes to mind" Jim finished with a half smile. "Six zodiacs circling the *Hercules* firing RPGs *'has'* a familiar ring to it. They took out two bridge teams and the Old Man with the first volley at 0345. Fire control, radars, and comms went with the second. Good thing you had to relieve yourself right after you were relieved as Officer Of the Deck! Combat was wide-awake when you came up on headsets from the Helmsman station and started issuing orders. You ordered the gunner to combat to man the main battery's local operations panel. The gunner took out two zodiacs with the first ten rounds from the 76mm, and you capsized one with the stern wake. The other three took off. I sure would have liked to see their faces when you and Greasey got *"flying"* and ran them down . . . and at 45 knots or so! Limping back on one barely running diesel and about enough speed to maneuver and the ensuing inquests were not very exciting though. They didn't even have the courtesy to call you "Skipper" after getting all of us out of that mess and home afloat. That's gratitude for you! At least you were promoted to Master Chief shortly after the proceedings."

"I try not thinking about the after action *BS* and funerals of six good men . . .," I said low and quiet.

Jim nodded his head in complete understanding.

I was a little subdued thinking about all those good men we lost but continued, "Yeah, I retired as Master Chief. We did very good work, but that was many years ago when we 'could' do good work. The PHMs were fantastic ships. Too bad the blue water Navy thought they threatened the destroyers and killed the program. Seventeen enlisted and four officers could do the job of three hundred men on a Tin Can, Spru-can or one of the new FFG7s!"

"I agree" he said and then added something that further roused my interest: "What is the smallest crew you can put to sea with and still be effective?"

"You mean run a PHM and fight it?" You have to be kidding… I thought, *"I may have to suspend disbelief!"*

"Yes," Jim said, "Don't look so incredulous!"

I took a swig of beer and couldn't help but think, *"Jim is CRAZY!" "What is he after?" "I know that all the PHMs are razor blades or museums frozen in cement." "What does he actually want?"* Several things crossed my mind and I did owe Jim a timely answer: "I really don't know, but I would guess you need…," I started to mentally count them off on my fingers; "one officer to be the captain and navigator and so on; at least two engine men with diesel and gas turbine experience but most of all EOS, (Engineering Operating Station), experience; one fire controlman for weapons systems; an ET for radar, comms and navigation systems. Two would be better. We must have a boatswain mate for general seamanship and care of the ship, gunners mate for the ammo, gun mount, and small arms. If we are going long distances, we should have one more of any of the disciplines for watch standing. Regardless, we would have to double up on some duties. I imagine we could get an apron for the bo'sun if we needed a cook."

"Nine crew members… Seems like a lot of people." Jim reflected.

"You could probably crew it with eight. And in a real pinch… six. But that means no twenty-four hour steaming: you don't have the watch standers. That could be overcome by lying low during the day and really 'flying' when it gets dark." I continued.

I took a long pull on my beer and waited for him to say something. He drained the last of his scotch, looked around, then suddenly stood up. It appeared that he made a decision.

"You up for a little side trip?" he asked.

I drained my beer and gave him an intentional hard stare. I sensed no threat. I felt no apprehension just a bit confused.

Under my breath I mumbled, "WTFO." To Jim I said, "I have nothing to lose, so yeah why not?" We stood up and dodged tables as we wove our way out the door. "This is going to be more fun

10

than mowing the lawn or walking the dog," I imagined. At any rate, it would be more exciting than anything I had planned for the foreseeable future.

"You mind if we make a quick stop to check on my fish?" I asked.

Chapter 3
The Ship

We left the bar and walked to his car parked across the street. I had no idea where we were going but I knew it would be interesting. My mind worked overtime as I thought about Gman and our time aboard *Hercules PHM-2*.

The PHM or "Patrol, Hydrofoil, Missile" ships were built by Boeing of Seattle. Six were built for the Navy and a few more for foreign allies. The first of the class, *PHM-1 Pegasus*, commissioned in 1977 served both Navy and Coast Guard until decommissioned in 1993. The Navy deemed the hydrofoil program too expensive. They needed the money to build more destroyers and other blue water ships. The *Aries, PHM-5*, is a memorial and the last one left. My ship, if memory serves, was about 133 feet long with a beam of 28 feet. She was outfitted with a pair of diesel water jet propulsion units and an LM-2500 gas turbine engine for propulsion while "flying" on the foils. She could make a good 12 knots hullborne and 48 knots on the foils. We always "flew" whenever we could and she could turn on a dime. Very few seagoing craft could outrun us! If we flew exclusively we could launch operations with a three-hundred-fifty mile radius. That gave us a seven-hundred mile effective operating range with a small fuel reserve for emergencies. An operation that combined hullborne steaming and flying could extend the radius to about seven-hundred miles. If we had fuel support along the way there was no limitation to our operating area. These limitations were more than offset by our ability to fly in sea states that slowed hullborne ships to a crawl.

Still deep in thought, my attention turned to the Fire Control System aboard the *Hercules PHM-2*. It was the first Mk-92 Mod 1 system installed on the PHMs. Keeping everything working and battle ready was a ball buster! The Combined Antenna System (CAS Radar), referred to by sailors as *'the egg'*, is capable of tracking simultaneously one air or surface target and two surface or shore targets. The MK 75, 76mm rapid firing gun, originally designed and built by **Oto Melara** of Italy, was accurate if not so reliable. Subsequent upgrades over the years increased *'Otto's* reliability and accuracy. We had no trouble shooting down scores of target drones and making flotsam of high-speed drug-running boats. That gun could shoot!

The short range and surface navigation system was built around the LN-66 radar. Its secondary task was identifying and warning about approaching low-flying threats. That was one if it's most valuable, endearing, and vital functions. Directing combat operations from CIC was exciting and rewarding but my real joy was driving **Hercules**. I lived for my watches as underway Officer of the Deck. Hullborne steaming wasn't all that exciting but flying on the foils was sheer exhilaration!

I managed to lose track of where we were. All those memories focused me elsewhere at another

time . . .

Jim pulled into a drive and up to a guard shack; that brought me back to the present and my mounting curiosity.

Gman flashed his ID and the security guard allowed us through the gate. He made a few turns, crossed over Lake Washington Blvd and parked at the end of a large industrial building. We exited the car and he led the way to a small door near the rear where we entered the building. We walked down what seemed like miles and miles of corridors with a myriad of cubicles and offices. Finally, we arrived at a garage door that opened with a swipe of Gman's pass and we entered. Just inside the door was another security guard; he waived us right through this checkpoint. I got the distinct feeling he was expecting us. Gman led me to the back of the building and yet another door. This was a large roll-up type door. Gman walked to the entry control panel, fiddled with it for a second, and pushed a series of buttons. The door opened. Unbelievable! Right before us, sitting on skids, was a Pegasus class PHM painted stark white with no hull number. She was beautiful but would look much better painted haze gray!

With the biggest ear-to-ear grin imaginable, Gman said, "Thought you would like this surprise!"

Almost speechless I answered, "Yeah, I'll be damned. I thought all of these ships were made into razor blades back in '93. Seeing one here, not stuck in concrete or relegated to a life as a museum is absolutely outstanding…Why?"

"Why is it here? Is that what you mean? Well, remember Boeing got the contract and built all of the Pegasus class PHMs. The contract with the Navy was somewhat iffy at times. It was cancelled once, restarted, and finally cancelled for good. Because of all the political crap Boeing never knew from one minute to the next if more PHMs were going to be built or not. They decided to build one extra, outfit it, and keep it just in case the Navy came to their senses. She just sat here and over time was simply forgotten. The Navy paid for this one but for some unknown reason let Boeing keep it. Boeing engineers did several upgrade tests of turbines and fuel capacity but nothing much more than that. You want to go aboard and take a look?"

"Hope to shit in your flat hat!" I exclaimed a little taken aback. "I want to see CIC and just what equipment is installed on this ship."

Gman led the way and we climbed up a makeshift brow to the main deck. I immediately noticed the Harpoon launchers were missing. I wondered why. We climbed aboard and entered the interior. CIC was our first stop and "lo and behold," there was my Fire Control system, intact. I looked around the machinery gray interior and everything seemed to be as I remembered, minus the Harpoon control and launch panel. Amazingly, all the publications were in their correct place including the maintenance-repair-cards!

After giving "combat" a good going over I said, "Let's check out the bridge."

"Lead the way" Jim replied.

I climbed the ladder and entered the pilothouse. Memories flooded back! I spent many hours on watch conning *Hercules*. Ah, to run one of these beauties in the open sea again would be the ultimate joy.

After a few minutes, I said, "Let's take a look around the rest of the ship. I want to see the engineering spaces and crew berthing."

We went aft to the CAS deck and passed the MK 34 RBOC (Rapid Blooming Off-Board Countermeasures) chaff and flair launchers then down to the main deck, inside and down to the diesel and pump machinery room. The space was spotless. In all

15

my shipboard experiences, I never saw an engine room this clean. Obviously, this ship was never at sea.

Gman and I examined the entire ship. I was impressed. She was fully equipped. Fuel her up and we could go to sea tomorrow. The only thing needed to restore her to a lean, mean, fighting machine was a crew, ammo, fuel, and food.

There it was again; the salvo alarm was buzzing. The reoccurring thoughts blasted through, *"Why me? What does Gman want?"*

Chapter 4
The Proposition

After several hours on the ship, we left her and retraced our path to the car. Once in the car Jim started the engine and twisted in the seat facing me and said, "Well, what do you think?"

I responded, "I just don't believe it. There sits a new hydrofoil all ready for sea trials." As an afterthought I continued, "After seeing the ship I'm quite certain you want me to crew her. When can we discuss it?"

He nodded his head a few times and said, "Partially right…I have answers for all of your questions, but first, let's go back to The Haven and have a drink. Scrambling all over that ship makes one thirsty."

I agreed and Jim backed the car out of the parking space and started to retrace our path back to the waterfront.

I went over today's events in my mind: *"Yacht captured, Somali pirates, government agent, and a PHM. This looks very interesting."* More thoughts crowded in, *"I have nothing planned, nothing in my life going on and no prospects. This just might turn into something I could really get my teeth into. I still have all my Navy skills plus those learned engineering for Boeing. There is no bigger thrill than pulling the firing key and destroying a target. I love weapons on navy ships and this could be a chance to tinker with them again."*

Gman glanced at me a few times thinking of striking up a conversation but could see I was deep in thought.

Of all the ships I sailed on **Hercules** was by far the most fun. PHMs were smaller ships and the crew worked together like a well-oiled machine. I switched focus from some of the obvious negatives and thought, *"This could even be very profitable! Living on a pension is fine for everyday needs: house, car, groceries, and entertainment. Having the money to travel, buy toys, and live large would be very welcome."*

At that moment, we pulled into The Haven's parking lot and entered the bar. Gman chose a table in the far corner away from potential eavesdroppers while I ordered a scotch for him and a San

Magoo for me.

We waited until they were delivered before I asked, "Okay, what is it you really want? What do you have in mind?"

I could see the wheels turning and after a slight hesitation he started, it was obvious that he was thinking aloud, "I did my homework Kensey, and you are the right person for this mission. You remember all the sea stories and talking we did on those long watches on drug patrol? I do… Every one of them. I am going to lay it out for you and you can give me your answer, OK?"

I nodded, "yes."

And he continued, "There is an important package on the *'High and Mighty'* and we, meaning the DEA, need to retrieve it before the pirates realize it is aboard. The package is well hidden, we hope, and extremely important. There is more and you may think twice about signing on when I tell you about it." He paused a second leaving room for me to back out. I didn't and Gman continued. "A Mexican drug cartel leader, Don Carlos Escobar, was onboard and it wasn't strictly for pleasure. He was on his way to meet with some Middle Eastern drug suppliers who are the main financing support for Al Qaida in that area. The meeting was to take place in Yemen. These terrorists are part of the group that almost destroyed the *USS Cole*. Escobar was carrying a package. Along with that, he had $20 million in cash as good faith money. The intent was to hook up with these terrorists who could use Cartel contacts to blackmail their way into the West and flood us with drugs. The results of this contact would be a global, well-financed terrorist group and drug cartel. The end goal is complete domination of the drug business." He stopped and stared at me. I got the significance of the stare.

I had to interrupt and ask, "How do you know all of this? It looks like their security wasn't particularly effective."

Jim gave that a thoughtful nod and continued, "That information, my friend, is above my pay grade. Understand we can't use government forces because it is just one small private yacht. We can't just pay the ransom because there is no guarantee that we could get the yacht back and doing so would draw too much attention. Same reason we can't use Black Ops: too much attention. We can't use mercenaries because of the Blackwater

18

investigations and besides: they are too easily tracked. The only logical conclusion is sending an unknown private group into harm's way to retrieve the package and destroy the yacht and anyone on board or near it. And that pretty well sums up why I'm drinking this fine scotch in Seattle, in The Haven, with you.

"Whoa! That's a pretty tall order." I said a little taken aback. "I've been in some tight situations but I had the entire navy and DEA at my back on those operations. I'm guessing this mission won't have those options. It will probably be 'off-the-grid' and the crew expendable. Does that about sum it up?" I asked trying not to look too incredulous.

Jim wasn't fazed in the least. He took up where he left off, "Listen, Chiefs run the navy and you were one of the best. We considered using an officer to command but using anyone on active duty would be inviting trouble. Ex ring-knockers are all too political with friends in high places and most Mustangs are pissed off at the system so they won't do it. That brings us full circle to the backbone of the Navy... *'Chief'*. We need this done. I've seen you in action. And besides, how hard could it be for you to recruit a crew of retired shipmates, get under way, and then run that PHM right up the pirate's asses!"

I was flattered and after a few moments, I said "What about the money... Do we return that?"

There wasn't a microsecond's hesitation in Jim's answer, "Chief, we are only interested in the package, period."

Chapter 5
The Mission

Twenty million is a boatload of money and well worth trying to recover. I was sure I would do it but I needed a lot more information before I gave Jim my answer.

"That pretty well explains our little outing" I mused. But I have to ask, "Will the Navy let us use their PHM? What about Boeing?"

He smiled and said, "DEA has a friend high up in Boeing that is donating that PHM. The Navy refused to comment. To me, that means they are with the program but want 'plausible deniability'. The ship will be delivered to any place in the US and turned over to you and your crew."

Jim continued on talking a bit lower and slower now. "As we see it, this is the mission: recruit a crew of your choice. Take delivery of the PHM. Outfit it with the necessary supplies and ordnance. Move the ship to the coast of Somalia. Retrieve the package and money. Once that is accomplished, we want you to destroy the yacht, anybody on board and any-and-all pirates that interfere. And, of course return home. Piece of cake."

"Yeah, right! Easy! Where am I going to get a PHM crew? They don't grow on trees!"

"Use the internet. Call old friends. Do whatever you need to … Chief." Jim was enjoying this I could tell by his swift, to-the-point answer.

A million things raced through my mind. I asked a few important, rapid-fire, and not so easy to answer questions. "What about all the 'hard to procure' supplies? First off: 76mm rounds and spare parts for electronics and engineering spaces. Small arms we will need, belted 7.62mm if you can get us a couple of M60s. I prefer 50 cal machine guns and that ammo ain't all that easy to get a hold of either. Even buying a couple cases of 5.56mm and M16s or five or six-thousand 9mm rounds will cause a stir. What kind of support can I expect for logistic problems of that order?"

"The DEA, as we speak, is calling in favors from several government agencies and services. Fuel will be supplied by the

Coast Guard, ammo, and spare parts from the navy, food you buy yourself. We will give you an advance of three million dollars for travel, crew recruitment, and anything else you might need. All of the logistics will be worked out later when your route is decided, training is started, and so on. This is not a small operation but we must keep it as quiet as we can. The fewer people who know what we are up to, the better. By the way, time is of the essence. We have to recover the package and destroy that yacht before the pirates find the cache. This last bit is for your ears only ***Chief.*** *'The package, we believe, is hidden in a secret compartment in the Captain's cabin'.* So do you want to take it on?"

I thought a few seconds and replied, "Count me in. How much time do I have to put this together?"

"Good, we have a deal. I can't give you an exact timeline but you might want to start recruiting a crew right after you take those salmon out of the smoker. You might not have time to eat both of them… Mind if I swing by on my way out and take one with me?" With that, he reached into his jacket pocket and pulled out a cell phone.

He handed it to me and said, "This is a secure phone, if you need to talk to me, discuss anything, want answers, call me with this phone... Only. It will get directly to me. I will call you right back. OK?"

"Yeah, got it." I stood up and said, "I have to go and think this through. Call you in a few days and lay out my plan for recruiting a crew and where, what, and when we need the ship and supplies, and *'special items'* delivered."

"Chief that is quite acceptable. I expect to hear from you in two days. As I said before, time is of the essence."

"Right! And Jim, catching those Chinooks was hard work. If you want some, you are welcome to one for the price of at least a half-rack of San Magoo. *"Cold"* San Magoo!"

Chapter 6
Plan of Action

Gman rose, turned towards the door, and said, "Call me with a plan real soon. I need a heads up to get started on assembling all the supplies and money."

"Will do!" I answered softly already preoccupied with details.

Gman left the bar and I sat there for a few minutes trying to arrange my thoughts. There were several questions I needed to answer: where and how do I get a crew? Where and how do I get a shit pot full of ammo and fuel? How do I get a PHM from Seattle to Somalia without raising interest from nosey people, especially the navy? There is a lot of water between here and there and it will be difficult to cross all that ocean without being detected or questioned. My head filling with hundreds of ideas, I left the Haven and raced back home.

I took just enough time to close the door, grab a cold San Magoo from the fridge, and check the smoker before sitting at my desk and firing-up the laptop. I thought the easiest way to keep track of the thousands of notes required would be designing a spreadsheet. The result looked fairly good for a two-Magoo project and I was ready to start in earnest. What first...

Finding a crew is of paramount importance so of course it should be number one on the list. Where do I get a crew? What better place to start than The Goat Locker! A smile crossed my face and I couldn't help but think about the first time I had to report to the Goat Locker and fetch the Chief. I was explicitly directed to knock on the door and under no circumstances open it until told to do so! I was about to enter god's-country and was apprehensive if not a little scared. I survived but will never forget the experience...

Ship's crews, especially seaman and seaman-apprentices, grumble about work assignments. Most scorn is heaped on the "Chief" who invariably assigned the task and who "drops" in on the job to make certain it is being accomplished correctly and in a timely manner. The men, more often than not, are skylarking and this usually leads to "rocks and shoals" discipline meted out to the men and Petty Officer in charge. Anyone with more than ten minutes aboard ship asks the pressing question before any detail starts: *"Where is the old goat..."* And the first place they check for the one person who can fix everything when a problem arises is the *"Goat Locker"* or Chiefs Mess.

Junior Officers trying to look good with the chain of command often butt heads with a gruff, stubborn leader, "the Chief," who always manages to get unpleasant jobs done. Ensigns and Jgs soon learn the "Old Goat" who's a pain in the ass gets the job done correctly and gets it done on time. They quickly learn the "Old Goat" protects them and makes them and their division look good. Respect is why they knock on the "Goat Locker" door before timidly entering. So...What better place to look for retired old goats than the Goat Locker?

I *Googled* Goat Locker, clicked on the first of 246,000 hits, entered the site, and started looking for familiar names. I was particularly interested in those with PHM experience. I never argue with lady luck. Member's names were listed alphabetically on the Goat Locker site. Within the first forty names, I found Bishop, John Henry. He would be an ideal candidate; I hoped he was available. Greasey, as I knew him, was the best gas turbine engine chief in the fleet. He served aboard several Spruance class destroyers, Fast Frigates (FFG), and best of all, the *Hercules* with me. I shot him an email hoping he would answer shortly. At least it was a start.

After I found a crew for the ship what next? Where do we do refresher training and run all the machinery and electronic systems through their paces? It would be fifteen or twenty years since most of the crew, me included, were at sea. I would have to hone my skills and I'm sure everyone else was in the same situation. So Cal might be the perfect area. I don't think anyone would give a white funny looking ship a second-look down there as long as we didn't fly until we were out to sea and away from coastal eyes. We could avoid all of the bases there, and scoot down to Baja to conduct rigorous sea trials. That would be a piece of cake except for the 76mm on the bow! I'll have to give that some serious thought. Right then, though, I had a dinner date with my current girl friend, Lois, to get ready for. I shut down the

24

laptop and as a second thought pulled the flash drive where I saved the spreadsheet that was part of my new log book. I needed to keep track of events and indulge in a bit of self-protection. I would log everything. Security awareness was already starting . . . or paranoia.

Dinner with Lois was less than satisfying. I was preoccupied and she wasn't impressed. Our banter consisted of me saying yes and no to a series of inane questions that had nothing to do with Gman or PHMs or out of town vacations. I like Lois and thought I'd apologize and see if we could take up where this night left off...on my return.

I hurried home, lit the PC off again and resumed planning. Next: how could I get the ship and crew to the coast of Somalia? It was just too far to steam there from the US; cost in fuel alone would be substantial and the time needed to set up refueling rendezvous points overwhelming! Gman said he would supply ammo, fuel, and whatever else we needed but at this early stage of planning I wasn't at all sure what that entailed. I thought I would figure that out after the ship was delivered, the crew was onboard, and we spent a little time at sea. On that fine thought, I hit the sack.

I arose early the next morning with PHMs and old men on my mind. Could I do this job? I reflected on my image in the bathroom mirror. What stared back was a man in his mid 60's in good physical shape, a shade over six feet tall, and still weighing around 180 pounds. My hair was gray, but I still had some! I kept clean-shaven and was in good health. I thought, *"What the hell... I can handle this assignment."* I dressed, and hurried to my neighborhood Starbucks for a good wake-me-up cup of coffee. The walk there was brisk. The walk home was invigorating! The wind driven rain stung my face; at least it wasn't snowing! A thought suddenly crossed my wind and rain battered mind, *"A vacation where the sun was shining might be a good thing..."* Once inside my warm, welcome apartment I checked my PC hoping Bishop found the time to answer. I should have picked up a $20 million Power Ball Ticket on the way home; you've got mail popped up on the screen and it was from Bishop! With great anticipation, I opened his email.

It read: **Ho Kensey you old Twidget! Good to hear from you.**

Yeah, I am single again so, why did you rattle my cage? Give me a call on the landline 224 555 4490 any time.

John Henry 'Greasey' Bishop

I glanced at the clock, it was early here, but what the hell, Greasey shouldn't be in bed anyway. I picked up the phone and dialed his number.

After a few rings, a gruff voice answered, "Yeah, what do you want?"

"Bishop this is Kensey. Are you still pressing the fart sack? It's time you got your lazy ass up and started earning a decent living."

He sounded taken aback and barely awake. I don't believe he really thought Master Chief Kensey was calling after all this time and at this hour but he started talking like we were still on *Hercules*. "Fuck you very much... Can't a guy get a decent night's sleep anymore? Nice hearing from you just the same. What's up shipmate?"

"Are you busy? I'd like to see you, *'TOMORROW'* drink a few beers, tell a few sea stories..." I lingered a second. He had no reaction so I continued. "I had an intriguing visit from a mutual acquaintance the other day. It may lead to a little adventure and profit. I think you may be interested. If I remember correctly you were always ready for the quick buck!"

Bishop's tone was a little cool, almost as if he didn't believe me. "You certainly got me curious and I could use some extra cash right now. This is a little short-fused ain't it Chief? It should be fine just as long as I ain't got to kill anybody... OK. Let's get together. I live in Waukegan, when... do you plan on coming; tomorrow?"

"No shit. Be there late tomorrow afternoon. I'll be flying in from Seattle; I'll call you at this number when I get to Waukegan. As far as killing somebody...!" I threw that last bit in to see if Greasey was actually listening.

"Roger that; I'll be waiting. And Kensey..."

"Yeah... What Greasey?"

"Bring money." He hung up and ended our conversation.

Things were looking up. This was exciting. I had to do something immediately. I called and booked a red-eye flight from SeaTac to O'Hare. It was a bit rushed and I wouldn't get into

26

Chicago before midnight but that would be fine. Waukegan is only thirty miles north of O'Hare. I could rent a car at the airport and drive there, find a motel, and get some sleep before meeting Bishop.

Another thought struck like a bolt of lightning. Money! I had a bit saved and a few thousand in cash. That would go fast if I started flying around the damn country. I wondered if Gman kept his word and deposited funds to my account. I turned slowly to the computer and clicked my bank icon. On-line banking came up and I checked both of my accounts. Well…three accounts. I had a new one. I was surprised the bank manager didn't call. My new account had a balance of three million dollars! Gman does his homework. This was going to be a profitable exercise if I survived.

I retrieved the cell phone that Gman gave me and pushed the 'call' button. It was programmed for one number only. I recognized the voice on the other end.

"Call you right back." Was all Gman said.

A few minutes later the phone rang and startled the hell out of me. I answered, "I am on my way. Going up to Waukegan to meet an old navy buddy. The job is well on its way. Thanks for that little gift." I wasn't sure anyone was on the other end but the line was live.

The detached voice replied, "Acceptable, you are welcome, the fish was superb, good luck!" and the line went dead. Short, sweet and to the point. I do hope the rest of my calls to Gman prove to be as satisfying.

On the way to SeaTac, I stopped by The Haven to ask Gunny if he would look after my apartment while I was gone. I could always count on him to clear up all the junk mail and shit that accumulates while I'm away on hunting or fishing trips. I planned to tell him I might be gone as long as a month… Maybe two or three. I told him I would be fishing with old buddies on the Great Lakes and perhaps the Chesapeake Bay. I might even swing by San Diego on my way back and chase some bonita and tuna with old navy buddies down there in the sun. In any event, I would be hard to reach. He agreed and I thanked him and departed for SeaTac.

27

Chapter 7
John Henry Bishop

I landed at Chicago's O'Hare right on schedule and made my way to the rental car counters. I stopped at the first one, it just happened to be Hertz, and waited in line. When it was my turn, I asked the bored, young lady who was chewing gum, for a nice midsize.

She gave me a muffled response not bothering to look up from the current issue of *"People"* she was reading and mumbled around her gum, "And how long would you need the car?"

"Two days, three at most." I grumbled.

I didn't expect the meeting with Bishop to take too much time. He sounded tense on the phone. I suspected he was eager to accept any paying job right now. I imagined anyone living in Waukegan would be happy to accept a paying job. The only thing the town had going for it was Jack Benny and that's because he was born there. AMC shut down right after their success with the AMX and Abbot Chemical was long gone. (Thank God!) You could cut the stench from that place with a knife and chew on it. I don't think anyone was sorry to see it go.

"Would you like the damage claim waiver insurance for the car, sir?" Gum chewer asked me, suddenly snapping me back from my thoughts.

"No." I handed her my credit card and patiently waited for the paperwork. This seemed to be taking a phenomenally long time. Finally, after signing a rash of forms, she handed me my copies, pointed to the garage, and said the car was in slot twenty-three. I walked to the car and found a Ford Taurus sedan. 'Perfect.'

I was here years ago. I attended an advanced electronics course at Great Lakes Naval Training Center. Memories of the extreme weather and cold came flooding back as I drove away from the airport and north towards Waukegan. As the signs rolled by, my past came rushing back.

Bombing down the Dan Ryan Expressway was a lot more fun in my 1966 baby blue, 389 Cubic inch tri-powered, four-on-the-floor stick shift GTO. Funny… We called it a goat. I learned to ice skate here. I wonder if they still flood the ball field in Lake Forest and let it freeze over. I spent a lot of time in the warming shed with the never empty pot of hot chocolate. The girls seemed to congregate there. I met a nanny from England at the rink. What was her name...? Mary! She and her inseparable friend Linda, another nanny, kept me and my buddy out of trouble. I wonder where they are... Probably back in England. Mary was a redhead. I've always been partial to redheads. If I ever get hitched again, it will be to a redhead. Hummmmm... Lois is a redhead. I continued north to the outskirts of Waukegan, then stopped at a La Quinta for the night. It was late and I needed to be fresh for my meeting with Greasey.

I awoke around seven, showered and had some lousy coffee provided by the motel. I'd kill for a Starbucks, but this motel-mud would have to do. I looked in my notes and dialed Bishop's phone number. He answered on the first ring.

"Yeah what do you want?"

"Greasey, it's me, Bob Kensey. I'm in Waukegan, where do you want to meet?"

"Kensey? How about Pierce's Corner? Still remember how to get there? Will be there in about twenty minutes, see you." He said quickly and just as quickly hung up. I thought it was rather abrupt but that was Greasey.

I made some wrong turns but found Pierce's Corner after a few detours. It is an old time coffee shop in downtown, or what passes as downtown, Waukegan. I spent a lot of time there just looking at the young women and drinking ten-cent cups of coffee. You could get a damn fine hot fudge sundae or a good sandwich that wouldn't break the bank. I had no trouble parking, unlike the days when 'cruising' was in vogue, and entered the cafe. Not much changed in the last forty years. The décor was the same shabby shade of orange. The long-legged waitresses were still mid-west pretty and the big window lined with booths gave a majestic view of a drab main street. The counter ran the full length of the coffee shop with the big windows opposite. I chose a booth along the window, ordered a coffee and sat facing the door. I just finished my first cup of passable coffee when in walked Earnest Borgnine: Greasey always struck me as Commander McHale of McHale's

30

Navy. He was short, slightly (pudgy!) overweight. His hair or what passed for hair was gray, and flecked with black. He had a very short gray mustache. His face always looked to me to be slightly out of whack, or asymmetrical. His ears were at different heights and his nose bent to the left. After forty years, I would still recognize him anywhere. I raised my hand to get his attention.

He sat opposite me and said, "No shit, it really is you. I can't believe these tired old eyes."

Greasey looked overworked as well as overweight. I noticed the grease under his nails when I shook his proffered hand. A bouncy waitress appeared with a coffee refill and asked if there was anything else... Greasey looked at her and ordered a full breakfast: ham, eggs, hash browns, toast and coffee. She gave me *"the look"* and I ordered some toast.

I turned to Greasey and said, "You still look the same, how are things?"

"Cut the crap, what do you want? Why are you here?" He asked his eyes glued to the waitress.

"Look, let's eat first before getting down to business. Cute waitress..." I said trying to lighten things up.

"OK" he said still staring at her.

We killed a quarter of an hour swapping lies before the "cutie" came back with our breakfast.

She delivered breakfast with flair and a quip, "Here you go Pops. I see you got a sucker to buy you breakfast..." She gave me a wink, laid out our chow, and sashayed all the way back to the kitchen.

"Thanks Marcie." Greasey barked in her wake. "What do you think of my daughter? She takes after her mother." He said as he turned his head towards me.

"Yeah." Is all I said as I put some strawberry jam on my toast.

We each ate and drank our coffee in complete and utter silence. I felt the tension in Greasey and wondered why. It seemed to me he had a distinct air of desperation surrounding him. I could see the little beads of sweat at the hairline and upper lip. Nervousness is something you would not necessarily attribute to Greasey. It bothered me but I really had no other option at this time.

After we finished eating and Marcie delivered refills of coffee

Greasey said "OK, you've stalled and fiddle-farted around enough. What gives?" He stared at me with his head tilted to one side and eyebrows raised.

I took a deep breath, sipped some hot coffee, and gathered my thoughts. "First of all" I started "You still know everything there is to know about the LM-2500 gas turbines? You are still the best turbine mech I know. By the way, did you keep up on diesel mechanics?"

His eyes lit up like a Christmas tree and his demeanor turned serious. He glared at me and said, "You bet your sweet ass! Not only 'was' I the best, I still am. I worked for General Electric on their gas turbine project and was the chief reason the LM-2500 received upgrades. I worked on the Fast Freddies, Spru-cans and PHMs before I called it quits. I finally had enough of the chicken shit military, the power-peddling bullshit of GE and just dropped out… I came up here to be with my one and only daughter. She threw me out a couple of years ago. The reason for that is none of your business. Why are you interested in the life story of a retired old fart, gas turbine, diesel mechanic?"

"I have a possible job opening. I can put you in line for some interesting and profitable work. But, I have to ask, can you get away soon for an indefinite amount of time?"

He nodded and said "Depends."

"Depends on what?" I didn't like the sound of 'depends'.

"Depends on how much it pays! Look, I'm gonna be honest here; I really need some cash right now. I kind of borrowed some money from Marcie and I really need to get it back to her." He uttered softly and looked down at the table. He absently reached for his coffee cup and took a sip.

"You remember the DEA agent assigned to the PHM squadron when we were in Key West?" I asked and he nodded. "Well, Gman looked me up a few days ago and laid out a proposition. He hired me and as an added bonus, I get to take a little sailing vacation in the IO. He has a line on a ship and I need to round up a crew. You came to mind right away. You interested?" I asked, rather casually.

I wanted to get his attention without divulging any real information. I did not want Greasey to make any side deals as he

32

very well could. He was a shifty kind of person but very smart.

Greasey's head came up, he looked me right in the eyes and exclaimed "No shit! You bet I am interested, lay some more on me, Kensey."

I stared right back and came to a decision. I would trust him only so far. How far depended on what I saw and felt as I laid out some possibilities.

"I need your expertise on the power plants and engineering controls. You know what a 'Q-ship' or better yet a 'raider' was? Q-ships were shallow-draft ships disguised to look like merchant men. We used them to defeat wolf packs in the Atlantic during WWII. Raiders were something else but neither were what they appeared to be. The most notorious was a wooden sailing vessel, the German raider *'SMS Seedler'*, captained by Count Luckner. *SMS Seedler*, *Sea Eagle* in English, sank over a million tons of Allied steel shipping during WWI! She had a couple of 105mm naval rifles cleverly hidden on deck and a diesel engine. Outwardly, she appeared as a three-masted sailing ship. It isn't an exact fit to what I have planned but I may have access to something similar. Not exactly a Q-ship or a raider but a good fighting vessel that is long forgotten and not expected.

I am going to crew it with retired chiefs who have experience on ship's systems. We are going to take that ship and do a little sight-seeing..., and other things. This *'mission'* is dangerous and we might not make it back in one piece. No guarantees, no warrantees, no promises except some money in your bank account.

I could see him mulling over everything I said and I was sure I had him hooked. After a few sips of coffee, he said, "Yeah, I'm in but I don't think you are telling me the *'whole'* story. How much money we talking? I really need to pay Marcie back."

"OK, I will give you ten thousand up front for travel expenses. That should get you out of any problems here in Waukegan. The rest of the money comes when we return. Is that satisfactory?" I said knowing he would jump at the offer. I could see all the tension and desperation leave his body.

He just kind of relaxed, looked dubious, and asked, "You can give me ten thousand right now?"

I nodded slowly watching him closely. He turned sideways in the booth and beckoned to Marcie.

She ambled to our table. I could see her resentment. Her voice was bitter and her questions pointed. "What? You can't pay? You want to put this on the tab like always?"

"Kensey tell her I'm gainfully employed and can pay her back before leaving. Please!" He pleaded.

"If your dad's debt is less than ten thousand dollars you are in luck. I am hiring him for a job." I stated as flat as I could. I did not want to be dragged into some kind of situation between daughter and father. I just needed Greasey and his expertise.

"Really? Well… Then, I can get back all the money Pops stole from me." She said as she turned to face me. "This isn't a joke or a scam my daddy thought up to get on my good side again is it?"

I didn't want to get involved in their problems and needed to head off a protracted conversation. I said, "No, not a scam. This is legit. Your dad is the best gas turbine guy around and I need him."

She stared at me her mouth agape. After a few moments she began to sob. Greasey got up and put his arms around her. Nothing was said.

Greasey stepped back a bit and said "Look, go back to work; we will talk later at your place. OK?"

She turned wiping away years of heartbreak and tears. Greasey turned at me and asked, "What's the plan? What do you want I should do?"

"I want you to clean up all your business here and be in San Diego by April first. That gives me one week to get the rest of the crew. I want you to stay at the Navy Lodge at 32nd Street. If you can't, get in a motel as close to there as possible. Leave your contact information at the front desk. I will use that to get in touch when I get down there. Rent a nine-passenger van for wheels. We will need it for the entire crew. Any questions?"

"No. Go to San Diego, stay at the 32nd Street Navy lodge, rent a nine-passenger van all on or about the first of next month. Got it!" He ticked off each point on his fingers. "Is that all?" he asked.

I told him, "Yes. For the moment." Then I asked, "Do you have anyone in mind that I could recruit for this adventure? I need a diesel mech, gunner, ship handler, boatswain mate, and an

34

electronics technician for comms. Any ideas?" I looked at him hopefully.

"You know, I do. Do you remember an old beat up senior chief engineman that we called Fritz the Nazi? The last I heard he is alone. The kids all moved away and his wife died. He is living on his Social Security and navy retirement. We kind of lost contact when I came up here but I'm sure he is still in Norfolk. A good place to look is the Chiefs Club at NOB. He always hung out there. He isn't into computers so the only way you going to find him is to go and look for him." He drank the last of his coffee and I drank the last of mine.

"Thanks for that. *'I'd planned on going to Norfolk next.'*. I've got to scoot. Give me banking info and I will transfer the funds into your account before I leave Waukegan."

He turned and called for Marcie. She walked over a much quicker this time. "Let's fix this right now. "Give Kensey your banking info. He is going to deposit some money into your account. I will explain later but we are a little pressed for time." He turned to me and said, "Right is right..." as Marcie left to retrieve her purse.

I replied, "Yeah, It's never too late to fix things. I have my computer in the car and will take care of this just as soon as I can.

Marcie returned and tentatively handed me a deposit slip torn from her pink, flowered checkbook. It showed the account was in her name Marcie Ann Bishop Vestry. What a handle! I decided to let it ride and not pursue any more information from or about Greasey. I got up, put a twenty on the table, and said to Greasey, "I will see next month on the first!"

I quickly left and started back to O'Hare. I wanted to transfer Greasey's retainer into Marcie's account and catch the next flight to Norfolk.

Chapter 8
Fritz Heinrich Schmidt

I arrived at the airport, turned in my rental car, and proceeded to the United counter to buy a ticket for the worst Navy port in the world, Norfolk, Virginia. I hated the place while stationed there back in the early 70's on the *USS Columbus (CG-12)*. Mosquitoes, cockroaches, and June bugs the size of marbles swarm everywhere. Norfolk, part of the 'The Tidewater' area, sits next to the Chesapeake Bay, the James River, and the Great Dismal Swamp. It has no socially redeeming values as far as I am concerned. I dislike the area immensely.

I landed at Norfolk airport late in the day. While on the plane, I completed the money transfer into Marcie's account and sent Greasey an email relaying that information. I tried to recall everything I knew about Fritz the Nazi. I conjured up a picture of a typical German: tall, blonde-haired, muscular, and very stern. His shipmates nicknamed him Fritz the Nazi because he was always clicking his heels together and throwing a mock Hitler salute. That's how I remembered him from Key West. He was a first class petty officer when he served on the PHMs and a wizard with diesel engines. That was someone I really could use. He was good with all the other engine room equipment and mechanical systems requirements. With both him and Greasey, we could get underway and operate the ship without problems.

I was closing in on this hunt and at this precise moment, I knew this scheme would work. There was still a lot of work to do before I finished recruiting a first-rate crew. If I managed to recruit all ex-chiefs for the critical jobs the mission would be, relatively speaking, a piece of cake. I felt the plane start its descend into Norfolk airport and that brought me right back to the task at hand; Find Fritz. I spent the remaining time before departing the plane mapping out a plan of action.

I rented a car and proceeded to "Norfolk Operations Base" or, as we call it, NOB. I followed the highway signs and it took a good two hours to get there. I got lost several times. Most all of the roads were changed since my last visit in 1973. I didn't see any

"Dogs and Sailors Keep off the Grass" signs so things must have improved a bit in the last thirty-five years. I finally arrived at NOB and found the Chiefs Club. The Club was a large room with many tables surrounding a small dance floor adjacent to a small stage. Two pool tables and a dartboard were over in an alcove on the left. The bar ran the length of the back wall. It was full despite the early hour. Happy hour was in full swing. I was starved so I ordered a beer, burger, and fries. I put my plan into action. As I ate, I observed all the chiefs in khaki uniforms. I was looking for the one chief that knew everybody and everything. There is *always* one Chief in every club who is the center of activity and thinks he is the center of the universe. He is not hard to spot. Here at NOB, he was a tall Chief in khakis with an Enlisted Surface Warfare Specialist badge over his ribbons. He roamed all over the club drinking with several groups from various ships and different commands. I watched him while I ate. When I finished I made my approach.

I walked over to him at the bar and asked, "Buy you a beer?"

He turned with a big question on his face and said, "Sure. Do I know you?"

I ordered another beer for him and one for me. Unfortunately, they didn't have San Magoo; Coors would have to do.

I didn't want to appear too eager so I shook my head and said, "No, but I think you might be able to help me locate an old shipmate. You seem to know everybody. Can you give me a hand?"

"Maybe. Who in particular are you looking for?" He seemed noncommittal.

"Fritz Schmidt. He's a retired Senior Chief Engineman. A friend in Illinois said he likes to hang out here. You know him?"

He nodded enthusiastically and said, "You mean Fritz the Nazi? Yeah I know him. He usually comes in around 1900 after the base traffic clears. How do you know Fritz?"

"I served with him in Key West. I'm on vacation in the area and thought I'd look him up. He always said he was going to retire in Norfolk, open an engine shop, and live high on the hog. I read in Navy Times that he made senior chief and a couple of years later saw his name on the retired list." That was noncommittal and should satisfy any curiosity about why I was here.

"Yeah… I remember him saying he wants to open an engine shop. By the way, my name is ETC Jack Hancock. Please no jokes! I am a 'Professor' at the Navy Instructor School here at NOB. Were you ever assigned instructor duty?" Hancock was fishing for information but I wasn't going to bite too hard.

"Bob Kensey retired Master Chief Fire Controlman, pleased to meet you. Yes, I graduated in 1974. Best school the Navy ever sent me to. I retired back in 1985, and the school served me very well. How long you been there?" I asked trying to engage Jack in some small talk.

That worked and he seemed eager to talk up his credentials. "Two years and got one more to go. I think they are going to send me to a carrier right here out of Norfolk when my tour is up. My real job is working the big search radars, IFF, comm gear, and test equipment. My detailer is a jerk. He says carriers are always short of chiefs, especially chief ETs, and short of 'voting with my feet' a carrier is where I'm going!"

"I understand. That's the reason I retired. My detailer was determined to send me to a carrier out of Norfolk. I hate this place and I didn't want to move again. I rather like Seattle, so I put in my papers." Just then, I saw Hancock's eyes light up and his head snap around toward the far end of the bar.

"There's Fritz. Come on I'll take you to him." We stood up and moved down the bar taking our beers with us.

Hancock waved his free arm and got Fritz's attention, "Fritz… Got an old friend of yours with me!"

Fritz stared at me for a few moments and tentatively said, "Kensey. Bob Kensey… I'll be damned! Never thought I would see you here in Norfolk." He seemed pleasantly delighted to see me.

He was exactly as I remembered. He still had all his hair and sat ramrod straight: Fritz was always at attention. His blond hair and blue eyes stood out. He was at least 65 but his arms rippled with muscle. I started to shake his hand vigorously and pat his shoulder. Chief Hancock butted in and said he had to get home to his wife. I thanked him and turned back to Fritz glad it was just the two of us now.

"What are doing here Kensey?" Fritz asked. He was staring at me and I could see the questioning look.

"Greasey told me where to look and here I am." I said.

"Greasey... Why did you go see him?" That question was obvious and I thought I'd sidestep it for the moment.

"Well it's a long story." Before I got into that I needed some information. "How have 'you' been? Greasey is fine and says 'howdy'. How is your health? You feelin' OK? You still look fit."

"I am in great shape. Best shape in my life. I take a few pills now and then for my heart but I am fine! Looks like the years have been good to you Kensey."

"You still married?" I didn't bite on the looking good query. I still needed to know if Fritz was available.

"No, wife died several years back. Kids moved on. I'm living here marking time till I die." He said kind of wistfully as if there should be something better.

"You own that engine shop you always wanted?" I asked watching his face.

"No. I never had enough money at one time to open it. Something always came up. Wife's cancer, kid's college, you know the score. I get a little ahead and then wham, a disaster comes along and wipes out my savings. Why are you here?"

The plan I devised on the plane from O'Hare was coming along nicely. "You miss the excitement of life in the Navy? If you do and you need some money, I have a job for you. I watched him closely but all I saw was curiosity. I took that for a 'yes'. I continued, "I have a ship at my disposal and a job to do. I need a crew and Greasey, who is already on board as my turbine guy, suggested you. Interested?"

He looked at me with a critical eye and decided I wasn't bullshitting and said "Jawohl. Count me in. What do I have to do? How much money? Who do I have to kill? Where do I go and when do I leave? Will I get enough money to open my engine shop?"

"Yes, yes, and yes." I answered. "First, I will advance you ten thousand to get all your affairs in order here. I want you in San Diego by 1 April. Stay at the Navy Lodge at 32nd street; if not there a motel close by. Greasey should be around there so keep an

40

eye out for him. Leave your contact information at the front desk of the Navy Lodge. Got that?" He was all smiles and nodded in the affirmative. "Give me your banking information and I will transfer the money into your account right now. Does this club have free Wi-Fi?"

Fritz gave me a blank stare and said, "Ja, I think so."

He got up and went straight out the front door. I got my computer out of the case, lit it off, and logged on. I waited for several minutes and ordered another beer. After a quarter hour, I started to get worried. What was taking him so long? I struck up a conversation with the waitress and the next time I looked at my watch, an hour was gone. Finally, Fritz returned, walked straight over to me, and handed me a check. Void, in black sharpie, was written across it. I logged in to the bank and quickly transferred the money.

"It should post to your account by tomorrow Fritz. OK?"

"Thanks, Kensey. Is that it? Be in San Diego by the first of April."

I said yes, closed the computer, and got to my feet. "I will see you then. I have a question. You know anybody else that might be interested in a little vacation to the IO?"

He thought a moment and answered, "Yeah. A guy I know works up in the Newport News shipyard. He is the disgraced ex captain of the *Gemini*. You remember: the CO who was caught fuckin' that young female sailor. He was court marshaled and served some time in Leavenworth. His name is Masters but I don't know where he is exactly. Ask around the shipyard and you should find him." I shook his hand again, thanked him for the lead, and left the club.

As I approached my rental car in the parking lot a voice from behind startled me.

"Hold on Kensey, I would like to talk to you." I turned to find Chief Hancock, still in uniform, shifting his weight from foot to foot.

"Don't sneak up on a guy like that! What do you want?" I asked very abruptly.

"Sorry, but hey listen; I talked with Fritz. He is an old friend and he told me you hired him to crew a ship of some kind. I wish I could go but I can't. However, I know an old retired chief ET who would give his left nut to be on your crew. He sailed on Fast Frigates and a couple of Spru-cans. He taught ET and crypto school. He put his time in and retired. Now he's wasting away working for the cable company. He is over 60, for Christ's sake and they are fixing to shit-can him. You interested?"

"Yeah, I am. Got his name and contact info?" He handed me a small piece of paper with a Norfolk address and a name, Simon Radisson, and a phone number scrawled on it. I would have to give this contact some consideration. I did need a comms and electronics guy.

I looked at Chief Hancock, held out my hand and said, "Thanks. Do you think I can talk to Radisson this evening?"

Hancock said, "Simon will be expecting your call." I thanked him again and got in my car. I couldn't believe my luck but decided I had to be a hell of a lot more careful. I made a mental note to send Chief Hancock a bottle of single malt for the lead. So far so good but I didn't want a lot of nosey people asking questions.

I drove out of NOB and navigated to an old bar I knew that used to serve San Magoo.

Chapter 9
Simon George Radisson Jr.

I was pleasantly surprised as I entered the parking lot of The Fouled Anchor. It was a single building painted haze gray with a 10 foot bronze fouled anchor over the door. This bar has been a hangout for Chiefs since before World War II. *'Imagine that… it was still standing and still in business. Will wonders never cease!'* I entered and sat in a booth at the far corner. The walls were covered with ship plaques and framed photos of Navy ships from *Old Ironsides* to the newest Arleigh Burke Destroyers. On the wall just above my head was a beautiful picture of *USS Pegasus PHM-1*. Appropriate, I thought. The place was littered with Navy memorabilia, ships patches, ships bells and clocks, inclinometers, and dogging wrenches filled the gaps between photos. A massive engine-order-telegraph sat at one end of the bar and a binnacle at the other. I looked around for the Fire Control Technician's rating badge symbol: a *'bar-stool'*. I was disappointed: not one range finder adorned the walls that I could see.

A very pretty waitress sauntered over and I ordered a cold San Magoo. She smiled and went behind the bar to get it. It didn't take long before there was a nice cold brew staring at me. I quaffed it with parched gusto! I debated with myself for a few moments then took out my cell phone and dialed Radisson's number.

After one ring, he answered. "Hello… Is this Kensey from the NOB Chief's Club?"

"Aye." I replied.

"This is Simon Radisson and if what Jack told me is true I would very much like to talk to you. Jack didn't give me any real information. He said an old retired chief was looking to crew a... ship of some sort… I *'am'* interested. How soon can we get together? You want to come here or I can meet you someplace?"

I said I was at the Fouled Anchor and asked if he knew where that was. He replied he did and would be there in about forty-five minutes. I said I would wait. That solved the problem of finding his house. I didn't relish looking for an unfamiliar address in a Norfolk I no longer knew and I didn't trust the Ford's GPS. I sipped my San Magoo and felt as if I was back in Seattle at The Haven. It was comfortable and I could feel myself winding down. Before I dozed off the door opened and a tall, thin, bald-headed, slightly stooped shouldered man entered. He was taller than Schmidt but did not weigh nearly as much. He spotted me and strode over to my booth. I held up two fingers to the waitress and she nodded.

He introduced himself. "I am Simon George Radisson Jr. retired Chief ET who is absolutely bored out of his skull. Glad to meet you."

The waitress stopped at our booth and deposited a couple of San Magoos. Simon spun his around slowly and eyeballed it closely before speaking. "Wow, haven't had one of these in a long, long time! Thanks."

"You know my name is Bob Kensey and I am on a recruiting mission. I don't have much time so I'll come right out and ask what I need to know: You free of any entanglements? You know like: my wife she. My kids they. My dog it..."

He guffawed and slapped the table, took a swig of beer and answered. "Naw, no attachments. No wife; none would have me. Hate the job. Own the house outright. Got rid of the damned dog; he kept pissin' on the door and made the whole house stink!"

I chuckled at his answers and continued, "I need to know a little about the equipment you've worked on. Are you familiar with the LN-66 and the comm suite on smaller ships, say a PHM or Fast Freddie?" I asked, hoping he was.

"Never was assigned to the PHMs but I sure know the LN-66. The PHMs were around during the late 70's to the early 90's right. If so, I know all of that equipment. Pretty much the same stuff as on the Oliver Hazard Perry class fast frigates or Fast Freddie's as we called them. I was assigned to tender duty, school instructor, and crypto instructor at Mare Island. If it involved ET shit, you name it I did it. I started my navy carrier as a radioman so I have the comms side nailed. I switched over to ET because I love working hardware! I was Operations departmental chief on my last ship, the **USS Kincaid DD-965** right here out of Norfolk. They wanted to send me to a carrier and I said no and put in my papers."

44

That seemed to be a recurring theme! I just smiled and said, "I know what you mean. I have a friend who refused a promotion to Master Chief Fire Controlman and retired rather than ride the **Enterprise**. It looks like you have the skills I'm looking for. If you are up for it, I am getting a crew of retired chiefs together to do a little job for a friend. I have an interesting little fighting ship and will be taking it into harm's way. This may prove to be very lucrative but it is also '*very*' dangerous. You still interested?" His eyes never left mine as he nodded yes. I continued with the standard 10K dollar advance and where he needed to be and when he had to be there.

He mulled it over a few seconds then added, "I am so fucking bored... I need a diversion before I croak. General Quarters, General Quarters, all hands man your battle stations! I really miss that. I'll be in San Diego on or before the first!"

"That's perfect. Check into the Navy Lodge at 32nd Street. Most everyone will be there by then." I said and accepted his blank check. I transferred funds right then and there. We finished our beers and stood up.

He looked at me and said "God Bless you! I really needed this. Thanks!"

I acknowledged his thanks and asked, "Got any leads on possible crew members? I still need a gunner and Boatswain Mate..."

He stood there for several seconds thinking and said, "No, but try the Chiefs Club at Dam Neck. Lot of Navy specialty schools out there and lots of old chiefs. You might try the club at Fleet Training Group. It's located at the Amphib Base in Little Creek. Nothing else comes to mind."

"Good idea. I will give them a shot. See you in San Diego." I paid the check and added a big tip for the waitress: Greasey's daughter Marcie popped into my mind these days whenever I tipped a waitress.

Simon started down the street in his shabby old pick-up truck and I got in my rental car. It was still early but jet lag was setting in and I needed a bed. I drove past a Radisson Hotel and thought, why not... I turned around in a service street, pulled into their parking lot and parked, checked in to a very nice room and hit the

45

rack. Before I went to sleep, I planned the next day's activities. I would try to find Masters up in Newport News before looking elsewhere.

Chapter 10
William J. Masters III

During my continental breakfast the next morning, I broke out the laptop and did an internet search on William J. Masters III. Eighty-three were listed. (I was certain only one 'the third' would be listed. Goes to show: you never know.) Only one lived in Newport News, VA. The information available on Masters was quite extraordinary. He came from a very wealthy New England family and graduated from the Naval Academy at the top of his class. He rose rapidly through the ranks and was known as an exceptional ship handler and leader. His last assignment was as Commanding Officer of the *USS Gemini PHM-6*. Lieutenant Commanders as a rule of thumb do not get command of a ship of the line. That was quite an accomplishment. Even though *Gemini* was a small hydrofoil, his getting command was impressive.

His one weakness was an affinity for the ladies. One day Masters was caught screwing a young female sailor who worked supply in the PHM transportable support vans. He was court marshaled, sent to prison, and kicked out of the Navy. After his release, he tried his hand at the merchant navy. That didn't work and he ended up working salvage operations. *"That's a giant step down for such a good ship handler..."* I thought. Nosing around the salvage operations in Newport News would be a good place to start looking for him.

I studied the scant pictures of him posted on the internet. I ticked off the important facts: Inch under six feet tall, full head of graying hair cut short, clean shaven, ruddy complexion with a face that showed his trials and tribulations. The internet pictures did not give me a clear picture of his eye color but one woman's description marveled at his blue velvet eyes...

With that picture fixed in my mind, I closed the laptop, finished breakfast and then motored north through the Hampton Roads tunnel, and on to Newport News.

Newport News is a fine old shipbuilding city and the shipyard located there is one of the best in the country. They have been building ships of all types since the Revolutionary War. I pulled into The Wheel House bar just outside the Shipyard gate. I entered a typical nautical themed pub and ordered a Samuel Adams Boston Lager. The bartender had never heard of San Magoo, Alaskan Amber, or Henry Weinhard! The place was dead. I could understand why… Before I came in the only customer was an old, weathered sailor who looked like he sailed on the Ark. I struck up a conversation with the bartender and asked where all the salvage boat crews hung out. *"Sure wasn't this place!"* He told me about a dive several streets over well within walking distance. That, he said, is where I would find most of the salvage crews. I finished my beer and left the change from a "fin" on the bar.

I left the Wheel House and followed the bartender's directions. Within a few minutes walking, I spotted a very large, very old tavern called Shoal Water. It looked like it was built from salvaged parts off shipwrecks. I went in, walked up to the bar, ordered a Rolling Rock and looked around taking in the crowd. It was not empty, but by no means full. I spotted twenty or so customers in small groups drinking beer.

I sipped my beer and started talking to the young woman behind the bar. I offered to buy her a beer; she gave me that all knowing 'Yeah right' look, but accepted the offer.

As long as I was on her good side, I thought I would do a little jigging for information. "Do the salvage crews come in here? I'm looking for an old friend who worked salvage out of Newport News."

She looked at me, made a mental assessment, and figured I was okay. "Yeah, mostly after five. Not much before then."

I looked at my watch and it was just approaching noon. I said, "Would you happen to know a Bill Masters?"

She kind of shivered and replied, "What do you want see him for? You're the wrong sex!"

I chuckled and told her we were old friends from the Navy. I don't think she was convinced but tilted her head and suggested I go get a good meal at the restaurant down the street and come back after five. That sounded good to me. I nursed my Rolling Rock until it was empty then left the Shoal Water and wandered around the waterfront and took in the sights.

The Seafood Inn was an upscale restaurant that appeared to

have quite a following: the parking lot was packed. It was only two in the afternoon and that seemed rather promising. After a twenty minute wait the hostess led me to a corner table. I ordered the New England clam chowder and grilled salmon. The salmon came with baked potato and salad. Not bad for around twenty bucks. I decided to really enjoy my meal and ordered a small carafe of wine. I gave some thought to Masters while waiting for my order. I never met him personally: we were in Key West at different times. I knew of him through scuttlebutt from various squadron shipmates I ran into over the years.

Masters' timing was impeccable. During his courts martial, the Navy was integrating females onto warships in large numbers. The Navy decided to make an example out of his "womanizing" and the punishment he received was harsh. He did time in Leavenworth. The Navy gave him a Dishonorable Discharge and he forfeited every benefit he ever earned. I figured he would be bitter and not speak to me at all. What did I have to lose? I needed him and he probably needed money. *"Good combination,"* I thought.

I tried to come up with some idea or plan of action of how to make my approach and get him to talk. In the end, I decided to improvise and simply enjoy my delicious meal.

At 1530 I finished eating and settled the check. I took my time returning to the Shoal Water. I wanted to be there, seated and drinking, before Masters came in.

They had Newcastle Brown Ale on tap and I just ordered my second when the barmaid signaled with her head indicating a table occupied by several guys. I acknowledged her signal with a nod and scoped-out the occupants. It appeared that there was some sort of celebration in progress with a lot of laughing, talking, singing, and backslapping. It was raucous but not out of hand. I studied each individual's face and none of them looked the least bit like the internet picture of Masters. I looked back at the barmaid. She shrugged her shoulders...

I got up and walked to the bar. I thought I'd ask her if Masters had a face-lift. "Masters is not there. Why the signal?"

"That's the crew he usually hangs out with. They're having a little birthday celebration for the big guy at the end of the table."

49

She said softly.

I thanked her and walked back to my table. I watched for several minutes but no one joined the party. It was beginning to get noisy as the participants got drunker. They were pounding down the beer. I was about to leave when a man entered and walked straight to the party. Someone handed him a beer and he drank it straight down in one quick gulp. JD, an old friend, is the only other person I know who can drink a beer like that. He could open his throat and pour a beer directly into his stomach. It didn't matter whether it was a can, bottle, mug, forty-ouncer or whatever, straight down it went. Then again, JD went out of his way to drink Schlitz…

The newcomer was tall and distinguished looking. He appeared to be in his late fifties. He could be Masters… His profile was a good fit for the internet picture but I couldn't be sure. I decided to wait a little while and try to pick up a clue to his identity.

My patience paid off and few minutes later one of the partygoers shouted to him, "Hey Bill why you late for the party? Banging a new chick maybe?"

"Naw. Busy on the ship. Couldn't get away. And don't you worry about who or what I am banging!" He yelled back.

That, no doubt was Masters, *"How do I approach him?"*

He wasn't there long when he got up to make a "head-call." I thought this was a good opportunity and after a few minutes, I followed. He was washing his hands when I entered the restroom. The most logical thing to do was simply introduce myself.

I cleared my throat, offered my handshake, and began, "Bill Masters, the ship handler? Ex PHM driver…" He looked a bit startled and examined me closely. I could see all sorts of messages in his eyes: fear, wariness, and dread.

I didn't want the momentum to shift so I continued, "I am not here to condemn or judge. I need your expertise. My name is Bob Kensey and I was a Senior Chief Firecontrolman on the **Hercules**. I left the ship before you came to the squadron." I took a deep breath and waited for a response. When none came I continued, " I have a proposition for you. Would you like to drive a PHM again?" Sooner or later, the entire crew would know our *'little fighting vessel'* was a PHM and right now I needed to convince Masters to sign on with us. A person can go overboard with

50

security. This wasn't the time.

His eyes got wider and he said, "Yes, I am interested. Why me? I haven't had anything to do with the Navy in years. I am just a pilot on an old salvage barge. I got nothing you want."

"Let's go some place quiet and have a beer. Can you leave the party without causing a bru-ha-ha?" I did not want to cause a scene in the tavern.

"Sure. No problem. They are probably all too drunk to notice or care." I could tell he was skeptical but his answer was good news.

We left the "head" (Navy for restroom) and he led the way to an empty table in the far corner of the tavern. He waived two fingers at the barmaid. She scowled but acknowledged his request. We sat down opposite each other and waited in silence for the beer.

Once it was delivered and we were alone Masters spoke up. "OK, what is it you want? You mentioned driving a PHM and that you needed me. I'm listening." He sounded a little tense.

I needed to pique his curiosity. "I know you were CO of the **Gemini**. You passed-over a bunch of senior officers to fill that billet because you were the best ship handler in the PHM program. I need a PHM driver! Simple as that. I don't care about your past. Don't care about your present. I'm only interested in your future."

"I am all ears." He said, "What's the catch?"

I knew he was ready to hear my offer. I made up my mind right after meeting him. I gave him the proposition: Up-front pay, where to be, and when to be there. Thus far, I was the only one privy to the twenty million and wanted to keep it that way. Two beers later, he was pretty well clued in on the mission and what was expected of him.

I was down to the last swallow of beer and Masters took the opportunity to get a few things off his chest. "Jim Billings huh? I remember him as a square straight up kind of guy. Never got in the way or tried to run our ships. He left that to the Captain and crew. He did a lot of work with the squadron concerning training and goals. I heard he got his hands *dirty* during the 'Clean Sweep' operation that turned into the 'Custer Debacle' and I'm assuming you are the Senior Chief Kensey that brought the **Hercules** back."

I had to answer honestly, if I wanted Masters as part of my crew. "Yes on both counts." I muttered.

Masters wasn't quite finished and nodded before continuing. "DEA was putting a lot of money into the operations out of Key West but Jim didn't push his weight around. I trusted him then so no reason not to trust him now. Tell you what Kensey; I tentatively accept your offer. I won't lie to you I really need that ten thousand as soon as possible. I will leave the job the minute someone brings up my past. I know you Chiefs and you don't forgive mistakes very easily. You are all navy to the bone. Sure, I messed up and I regret it, but I don't want it thrown in my face. You had a little run in with the UCMJ didn't you? You know how it goes... The 'Custer Debacle' and my indiscretions aren't in the same boat but we both know how *'difficult'* the chain-of-command can be."

"You got a deal. I will try to keep the others off your back. You have to accept the fact that they will be hard on you if you make a mistake." I informed him.

The mood shifted to a more businesslike manner. I knew Masters had questions. I wanted to make sure he had the right ones. "How you going to get that PHM to Somalia? Flying it there on the foils would take a month and a shit pot full of fuel stops. All that time lays you open for someone to stick their nose in. It is very hard to hide a ship with a big damn gun on the bow! That will invite attention, not just from our Navy, but every Navy in the whole fuckin' world."

"Got any ideas?" I asked. He brought up the same points I had been worrying about.

"No, no ideas." He answered.

"Gman could have Boeing deliver the ship anywhere in the US. We need a place to deliver it, outfit it, and take it on sea trials. We need a little training time to get back into shipboard routines." All of these problems had been on my mind since accepting this mission.

"You know, I might have an idea," Masters said, "Tell you all about it in detail a little later. I assume Jim will deliver the ship to San Diego. I know a small place down in Baja we can work out of. We will need enough food and fuel to get us to Cabo. Oh, if you don't have small arms aboard yet see if Jim can get some M16s and two M60s."

52

"Sure, that will work. The ship will be delivered about the first of April." I said. "On a different topic, do you have any crew friends left from the days aboard the PHMs? I still need a few crew members."

He hesitated then said, "Yes. Do you remember Boats Clark? He was the Master Chief of the PHM squadron?" I nodded and he continued, "After he retired he looked me up. I had just been released from Leavenworth and Boats showed up on my doorstep. How he found me, I don't know, but he did. He has been tagging along with me ever since."

I was shocked. I remembered Boats Clark; he was a hard, down the line, Master Chief Boatswains Mate. There wasn't anything about seamanship that he did not know. He was a perfect choice for our mission.

"Can you recruit him for us?" I asked hopefully.

"I will talk to him and am pretty sure he will want to come along. If nothing else to give you guys a hard time. How do I get in touch with you?" He asked.

I gave him my number and email address. I told him to send me his banking info and Clark's when he recruited him. It was getting late; I was tired but satisfied. I had my ship handler, and as a bonus a damned good bo'sun.

I stood up and said, "See you in San Diego and let me know as soon as you get Clark onboard. Good night." I stopped by the bar, paid my tab, left a nice tip for the young lady, and left. I navigated back to the Radisson for a good night's sleep before recruiting a gunners mate. Preferably one who had experience with the Mk 75 gun.

Chapter 11
Joseph Meechum

Breakfast at the Radisson was nothing to write home about but it did fill me up and the coffee was passable. Starbucks would call it 'floor sweepings!' I needed to notify Gman of my progress and have him make the necessary arrangements to deliver the PHM to San Diego. Once again, I picked up the one-number cell phone and punched the call button.

On the first ring, Gman answered. "Hold!" The line sounded dead to me. No noise; no nothing...

A few seconds passed, twenty or so, then Gman came on the line and said, "Report"

"I'm on target and track. I need one more to fill the crew. Equip our yacht with at least two M60s and a dozen or so M16s. Don't skimp on the ammunition. Deliver it to San Diego about the 2nd." I thought I'd give Gman a bit of his own medicine.

"Shit! Fuck! I said time was of the essence but I figured on a few more days!" That broke the, 'report' 'good by', I don't have time to talk, logjam.

Now that we were communicating, I could get down to business. "Thank god! I thought R2-D2 was on the other end of the line. I'll have most of the crew at San Diego 32nd street Navy Lodge by 3 April at the latest. For the moment, Bishop is your contact until I finish up here and get to San Diego myself. I think delivering our yacht to one of the small shipyards will work. I would shy away from 'Nassco'. They have a cozy relationship with the Navy. 'Triple A South' would work and there is a small yard in Chula Vista. If it is on the seaward side instead of in the harbor it would be the best bet. If we are OK with the Navy I would prefer to be pier-side at the degaussing pier on Point Loma." I paused in case Gman wanted to jump in with details. "I'm assuming the silent treatment means you've got a handle on everything. I'll report when I recruit a gunner. Once I do that I'm going dark-and-dirty until I have a delivery destination. You there? Guess so... TaTa." I still had an open line. I thought I'd wait for a response before hanging up.

"TTFN Kensey." And the line went dead.

That made the hunt for a gunners mate even more pressing. I opted for one more shot on the computer before trying Dam Neck or Little Creek. I was tired of bars and clubs for now: it was getting a bit tedious. I booted up the laptop and navigated to the crew listings of the *Hercules*. I scanned it again and a familiar name jumped out at me. Joe Meechum or Preacher was stationed aboard *Hercules* during the Custer Debacle. He could make 'Otto' talk with precision! I dug in my memory for everything I could remember about him. He was called Preacher because he was a deacon in the Southern Baptist church and was always quoting scripture. He never swore or used salty language but he did say the gun was haunted sometimes! I remembered he lived somewhere down south but could not, for the life of me, remember exactly where. One way to find out was do a people search on the internet. After a few minutes, a Joseph Meechum, age 62, Olive Branch, Mississippi popped up along with a phone number. Nothing ventured nothing gained... I dialed. On the third ring a soft, male voice answered, "God Bless you, how may I help?"

"Sorry to bother you, but I am trying to locate an old shipmate, Joe Meechum." I said with the most respect I could muster.

"This is Joe, who you be?"

"Joe, you moth eaten cannon cocker! This is Bob Kensey from the *Hercules*, remember me?"

"I do! We had some good times on the *Herc*... Why you calling me?"

"I got a proposition for you, but I can't tell you over the open line. Can I come there and talk face to face? I could be there tomorrow depending on flights. I am in Norfolk right now."

"Sure, but I don't know why you would want me. I been long retired and a landlubber now. I guess it don't hurt to talk and I would like to see an old shipmate. You got my address?"

"No, just Olive Branch, MS. What's the rest..."

"Once you get to Olive Branch drive to the intersection of Desoto and Center Hill Road. There is a little white church or what used to be but now is a burned pile of rubble. When you get to the city call me at this number and I will meet you there."

56

"Got it. Intersection of Desoto and Center Hill. Be there tomorrow or the next. Good to hear your voice Preacher!" I said with enthusiasm and hung up.

I checked flights for Olive Branch, MS but none were available. There was a flight this afternoon to Memphis. I booked a seat and rental car online. I had about two hours to get to the airport and turn in my car. I checked out of the Radisson and made a beeline for the airport. I couldn't help but think I was well on the way to recruiting my last crewmember. If I convince Meechum to join us and Masters recruits Clark, I would have an exceptionally capable crew!

I didn't dally once I reached the airport. I turned in my rental car and went directly to the departure lounge. Once through security and comfortably seated in the lounge I checked my email. Nothing from Masters yet... Nothing from anybody.

The flight departed on time and arrived in Memphis five or six minutes late. There are numerous Navy schools in Memphis but this was my first time in the city. I picked up my rental car and followed the on-board GPS directions to Olive Branch. I arrived there in short order. It was too early to call Preacher. I decided to look for some place to have a good meal then crash. Most any motel would do as long it wasn't the "Bates" or a dilapidated three-ple in a citrus grove. I passed a Motel 8 with an all-you-can-eat catfish restaurant and a rib joint, *'Johnny Rib's'*, across the street. This wasn't the Radisson but it would do tonight. No doubt *'Johnny Rib's'* had cold beer...

I was up bright and early the next morning. I took advantage of the motel's continental breakfast and watered down coffee and then got directions to Desoto and Center Hill road. I waited until I started the car before calling Preacher. I told him I was on my way to the church and was eager to see him. He said he would be there. I followed the desk clerk's directions and soon came to the intersection. On my left was the hulk of a burned out church. The walls or what was left of them, were the only things still standing. The fire-charred steeple was barely recognizable in the pile of rubble. I saw a tall black man wearing a long, frock coat standing with his hands clasped in front. He reminded me of an old cowboy movie *'Parson'* from the 1880s. Preacher looked the same as I remembered but his raven black hair was replaced with tight white curls. He still looked fit enough to power-buckle a two ton 16" shell without breathing hard! I was impressed…

I jumped out of the car and as I approached him, I saw sadness and sorrow in his eyes. "It's good to see you Preacher." I offered my hand.

He grasped it firmly and replied, "Good to see you Kensey can't wait to hear what you have to say. Got my curiosity all riled up. Good Lord says it all comes to he who waits and I'm sure tired of waiting!"

"Can we go inside or somewhere private?" Was about all I could think of to say at the moment.

"Sure follow me." He said. We skirted the rubble and went around and to the back of what was left standing. As we walked he said, "Church was a victim in the last rash of church burnings. No money to rebuild. Had to stop all the programs for the kids around here. Ain't no money…"

"Yeah I know times are hard and there isn't a lot of money anywhere. Remember Bishop? He got bit by the same bad economy. Maybe I can come up with a solution to some of your money problems like I did his. Interested?" We entered a small cabin with a desk and two chairs, coffee pot, two cups, and a Bible on the desk. It looked like he was ready for me. "Preacher, I need you. I need your expertise on the 76mm gun you used to dote on. What I am about to tell you is in the absolute strictest confidence."

He suddenly picked up the Bible and said, "I swear on this holy book!"

"That is not necessary. I trust you." With that said, I laid out a sketchy plan for a lovely vacation cruise in the IO.

"You know," he lamented, "I thought the day I made Chief was the best day of my life. The worst day was giving it up and retiring. The Good Lord going to give me a chance to relive those days and rebuild this church! I can't believe it. Kensey, you a messenger from God. I accept your offer. Where and when do you need me?"

"I left out a few pertinent details Preacher. This vacation is short fused and dangerous. I don't need a 76mm gunner because we are going fly-fishing! I need you in San Diego no later than 2 April.

Can you make the deadline?" I asked afraid he would back out.

"Ain't never been a fool Kensey. You know that. This gonna be worse than "Clean Sweep"? He really wanted to put his church in order and wasn't afraid of a little 'action'.

"I don't expect this to end like the "Custer Debacle, but aye… it could be worse." I had to be straight-up and honest. I didn't want Preacher signing on then backing out later.

"Like I said; I ain't no fool. All I need is assurances that the Church will be rebuilt if I don't make it back, and yes, I can be in San Diego by the second."

"Were you still around when the CO of the *Gemini*, Masters, was fired?" I asked with a little trepidation. If anything caused Preacher to back out sailing with Masters would.

"For a bit. Didn't he get caught havin' carnal knowledge of a young woman under his command? Yeah… that's him. You need a ship handler and I can work with him if I have to. You gonna tell me I have to. Ain't you?" He wasn't happy but I knew I could count on him to fill out the crew.

"He is our ship handler. He has to be. We have a brand new PHM to play with…" I informed him.

"Hell and damnation! Count me in! Masters and all! Preacher couldn't hide his excitement and that cinched it. I had my crew…

He opened the desk drawer and removed an old-fashioned double entry checkbook. He wrote void across the check and void on the stub, handed it to me and said, "Put the advance in this account. I can get started on rebuilding the church. My retirement checks will get me to San Diego so I won't need any of this money. Is that alright with you Kensey?"

"Fine with me as long as you are in San Diego no later than the second." I said with relief. I had my gunners mate! We both stood up and shook hands. I turned and started back to my car. I glanced back at Preacher. He was kneeling by the remnants of his church saying a prayer. At this juncture, a prayer could not hurt!

I returned to the airport and booked a flight back to Seattle. I thought better of it and changed my destination to San Diego. The San Diego flight departed in a little over an hour. That worked out for the better. I cleared Memphis airport security and found a table in the departure lounge. Things were looking up . . . The lounge carried beers-of-the world including San Magoo. The waitress wiped the dust, *"How does a bottle of beer get dusty in a cooler?"*, off the bottle, popped the top, and expertly filled my frosted glass.

"I've worked here nearly a year and a half and this is the first San Miguel I've ever poured." She said eyeing the bottle to see where it was brewed.

"That's 'San Magoo' sweetheart and it's brewed in the Philippines." I added, "You need to get acquainted with more sailors."

"Oh . . ." Was all she said and took up her station behind the bar.

I checked my email for news from Masters. None . . . I hope he was good to his word. I could use a good bo'sun but Clark wasn't *'mission critical'*. If Masters didn't come through, I was pretty confident I could recruit a boatswains mate in San Diego.

I brought up the spreadsheet, updated a lot of information, and looked over planning for the next phase of the mission. I needed a name. *"The mission"* rang hollow. I'd have to think about it on the plane. The flight attendants were opening the departure gate and the purser announced our flight was now boarding. I closed up the laptop and joined the other weary travelers in queue.

Chapter 12
Point Loma

Modern travel is efficient if not all that comfortable in business class. 0200 30 March found me, tired, hungry, and needing a hotel. I grabbed a cab to Broadway and stopped at the 'Pixi Kitchen' for the best all-night grilled ham and cheese sandwich on the West Coast! The cook, bottle washer, owner, and proprietor put my meal together rather quickly. Forty-five minutes later, I was turning out the lights in my San Diego Hotel room.

I awoke at 1100, got up still a little travel weary but pleased that everything was coming together nicely. My 'Pixi Kitchen' late night grilled ham and cheese wasn't sitting that well. I decided to skip breakfast in favor of a brunch at a reputable restaurant. I took a leisurely 'Hollywood' shower relaxed a while then checked my email. There in beautiful black and white text was an email from Masters. The email was short and to the point: **Clark is a go. Below is banking info. Bearer of good news when we meet in San Diego. Masters.** What followed was all of the banking info for both Masters and Clark. What surprised me was that the Bo'sun had a bank account! Beyond recruiting a boatswain mate not much new information was in the email. I wondered: "What 'good news'?" That concluded recruiting a crew to steam and fight the ship. They just needed to get here...

This was a good time to check in with Gman. I punched 'call' on the one-number cell phone and got the usual, "Wait!"

Seconds drug by and finally Gman came on the line. "Kensey, glad you called. Report." He said rather brusquely.

"I am in San Diego, where is our yacht?" I said and continued, "I have a full crew recruited and am ready to take possession of our gem. When will you deliver it and where will we operate from?"

Gman sounded tentative and a bit annoyed. "I've been in perpetual meetings, and I had to call in a lot of favors, but I have an agreement to use the degaussing pier at Point Loma. The Navy and DOD were very reluctant. DEA and State aren't happy either. I hope all of the wrangling, arguing, ass kissing, and shit eating is worth it! There are a few conditions for using Point Loma. You can only operate at night. You must cover the guns at all times until you are in international waters. I had tarps rigged over the fo'c'sle and fantail so you are covered there. You can only practice flying beyond the damn twenty-mile limit. Oh, and the security at Point Loma wants pictures and clearances for you and your crew. I'll take care of that once you give me their names. I can get photos and security information from their old records." Gman said.

I gave him all the names and social security numbers, and informed him I would run out to Point Loma and inspect and familiarize myself with the area.

I had one more question. "Thanks Jim. I know how much trouble arranging all this is! Operating out of Point Loma is perfect. When do we take possession of our yacht?"

Gman hesitated then said, "She will be in the area late on the third. Is that soon enough?"

"Yes, that's perfect!" I replied.

"Loose lips sink ships, Kensey. Take care." Dead air followed.

This mission was on track. I knew approximately when we would take possession of our ship, and where we would dock her and the area I would use for sea trials. The next big hurdle would be getting to the Indian Ocean from here! I would need to contract a heavy lift barge or something similar. Jim would have to be involved. I was sure that would not make him happy . . .

I was in San Diego two days earlier than planned. I could see Horton Plaza from my room and thought I'd better pick up some new clothes and other essentials. San Diego Stadium was just a short walk from here. *"Oh well . . ."* I thought, *"Another time."* I could check and see if Greasey was here yet. I thought I'd buy him an authentic Mexican dinner at Cheuy's and bring him up to speed. I dialed Greasey to see if he was here or on his way. His phone rang and his voice mail picked up after four rings, "I have gone fishing. Be gone about three months. Call back." Greasey was not one for manners or pussy-footin' around. I the called the Navy Lodge and John Bishop hadn't checked in yet. He was probably in the air right then.

I was dog-tired, jet-lagged, and still on right-coast time. I went up to my room thinking about a power-nap. I was traveling very light. Tomorrow I would need to go shopping and then out to Point Loma…I woke from my ten-minute power nap a little before 2000. I felt rested but still somewhat punchy. I was hungry so my body, at least, was catching up to left-coast time. I hailed a cab to Chuey's and downed several Dos Equis and one of their mucho excellent dinners. I nearly dozed off on the way back to the hotel and was happy to see my room and its comfortable queen sized bed.

I rose early and opened several stores at Horton Plaza. I didn't spend more than an hour purchasing some khaki shirts, pants, socks, underwear, and renewing items in my spit-kit. I dropped everything off at the hotel and had the front desk call me a cab.

I had the cabbie drop me at the National Cemetery on Point Loma. A dear old friend, a retired Senior Chief Firecontrolman, passed away several years ago and I hadn't paid my respects. I located his grave, placed fresh flowers on it and then touched the marker and said, "So long Arf. . . fair winds and following seas. We may be tearing up heaven's 'Silver Bullet' together if things don't go right on this mission . . ." I saluted, executed a precise about-face and retraced my steps to the reception center. Along the way I thought, *"Sure could use you on this one . . .You knew everything about five-inch and 76mm guns and the Mk-92 fire control system and could 'grab the bull by the horns' and get things done."*

I hailed a cab that just dropped someone off and instructed the driver to take me to the degaussing pier. He wasn't happy; it was a mile or less down Point Loma. He dropped me off with a scowl and I approached the security guard, showed my retired ID, and entered the base. I used a base cab to get to the personnel office and spent the next several hours being shunted from one person to the next. I was finally directed to an office occupied by a little old gray haired lady. Her badge identified her as Gemma Grace: NCIS. She instantly reminded me of the old frontier woman who runs the only bar, Dirty Dicks, in Belmont, Nevada. I quickly looked around expecting to see the 'peacemaker' she always wore strapped to her hip. She looked at me as I entered and said, "Kensey, right? Been expecting you today. Our mutual friend, JB, sent me all the particulars for you and your crew. I have everything you require right here." She held out a manila folder filled with badges and passes. "These will allow you and your crew access to the base and pier without much hassle."

I took them and said, "Thanks. Why did it take forever to get to you? I've been here several hours wandering around and no one seems to know anything about anything!"

"Sorry, but there just wasn't time to notify 'everyone'... The word was late coming down from on-high. Quit your bitchin' Chief and get on with it. I'm busy." She said abruptly. Her abruptness startled me; I nodded acknowledgement and left.

This day was not a complete loss. I paid my respects to an old friend, reconnoitered the base and pier, cleared security hurdles, and found the one person, the little old lady in tennis shoes, who could get things done if needed. The gate guard called me a cab and I had him drop me off at Old Town for an early supper. I was weary but gaining on jet lag. I was back in my hotel room by 1630. I spent the evening updating the spreadsheet and making plans.

Other than it being April Fool's day, Friday was shaping up to be a day of rest. I Googled West Coast marine salvage and came up with 450,000 options . . . West Coast Marine Salvage Inc. of Los Angeles appeared to have the capabilities but was not interested in transporting a 133-foot ship to the Indian Ocean. I crossed them off the list and tried Global Diving and Salvage of Seattle; they didn't have the capabilities. Orion Marine Group of Tacoma had possibilities but it would be tomorrow before I could talk to their worldwide coordinator. Wilson Brothers Inc. out of San Francisco had heavy lift capabilities but didn't answer their phone. I gave them an asterisk and thought I might try later.

It was a beautiful day, I was feeling great, and decided down time was in order. I walked to the G street pier and had a two and a half hour lunch. I toured the Star of India then caught a bus to Sea World. I rounded the day out with dinner at Fuddruckers, returned to the hotel and called it quits.

Chapter 13
Crew Meeting

2 April at 1000 I dialed the Navy Lodge and asked the attendant to ring John Bishop's room. He picked up on the second ring. I told him I was at the San Diego Hotel downtown and had a few things to do and I would see him later in the afternoon. Greasey informed me that a reservation was waiting at the Lodge and I was all set and to check in as soon as I could. He had everything under control. It was so good to be working with Chiefs! I did not have to micro manage things. They could function on their own as long as they knew the goals.

I was antsy. I was rested and over jet-lag; it was time to get a move on it. I finished a decent turkey club, drank one last cup of English Breakfast tea, settled the bill, hailed a cab, and set out for the Navy Lodge at 32nd Street Naval Station.

I paid the cabbie and noticed the close proximity of the Chief's Club to the field event track. Anyone needing a workout could use the track and the rest of us could cheer them on from the Chief's club. I couldn't get that vision out of my mind as I approached the front desk. Before I could ask about Masters, a voice from behind hailed me. "Ahoy, Kensey over here!"

I did an about-face and found Greasey, Radisson, and Schmidt, standing together at the doorway to a meeting room just off the lobby.

"Let me check in and ditch the ditty bag and I will be right down. Good to see all of you. I see you met Simon Radisson, our ET." I said with enthusiasm.

"No problem. We're set up in the Cruiser Room. See you in ten." Greasey replied.

I checked in quickly, hurried to my room, threw my bag on the bed, used the head, then went below to join the others. As I walked into the Cruiser Room, I took stock of who was present. Seated around the table were Greasey, Fritz, Preacher, and Simon "Sparks" Radisson.

All eyes were on me and I said, "So good to see all of you. Hello Preacher. First order of business is coffee. We have any?"

Greasey went to the door stuck his head out and shouted "Coffee" to the desk clerk. He turned to me and said, "Taken care of Chief. If these feather merchants are on the ball it will be here in a minute." He beamed that sly grin of his.

"Thanks, Greasey. While we are waiting, I want to make sure everybody knows everybody else. I'll start with 'Sparks' Radisson. All of you meet our ET. He is an expert on the LN-66, communications, and MK 12 AIMS IFF. He has a good background in crypto and has kept up on modern satellite communications security. He can do all of the electronics on the ship but has no PHM experience. We'll have him stand on his head in a corner while foilborne. That should bring him up to speed."

"Yeah right!" was unanimous as was the mischievous all-knowing looks from those who had been flying on a PHM.

"Hey . . ." Greasey said, "Why does an ET have a Radioman's nick name?"

"Actually 'Sparky' is what you're thinking of." Sparks said. "I had a micro managing, first class supervisor, Dilly was his name . . ., and he was one! He always looked over my shoulder and I couldn't do anything right. I was adjusting a high voltage power supply and Dilly was right behind me. I could feel his breath on my neck. The ship took a roll, Dilly bumped into me, I got the shorting bar across the high voltage. When it flung me back I blacked both of Dilly's eyes and broke his nose! The guys said *'sparks'* flew from my fists! I'd been a radioman striker so the name instantly stuck and I haven't been able to shake it since . . . I have no idea how that handle followed me here . . . Kensey."

That had everyone's attention and I continued. "One of the things we got to teach him is standing watches on the bridge." There was a knock on the door and Greasey jumped up and took the tray from the waiter. On it was a full thermos pot of coffee, cups, milk, phony sugar packets, and stir sticks. No expense spared...

When all the cups were filled, I got back to business. "Most of us here know each other from the PHMs. Greasey, Preacher, Fritz, and I served together in PHMRON 2, the squadron out of Key West. Sparks served on Fast Freddies and Spru-cans. I also want

66

to tell you that I recruited Bill Masters, ex CO of the **Gemini**. He should be here tonight and he is bringing Boats Clark with him."

"No shit!" Greasey chimed in. "Masters is a fuck-up and skirt chaser. He landed himself in Leavenworth for doin' that shit! Why you bringing him in?"

"Forgive your brother's sins. If I can tolerate Masters so we can accomplish this devilishly hard job I expect every one of us can." I silently said a prayer for Preacher's insight.

"We need a PHM trained ship handler. He is the best one available. I have his word there will be no problems. I gave him my word that we would not ride him or cause him any grief. I expect to keep my word. Anyone wants out... Now is the time!"

"You still gonna be in charge or is Masters takin' over?" Greasey said in a low whiney voice.

"I am in charge. This is my mission, my ship, my orders. Period." I said.

After a few murmurs, furtive glances at Preacher, and silent and not so silent swear words, "You got it, Kensey. No problem!" Greasey said very quietly. The others all nodded in agreement.

The mood changed appreciably when Greasey said "No shit! You got Boats Clark. He's a hard man but the best Master Chief Boatswains Mate in the Navy. Sure won't be any nonsense with him around."

"God help me, the heathens are a comin' to get me. O' Lord, protect me from the sinners!" Preacher said with his palms together as if praying.

I saw the little smile on his face and so did Greasey. We knew Preacher. The others would have to get to know him.

"I know Boats Clark! We were shipmates for a short time on the **USS Stark FFG-31**, if it is the same Clark. He was president of the Chiefs mess. Hard man is right! No nonsense at all. Got to be the same man." Radisson exclaimed. "Who was or is Masters?"

I took the opportunity to bring some of those not in-the-know up to speed. "Masters was the CO of the **Gemini**. He was court marshaled then kicked out of the Navy for bangin' a young female storekeeper. He paid for it with time in Leavenworth. That's the last we hear of it or bring it up... OK?"

"Aye aye!" Came back to me as almost one voice.

"Enough of that shit, now on to the task at hand. The ship will be delivered here within the next few days. I don't have specifics yet but will let you know as soon as I can. Your jobs, until the ship gets here and we move aboard is to buy the provisions you want, get all your prescriptions filled, and any other personal business. I think we have about two days, maybe three at most before we move aboard. As it stands now we will operate out of Point Loma. That will keep us out of San Diego Harbor" I held up the manila envelope from 'grandma', dropped it on the table and continued. "Security Badges to get us on base and a vehicle pass are here. We need to keep a low profile. No one here wants to own us or acknowledge our presence! As for the ship, I want to take possession and board her at sea and then steam south for sea trials and refresher training. All of us have a few more years under our belts now so it will take a bit longer to get back in the swing of things. I want to be on our way soon. The more time we spend around here the easier it is to be detected. Any questions or comments?"

Greasey stood up and hesitatingly asked, "Is there any room for one more?"

I nodded and said, "It depends on who he is and if his skills are needed. I don't want just anybody. Everyone here has critical skills and any addition to the crew must fit that criteria."

"Well Kensey, I've been here a day or so and wanted to check out some of my old haunts. I went to my favorite taco stand and found it had a new owner. My old shipmate Chief Corpsman Sanchez. I couldn't believe my weary old eyes! He was assigned to the Squadron and qualified as a watch stander on *Taurus PHM-3*. I started shootin' the shit with him and playing the you remember so and so and what happened to blah blah? He mentioned that he wanted to open up his own high-class restaurant instead of the taco stand. I thought why the hell not? I figured I would talk to you first Kensey. Honest, I didn't spill the beans. When he asked why I was here, I kinda lied and said company business."

"Greasey, hope you didn't say too much but if he is a qualified watch stander and he is a chief and he is available. Yeah, go and get him. Bring him here if you can and I will have a word. I'm sure
68

I remember him and he was an OK guy. We used him as one of the translators whenever he rode the ships. He was pretty good at interrogations and helped us out a few times. Wish he was with us on 'Clean Sweep'. We might have come home with a few more men... Yeah a corpsman, or *Corps-Man* as our President says, would be good to have along."

Greasey got up and said, "On my way. It'll take about thirty minutes to get to Chula Wanna, pick him up, and get back here. You gonna wait?"

"Sure, in the mean time I'll give Gman a call and check the status of the ship." I said to no one in particular.

Greasey departed and the rest started telling 'this ain't no shit...' sea stories. I got on the cell phone and rang Gman.

He called back immediately and said, "The ship is going to be about three miles southwest of San Clemente Island. On the third of April at 2200. Be on the old fishing pier right next to the *USS Midway* museum complex at 0600. A charter boat called '*Lucky Lady*' will lie too and pick you up. The skipper will be expecting you and your crew. He will take you to the rendezvous. The ship will be put in the water when you get there and then she is all yours. Inspect her thoroughly! Some interesting equipment has been added since we last talked. Then take her into Point Loma. Do you have any questions?"

I repeated the instructions and told him we would steam four or five days before returning to Point Loma, and added a thanks! I hung up and turned to the crew and repeated most of what I just learned.

Fifteen minutes later, my personal cell phone rang. I was a bit surprised; I answered it, "Kensey."

"This is Bill Masters. Boats and I are in San Diego and will head straight over to the Lodge."

"Excellent! We are in the Cruiser Room right off the lobby. The rest of the crew is here so we will wait for you and Boats. And Bill, glad you could make it. Same for Clark." With that, I hung up. "That was Masters. He and Boats are on their way here. Hang tight until they get here."

A few minutes later Greasey returned with a Latino man in tow. He looked to be in his late 50s or early 60s, and had a relatively slight build. He couldn't have weighed more than 135 pounds. I was immediately jealous because he had all his rich black hair and it was perfectly coiffed.

Greasey introduced him, "Kensey, this is HMC, retired, Roberto Sanchez. We all called him José."

"Bob Kensey," I said shaking his hand, "I remember you from *Hercules*. You rode our ship as a translator and extra watch stander. Why do you want to join us?"

"I do not know where you are going, what you are going to do, or how you are going to do it but Greasey and I got to talking and he said a bunch of retired Chiefs are getting together for some fun in the sun. I'm retired, running a taco stand I don't much like, and Greasey said there is a possibility of earning a few off-the-books bucks. If this is, as I suspect, a throwback to the past where I can function as Chief again I want in! I saw the excitement in Greasey's eyes, and I see it in the others too. This could turn into a new lease on life for me. I get no fuckin' respect for being a street vendor! I want to be part of the action again not just a taco bender!" With his last statement, I could see his excitement and determination.

I mulled over José's qualifications for a moment then muttered more to me than anyone in particular… "We are all over sixty. Most of us on some kind of meds for ailments ranging from heart problems to diabetes. Might just be a good idea to have a pecker-checker aboard especially one who can stand bridge watches! OK. Fine with me Sanchez. Anybody object?" A few heads nodded up and down and a few said nothing or just aye. That cinched it. Sanchez was in.

"Welcome aboard José, can you be ready to leave by tomorrow morning?" I asked.

He smiled at me, lowered his eyes and said, "Amigo, I can be ready tonight if you want!"

"That won't be necessary," I said with a little smile on my face.

Greasey and Sanchez sat down and immediately joined in telling sea stories. Sparks and Fritz brought out an Acey-Ducey game, probably liberated from the Chief's Club, and started playing. A knock on the door startled me and a waiter with a huge plate of horse-cock sandwiches and potato chips, a tub of ice with

70

soft drinks and another pot of coffee entered. He placed everything on the table and started to leave. I thanked him and tipped him handsomely…

After the waiter left I asked, "Who is responsible for ordering chow?"

Greasey looked up and said, "Who the hell do you think? I did it."

José piped up, "What, no tortillas?"

Fritz couldn't leave well enough alone and took up where José left off. "Wo ist die affle strudel? Can't haff coffee mit out affle strudel. Dumkopf!"

Preacher said, "Grace…" and grabbed a couple pieces of bread and put a rather sizable ham sandwich together. That put an end to the ribbing and got Greasey off the hook. Everyone agreed a Bravo-Zulu was in order.

I announced, "Afternoon snacks are served."

The cold-cut plate was pretty much empty and our newest member, José, volunteered to refill the coffee pot when the door opened and Masters and Boats walked in. Those who know either Boats or Masters mumbled greetings while Greasey quietly ate the last of his sandwich.

Sanchez, on his way out the door, stopped, greeted and shook hands with Boats and Masters and said, "I can't seem to get away from serving people. I'm getting a refill on the coffee. Anything you guys want besides what's left of the horse-cock and bread?" Both men said what was left was fine with them.

This was my first meeting with Boats Clark. He was a large barrel-chested muscular man in his mid 60's. I sensed his leadership strength and Navy know-how. He carried himself with a palpable air of authority. There was no doubt that Boats was all Navy!

"Bob Kensey," I introduced myself to Boats. "Good to have you onboard. Going to need your expertise with hydrofoils. You joined the squadron after I left but I heard lot about you. You earned a good deal of respect and became somewhat of a legend in the Squadron. I'm more than happy to welcome you aboard and include you in this adventure."

In a gruff but pleasant voice Boats replied, "Heard a lot about you too Kensey. I am here to give you one-hundred percent. I don't know why the Navy tried to keel-haul you over 'Clean Sweep' but I know you fought **Hercules** very well under near impossible conditions then got her home after taking a beating. You're in charge *'Skipper'* and you can count on me to follow you into hell if need be. I've got your back, your deck , and I promise to keep all these over paid chiefs in line as an added bonus!" He finished with a wink and an impish grin.

"Boats and I got here as fast as we could. We miss anything important?" Masters asked.

I introduced everyone around to the newcomers. Boats remembered Sparks from his days on the **USS Stark** and Sanchez worked directly for him in the Squadron. It felt like a ships reunion. I quickly brought Masters and Boats up to speed and invited them to sit down.

José returned with fresh, hot, coffee and set the pot in the middle of the table and announced, "My taco-bending days are over; serve yourselves."

Everyone filled coffee cups while Masters and Boats built themselves sandwiches with the remaining cold cuts then sat down.

I rehearsed this scene in my head a thousand times. It was time to get everyone on the same page. Now was the time to inform them about mission details: where we were going, how we were going to get there, what we were going to do once we got there, and what the payoff was. I debated on telling them about the twenty-million. *(Play it by ear was the decision.)*

I stood up and said, "Listen up. Don't take notes. This is what we are going to do. This isn't a garden party and it sure isn't a cakewalk! Most of you have some details. If anyone doesn't want to take a lot of risks leave now before I fill in some of the missing pieces…" I paused and deliberately looked at each man one at a time. No one backed out or looked away.

I breathed in slowly and began. "A few days back I was approached by an old friend, DEA agent Jim Billings, Gman, whom most of you know and trust. Seems some raggedy assed pirates hijacked a private yacht off the coast of Somalia. The yacht was carrying a Mexican drug lord, Don Carlos Escobar, and a few

72

bodyguards along with a package that our government wants. Escobar was going to join forces and help finance an Al Qaida terrorist group. The DEA wants that package. CIA wants in on it to insure no compromising of any Mideast operations. CIA, DEA, State, and Justice have their hands tied.

The government can't go after a Mexican registered yacht and can't hire mercenaries because they are too traceable and untrustworthy. A lot of us here ran joint operations with Gman out of the Keys. He convinced Washington that a bunch of old chiefs could fly under the radar and get the job done. Nobody gives a shit about a bunch of old retired Chiefs drawing pensions! Jim contacted another old friend, someone high up in Boeing that lost a kid to illegal drugs. This person gave him a brand new Pegasus class hydrofoil! The PHM is outfitted with Mk 75, 76mm gun but harpoon has been removed. She has an LN-66 surface search radar, CAS fire control radar, stable element and laser compass, a complete comms package, and IFF suite installed. No crypto as far as I know. Of particular interest to Greasey and Fritz, the engines have all been upgraded and additional fuel tanks installed. Preacher you have some goodies too. You have a full magazine. You'll have to check the mix but I'm certain you have a bunch of HEPD and VT Frag, maybe even a star shell or two. I specifically said 'no' BL&P. I want every round to go boom and raise hell! You should have a good mix of small arms and a couple of M60s. Again, you'll have to inventory and report what you have. Our job is to get our ship to Somalia, seize as much Cartel information as possible and recover a 'package' for CIA and DEA. I assume that means documents…And now the interesting part. We are to destroy the yacht and if possible dispatch Carlos and as many of the pirates as we can… How we accomplish the mission is our responsibility. Are there any questions?"

"Whoa! Fuck me to tears!" José gasped.

"This is some picnic." Boats finished.

"Yea as I walk through the valley of the shadow…" Preacher started

"We will fear not 'cause we'll be the meanest mother fuckers in the valley with all that fire power!" Greasey finished.

"Jawohl" Was all Fritz could muster.

73

There was a pregnant pause then everyone started asking questions all at once.

I finally pointed to Sparks; he hadn't said much so far. Everyone else fell silent and Sparks spoke up.

"What are the comms on board? What radios? What about satellite comms? Do we have any long-haul capabilities?" He ticked important issues off on his fingers and finished with, "Any secure cell phones?"

"I really don't know, Sparks, have to wait and see. I did spot an HF whip so we will have MARS as a fallback. According to Gman, there is satellite communications. I asked for a satellite link to the internet. I'll bet it is available. I'd like to be on line the entire mission." I said.

"Dear Lord, how much ammo did you say?" Preacher asked.

"Full load out as far as I know. To me that is in excess of two hundred rounds. Not a lot but an ample supply." Greasey and Fritz were in an animated conversation and Sanchez moved over and joined them.

"I am risking my life and so far I've only seen about ten thousand. What else is in it for us, Kensey?" Greasey asked defiantly.

"Gentlemen. We have three million dollars on hand to complete this mission. Each of us has been retained with ten thousand except José and I will correct that later. All the money left after expenses are paid will be divided equally among crewmembers. In addition, I have an understanding with Gman. He said we could keep any and all money found on the yacht. He believes it is a substantial amount. My plan is to split whatever we find. If any one doesn't make it for any reason, his heirs get his share. Any objections? And that brings up an important decision. Who volunteers to be Suppo and Disbursing Clerk?"

I fully expected Greasy or Masters to speak up but I was greeted with complete silence. I hadn't fully thought this through so I just said, "Looks like I'm still on the hook. . . I'll think about collateral duties and let you know who's assigned to what after we take possession of the ship."

"Aye aye," was the consensus and we moved on to other items.

"How do you plan to get the ship to the IO?" Sanchez asked.

"I have feelers out for two, maybe three, outfits who have the capabilities to get us there, but nothing solid yet." I answered. Masters stood up and addressed me, "Could I offer a solution Kensey?"

I nodded. "Sure, go ahead. I have several plans in the works but I'm always open to ideas. Better ideas are even better!" I was surprised and curious.

"First, my family has a villa that they use as a vacation spot. It is located on the Isla de Cedros off the coast of Baja. It has a deep-water protected harbor and is away from all prying eyes. We can run the ship down there and use the transit time to run sea trials. On or about 5 April, a Wilson Brothers salvage ship, *'Scrap Dealer'*, will arrive in the area to conduct some family business. The Wilson's are willing to load our ship on deck, cover it, and transport it anywhere in the world. They are willing to lay-to and wait a few days for us to complete our job. When we finish, if we survive, we can rendezvous with *Scrap Dealer* and she'll load us back aboard to steam for home. *Scrap Dealer* has a fully equipped machine shop, and several JP5 tanks to keep us fueled. The only problem is Kensey, I promised the Wilson brothers two hundred thousand dollars up front and another three hundred thousand when we return to Isla de Cedros. The three hundred thousand will have to be on deposit somewhere in case they make it back and we don't…"

He looked straight into my eyes and I thought, *"This will work!"* One major hurdle was cleared. Half a million dollars to transport us there and back was steep for sixty or seventy days work but would get us half way around the world without raising too many questions.

"Masters… I think that will work. How trustworthy are the Wilson Brothers and their skipper and crew? Are they willing to stick around in pirate-infested waters like a sitting-duck and wait for us? Are they aware of the mission details I gave you?" If the answers to my barrage of questions was *'yes'* the Masters plan would become plan 'A'. It had merit.

"I spent some time sailing with Captain Jacob Shaw on *Scrap Dealer*. He's solid as a rock and unquestionably loyal to the Wilson Brothers. The Wilson Brothers pretty well owe their livelihood and 'lives' to the Masters and their villa. Villa is a little unassuming; it is more like a fortress. I trust them with my life. *Scrap Dealer* and crew can handle anything short of a pitched battle with war ships so a few pirates in zodiacs would be well advised to steer clear of them! They will wait for us until they know for sure we are not returning . . . I could keep you entertained with *Scrap Dealer* stories but the short answer, Kensey, is definitely 'yes'!" Masters ended with, "I think this is a good option."

"Give me a few minutes. I like this plan but I need to make sure Gman can cancel ours without stepping on toes." I already made up my mind. The call to Gman was a courtesy.

I stepped out of the Cruiser Room and called Gman. The noiseless connection engaged and Gman said, "Hold."

"Can't this time. I have alternate plan of action but will rendezvous with the barge on schedule. Call me for details." I broke the connection and reentered the Cruiser Room.

"We're a go on Masters' plan." I informed the crew. "Gman likes it, Masters. Thanks for the leg work. That really is good news. I can transfer the money to them if you have the banking information." I said.

"Figured that would be how you worked. Here are all the numbers you need. As soon as the money posts, *Scrap Dealer* will set course for Isla de Cedros. They need the money quick if *Scrap Dealer* is to arrive on time."

"I will transfer the money as soon as we are done here." I stated. It was time now for some mundane but necessary business. "Greasey, take the van you rented and load it with all the supplies, deliver it to the pier ready to load on *Lucky Lady* at 0600 tomorrow morning. Notify the rental company that their van will be at H&M Landing and we have no further use for it. Everyone else, get your shit ready, I want you all on the pier ready to sail by 0530. It is going to take about sixteen hours to get out to where Gman has the ship, so that means 2200 or thereabouts. We are going to make the transfer from *Lucky Lady* to the PHM in pitch-blackness. Tricky, but we can do it. Masters, can we provision the ship at Isla de Cedros?"

"Yes. My family has a well-armed villa. Stores and ammo

galore. *Scrap Dealer* will have fuel and fresh water, so I say no problem."

Greasey broke away from Fritz and approached me, deliberately turning his back towards Masters. "Do I gotta take orders from this guy?" He whined.

"Only when he is on the bridge," I said as gently as I could, "This ship only has one skipper. We already settled that!"

"OK... OK" He said curtly. That seemed to placate Greasey and set the tone. Masters wouldn't be a problem and Boats would soon insert his natural born authority to keep everyone in line.

Fritz who had been silent until now piped up, "Kensey, what about pubs on the PHM? I can't remember all of the operations and maintenance required. And do we have a name for this ship? PHM don't get it!"

"Good questions, Fritz. When I saw the ship at Boeing, it had all the pubs and MRCs on board. Looked like a full set of required tools, everything we need. I said it was ready to go and I meant it. We'll have to think about a name but right now this meeting of the *Goat Locker* is officially finished."

"*Goat Locker* is what we are and *Goat Locker* is what it should be." Boats stated.

"I christen thee '*Goat Locker*'. Preacher made it official.

Any more questions?" I asked. There were none so I said, "See you tomorrow on the pier at 0530. If you're not there you're not going." It took a while but soon the place was empty except for me. I left the Cruiser Room, closed the door, and thought, "Hope this isn't my final chapter..."

I went up to my room, logged into my bank account, and transferred the required funds to the Wilson Brothers Salvage Company, Inc. When that was completed, I called a cab. I decided to visit the Navy museum, have a good meal at Tom Ham's Light House and be in bed by 2200. Tomorrow would come soon enough. The one number cell phone chimed. That just had to be Gman.

"What the fuck Kensey? I was in a meeting with the movers and shakers when you called and I had to BS them about what's up... They went to a lot of trouble to get people on board with our plans. Your changes better be goddamn good!" Gman was pissed; his voice betrayed his agitation.

I had to placate him. "Sorry mate. I got the entire US government off the hook and needed to finalize details right then." I spent ten minutes going over the particulars and in the end Gman agreed this was a plan worthy of a pallet of San Magoos!

Chapter 14
Goat Locker

At precisely 0530 the entire crew was assembled on H&M Landing. To the best of my knowledge no one mentioned a dress code, but we did appear to be in uniform. Each of us retired Chiefs wore khaki chinos, khaki one or two pocket shirts, black socks and shoes, and a blue baseball cap. Most of the ball caps sported a fouled anchor with rating symbols. Preacher just had crossed cannons with a cross through the middle on his and Boats' hat had crossed anchors. I felt left out until Masters, dressed much the same except for brown shoes and an eagle on his cap, handed me a ball cap with a bar stool (range finder), on the front, scrambled eggs on the bill, and MFWIC blazoned across the back.

Before I could comment a grizzled old man with a limp and a filthy 'dixie-cup' hat approached our group and said, "I'm Skipper Dan of *Lucky Lady*; which one of you yahoos is Kensey?"

Greasey quipped, "MFWIC is beside you." Before I could answer.

I glared at Greasey, extended my hand to Skipper Dan and said, "I am."

He firmly shook my hand and uttered, "Better start loadin' your provisions and gear. I've cleared a spot for it. It's gonna take over sixteen hours to get to the rendezvous so let's get a move on."

I turned to the others, gestured to our things and said, "You heard the man, let's go."

Everyone picked up their gear and moved it to the *Lucky Lady*. After all personal gear was aboard, we loaded provisions. There wasn't an overabundance, but enough to last us a week at sea. I didn't think we would be underway for that long but it was better a penny wise than a pound short.

After all of our gear was on board and secured *Lucky Lady* steamed out of San Diego Harbor. As we cleared Point Loma then buoy 1-SD I couldn't help but remember the last time I left a safe harbor and headed for the unknown. I was sure that the others felt the same.

Our course was West by Northwest and we were running into quartering seas of ten to twelve feet. The California Coast was a soft blur on the horizon when Preacher and Sparks fed their breakfasts to the fish! Skipper Dan said he could give them the latitude and longitude if they wanted to pick it up on the way back. Seasickness would subside in a few days; in the mean time we would all need to regain our sea legs. Boats immediately started badgering Preacher and Sparks about shipping out with a boatload of feather-merchants and lard-asses. They took it in stride even though both were a green around the gills!

Sixteen hours later Skipper Dan said he had a radar contact four-thousand yards off our starboard bow. I stepped out of the pilothouse; it was pitch black with a few stars showing above the mist. I brought my lucky Mk1 Mod2 ten-by fifty TDT glasses, (A gift when I helped remove the last known TDTs still in action from the *USS Bainbridge*), to my eyes and searched an apparently empty sea. About two points off the starboard bow I could barely make out running lights. This had to be our tug pulling a heavy-lift seagoing barge. *Goat Locker* was nearly ours! Tension mounted as I pointed out the lights to the rest of the crew. Seasickness, aches, pains and other worries melted away in the darkness. Up until now, this adventure seemed like a lark: a bunch of old guys dreaming about fighting ships and being at sea. Now it was real and everyone was lost in his own thoughts and maybe regrets at signing on. Preacher was a bit aft of us, back turned and head bent down.

I walked aft, tapped him on the shoulder and said, "Say a prayer for all of us and ask Neptune to watch over us too."

"Amen Skipper. Praise the Lord and pass the ammunition!" Preacher whispered.

"Kensey I have the tug master on VHF. He has your yacht. Make your preps we'll be along side in ten or fifteen minutes." That was the signal from Skipper Dan to get the lead out.

Lucky Lady drew alongside the heavy-lift barge. Skipper Dan's First Mate shot a line across to waiting deck hands.

We maintained zero speed relative to the barge and waited a few minutes until all its speed bled off. Boats was in his element. In less than ten minutes he and the first mate had a high-line rigged and was transferring our supplies and personal effects to the barge. Their crew transferred our meager rations and personal gear somewhere under the tarps. I worried about the work lights. They lit up the barge and surrounding area like it was downtown San Diego! *Lucky Lady's* radar had given us a picture of the entire area out to about a hundred miles; no other sea craft, Navy ships, or any aircraft could be seen in the area. We were free to take possession of our ship.

A heavy-lift barge works by filling its ballast tanks with water, submerging deep enough to float off whatever is on deck. Cranes and wenches on the barge are used to maneuver the cargo and keep it under control until it is fully afloat. As the ship settled in the water, the thin Mylar-like coverings over the bow and stern were removed. We all stood stalk still and gazed at the beautiful ship bobbing in the sea tethered to the barge's port side. On close inspection, we could read the name painted on the bow: *Goat Locker*!

"Damn! Gman was good… It was less than twenty hours since I told him we named our ship *Goat Locker*. I told no one in particular.

The others crowded around and Masters uttered, "Beautiful. It's more than official now!"

Greasey said, "Yeah, I don't fucking believe it!"

Preacher kneeled and prayed aloud, "God bless *Goat Locker*. She be the finest ship in the world to go into harm's way. God, protect her and she will protect us!" Then he recited the Navy Hymn:

"Eternal Father, strong to save,
Whose arm hath bound the restless wave,
Who bidd'st the mighty ocean deep
Its own appointed limits keep;
Oh, hear us when we cry to Thee,
For those in peril on the sea!"

"Awesome," was all Sparks could say.

"Alright let's get a move on and finish transferring the gear and food to *Goat Locker*," Boats exclaimed and I could hear the pride in his voice. "Skipper you should be first aboard. I am sure there is something on there that you need to take care of. I will see to the rest. OK with you?" he added as an afterthought.

"All right, someone help Boats and finish this…UnRep. Greasey and Fritz go aboard and get the Ships Service Power Units and generators fired up then get main propulsion on line. Sparks you work with Masters and make sure we have comms and bridge controls. Preacher… Preacher! Quit standin' there with your mouth hangin' open. Help Boats and if he doesn't need you go check out those beauties on the fantail you're so infatuated with. You old farts take care and go slow. Remember you aren't young seaman and this is going to be hard work." I yelled.

We were in the lee of San Clemente Island. The sea was calm here and Skipper Dan instructed his crew to rig a series of large orange floats along *Lucky Lady's* starboard side. Thank God! I didn't look forward to a Bo'sun Chair ride to the barge. With the barge 'sunk' our main decks were about the same height and an easy jump even for old goats.

I jumped from *Lucky Lady* to the barge.

"Kensey? A man stepped out of the deckhouse and approached.

"Make it quick. I'm busy." I didn't have time for social meetings with the barge crew.

"I'm Richard Kopf. I'm here on Jim Billings' behalf. I'll be riding with you."

He extended his hand. The hackles on my neck stood up. I wasn't pleased but I shook his hand and stared hard at him. The thought that ran through my mind was Danger! Jim would have told me about this the very instant the decision was made to have a rep on board.

"I don't have time for you right now. Wait until Bo'sun Clark is ready to board *Goat Locker* then come aboard with him. He'll probably be the last off *Lucky Lady*. We'll talk later." With that said, I scrambled up a rope ladder to the main deck of *Goat Locker*.

Greasey and Fritz were close behind; both were giving me puzzled looks but neither asked the obvious question.

"Beats the fuck out of me. Worries me that a stranger shows up and wants to ride. I'll discuss this with Boats and Masters and we'll get to the bottom of who this pencil pushing, needle dick, interloper is and what he's after. We have work to do now. Let's

82

get to it!" That's all I needed: an unexplained crew member.

I turned on my flashlight and worked my way to combat while the other two went aft to the engineering spaces. Lying on the MK 92 console was a large sealed manila envelope. Written on the front in big, black, bold letters was, "For your eye's only Robert Kensey." I picked up the heavy envelope. *Goat Locker* shivered and shook a bit. She was coming alive! I opened the envelope and started to remove the contents when the lights flickered then came on steady. Greasey and Fritz made short work of that job. In the envelope was a letter, it read:

Kensey, if you are reading this you are aboard *Goat Locker*. Hope you like the quick paint job. This envelope contains the coordinates and latest satellite photos of the target area. So far, the target appears to be fully intact. We have a native in the village who is acting as our eyes and ears. If there is any change in the current situation I will contact you by secure SatCom installed in CIC. Radisson should have no problem getting it to work. I was very fortunate to pick up two 20mm chain guns and had them mounted where the Harpoon launchers were. Have your crew rig up twelve volt batteries to get them to work, just wasn't time. In the armory, are ten M16s, two M60s, three twelve-gauge pump shotguns, and ten M72 LAWS equipped with the new laser sight module, ten updated FIM-92G Stingers, along with several Glock 19 handguns and enough ammo to fight World War III! Pay very close attention to the small yellow paper stapled to this letter. Guard it with your life. The paper contains the communication codes for the SatCom and combinations to all of the Sergeant Greenleaf security locks and safes. Of particular importance is the location of the hidden compartment aboard the yacht and the combination to open it.

Good luck to you and your crew.

JB

I carefully removed the yellow paper and placed it in my wallet. I would find a good secure spot for it after I had a chance to get settled. I quickly perused the rest of the papers: Satellite photos of the target area, and exact coordinates of the target among other pieces of information.

"Absolutely no mention of Needledick...That's not good." I thought.

Greasey entered CIC and reported, "Fritz is standing watch in EOS. Fuel is hundred percent, fresh water hundred percent, and there are two huge fucking guns stuck on the fantail! As far as engineering is concerned all good to go! I sound like eight o'clock reports!"

"Aye Greasey. The guns are a gift from Gman. Could you go and help the others?"

He nodded and departed CIC. I went over to where classified data was stored on the PHMs. It took a few tries to open the Sergeant Greenleaf combination lock. I placed the folder in the heavy metal file cabinet, relocked it, and then I made a decision. I walked across CIC entered the magazine and opened the door to the armory. I selected a Glock 19, loaded the magazine with fifteen hollow points, inserted the clip, jacked a round into the chamber, set the safety, and started topside to organize stowage of supplies and gear.

Boats had things on deck well in hand. I'd been leery about high lining our chow and personal stuff to the barge but having the barge crew do all the heavy lifting and loading aboard *Goat Locker* was paying off now. Even so, the job of stowing everything took an hour or better. Old men don't move very fast...

I spotted Boats coming from the bow on the port side. He must have come aboard there and missed our 'guest' amidships.

"Boats, we have a major problem." I said in a whisper as I removed the Glock from my waistband and handed it to him. "There's fourteen in the magazine and one in the pipe." I pointed to the safety and said, "Remember, if it's red your dead!" His eyes suddenly got bigger as he tentatively took the gun.

"What's up Kensey?" He asked in a hushed voice.

"There is a guy who approached me on the barge. He said he was from Gman and was going to ride with us. I didn't get word of a 'supposed' rider from Jim. If he tries to board *Goat Locker*, you have my permission to put him in the water..."

Boats gave me that big grin and said, "Fuckin-A! He isn't coming aboard my ship!"

84

"Aye Boats and thanks." I said.

Masters called down from the bridge, "Skipper Dan is clear of the barge and bids us fair wind and following seas. The tug Master suggests we single up and prepare to back away from the barge so he can get some way on and get the barge under control."

"Aye make it so." I yelled up to the bridge and turned to Boats who was already taking charge of getting us under way. "I'll be on the bridge Boats. You need anyone besides José to handle lines? Did you have any trouble with the needledick I warned you about?"

"Negative on the help Skipper. I'll have us attached with the bow line only in about five. The jerk tried to board on the high line and I dropped him in the water. Last I saw was the barge crew laughing their asses off as they threw him a life jacket and line. If you go aft a bit they should be plucking him out of the sea about now." He gave José some instructions then headed for the bow.

I made my way to the bridge and found Masters and Sparks making final checks.

Sparks announced in a loud voice, "Skipper's on the bridge!" I told him that wasn't necessary but thanks.

I nodded to Masters and said, "You're on. Boats is gonna single up and leave the bow line attached. You need to swing us away from the barge and back out about two hundred yards so the tug master can get under way."

"Aye aye Skipper." Masters was already on the blower with EOS manned by Fritz and started issuing maneuvering orders. Sparks took the helm and strapped in. "On my mark port back slow....Mark! Helm hard starboard!" *Goat Locker's* stern slowly swung away from the barge. "Helm amidships port stop." Masters stepped out on the CAS deck and yelled down to Boats, "Release the bow line." And to EOS, "Both back slow." *Goat Locker* backed away at a perfect ninety-degree angle.

"Masters must be showing off... we have a steerable bow thruster." I thought.

At 200 yards from the tug and barge, Masters called all stop and turned to Sparks, "You've now officially completed your first helm and bridge training Sparks. Don't be so timid with that joystick. Hard starboard means 'full' right rudder. We are now going to settle on our southerly course. Fritz, all ahead one third. Helm come port and settle on course 180 degrees true." Sparks missed the course three or four times but *Goat Locker* finally was making six knots on a heading of 180 degrees true.

As soon as the tug and barge were well in our wake, Masters called down to EOS, "I've got throttles here Fritz. Is there any reason I can't bring the engines up to two thirds power?"

"Negative. And I'm gonna secure EOS if you are gonna stay hullborne." Came back immediately.

"Here let me show you a trick." Masters said to Sparks. He set the Hydrofoil Collision Avoidance and Tactical System (HYCATS) or autopilot to a heading of 205 degrees true and advanced the throttles until *Goat Locker* was making ten knots.

Boats entered from the starboard side and informed Sparks he could un-buckle from the helm. He only chuckled, gave Masters and me a stern look and said, "Sparks you don't have to strap in until we are flying…"

"We'll cruise hullborne for the next several hours, until sometime after sunrise before trying out the sticks. Everyone needs to get a few hours sleep before we put *Goat Locker* through her paces. I will get the LN-66, and MK 92 radars up for navigation and set up a watch bill for tonight and tomorrow morning. By then, we should all be rested and ready to fly." I said to Masters.

He replied with a slight grin on his face, "Sounds good to me. I would like Boats to tour the ship and make sure she is ready for sea. And Boats can you set Condition Yoke and get someone to make coffee? I can run the ship from here on autopilot but need someone in CIC to monitor the radars and Fritz or Greasey near the EOS. It's been a long day. We are about half way through the midwatch and first light is around 0630. We should have most everything sorted out by then and…Oh, who was the guy Boats dumped in the water?"

"He said he was from Jim and was going to ride with us. Nothing in any communications from Gman mentioned him. I don't like surprises."

Masters laughed and said, "Me either, Kensey. I know Gman and he sure as hell wouldn't send anybody without notifying you.

Security, I guess, is not what it should be."

"I agree. Well that's my problem. We'll have to wait and see. I'll inform Gman when I get a chance." I continued, "I'll get Sparks settled in CIC. Fritz can stay in EOS. I can relieve Sparks in six hours, and Greasey can relieve Fritz. Boats can relieve you but I want you on the bridge when we first go foilborne." With that, I left the bridge and made my way to combat with Sparks in tow.

I found José and Preacher standing in CIC, looking around, reacquainting themselves with ships gadgetry.

"Sparks, get CIC up and running. You got the first watch; I will relieve you in six hours. Preacher, get some sleep. You'll have plenty of time tomorrow to check out the gun and magazine." Aye aye was the only response.

I left and went to the crew quarters, found Greasey and Sanchez talking, butted in, and told them the watch schedule. Sanchez turned and left for the galley, Greasey departed for EOS to set steaming watches up with Fritz.

I was fortunate and the guys put all my gear in the Captain's cabin! Pretty good digs for a beat up old Chief! I felt a keen sense of ownership and responsibility that was almost overwhelming. It kind of took my breath away! Before I put the yellow piece of paper in the captain's safe, I copied the SatCom codes and took them to Sparks. He said he'd have it up and working in no time. While talking to Sparks, I felt the ship pick up speed and heel over slightly as she made a turn. We were underway, the watch was set, and **Goat Locker** purred, and gently pitched and rolled in a following sea.

"Happy Birthday Skipper!" Sparks greeted me as he prepared to assume the CIC watch.

"Thanks but my birthday is in November . . ."

"Oh I just assumed it was your special day. Gman sent this message." Sparks handed me a yellow teletype sheet.

Comms check:
4-05-2011 mega happy birthdays:
 Hope all is well:
Jim:

"Sparks is this all that came through? I don't see a date-time-group anywhere here. Are we sure it is actually from Gman and not some guy named Jim?" Sparks gave me a questioning look as I handed the message back to him.

"No . . . I'm not 100% certain Gman sent this but it did come in over the secure satellite link. You want me to file this or destroy it?" Sparks asked a little puzzled.

"Destroy it . . . On second thought file it. Call me paranoid but this doesn't feel right." I returned to the complexities of setting up a watch bill and dismissed Gman's, or Jim's, or whoever's cryptic birthday greeting.

Chapter 15
Sea Trials

Six hours later, there was a light knock on my cabin door and Sparks stuck his head in, "Rise and shine! Time to take over the watch."

"Give me ten minutes to shower and dress." I said wearily. He nodded and left. I arose, showered, and dressed. When I left my cabin I looked in on the bridge. Boats was the only one there and I asked him, "How's it going? Masters take a break?"

"Aye and all is well. We are heading south at about ten knots, kind of wasting time till everyone is rested and we can go foilborne." He said in a flat voice.

"Did you get any sleep?" I asked. He nodded his head in the affirmative.

I proceeded to CIC where Sparks was sitting in a chair next to the LN-66 repeater. I glanced at the scope and no contacts showed. I looked around combat and took it all in. A satisfied feeling overtook me. I was where I wanted to be. There was no question about it. I sat at the MK 92 WCP (Weapons Control Panel) and went through the procedure to get it running. I looked around for the Data Exchange Auxiliary Console (DEAC), the device used to load up the computer. I was mildly surprised to find the DEAC replacement, Shipboard Peripheral Replacement System (SPRS) instead. The SPRS was far easier and more reliable than the DECA. Next, I loaded the operational program into the UYK-7 computer and ran a DSOT, (Daily Systems Operability Test). It passed with no glitches. With those chores completed, I got up, walked over to Sparks, and said, "Report."

He looked at me, smiled and said, "LN-66 is up and running no problems. Comms plan is set and we are monitoring marine traffic and military frequencies. Nav and GPS are up and running. IFF up as far as I can tell with no mode four. SatCom codes input and link established. I found a couple laptops and a scrambler in the safe over there, booted them up, hooked up the scrambler, and connected to the internet. We have comms, we have radar, what more do you want?"

I laughed and said, "Bravo Zulu! I don't want anything more! Did you get any rest?"

"If you mean sleep, yeah, I catnapped all night and feel great. I'm ready to share combat with you and get to work. I am really lookin' forward to flying! New experience for me. I never been on one of these things before. Pretty exciting." He said with a big fat grin.

"Yeah great, can you take the watch a little longer? I want to go aft and check on Fritz and Greasey." I hoped one or both were rested. Flying after all these years was going to take some concentration...

"Aye. I don't see any radar contacts and everything else is pretty much running in auto."

I left combat and headed aft thru the galley. Sanchez had fresh brewed coffee ready. It smelled great and I grabbed a cup. A tray of eggs, bacon, and toast, was laid out on the mess table ready to be eaten.

I looked around and spotted José who nodded and said, "Go ahead and eat it. That breakfast was for you anyway." I dug in and finished in short order. I took my empty tray and silverware to the scullery and looked at José. He said he would take care of it. I continued aft to engineering. Greasey was monitoring the EOS and Fritz was asleep in the chair next to him.

"Ahoy, Greasey. Any problems?" I called as I entered the cramped space.

"Mornin' Kensey. Not a fuckin' thing! It's working so well I ain't got nothin' to do but watch these dials. Looks like they really filled her up with JP-5 because we have used only about two percent in the last six hours of running on the diesels. Fritz has been asleep for the last couple of hours and I got some good sleep last night. José made breakfast for everybody and we all ate. Masters came off the bridge and hit the rack in officer country. I might change my mind about him... Don't know yet."

"No problems are a good thing, Greasey. And don't worry about Masters. He will probably save our ass when the shooting starts! We're going to bring her up on the sticks soon. You ready?" I asked.

"Yeah, Aye aye we are ready!" Greasey said with enthusiasm.

I retraced my path back to combat. As I entered, Preacher stood up and greeted me. He looked a little ragged around the edges but ready for action.

He said, "God bless you Kensey. I sure am surprised! That magazine is filled with HEPD (High Explosive Point Detonating) and VT Frag, (Variable Time Fragmentary) rounds. Both rings and magazine are filled to capacity with over three hundred rounds! The armory is loaded with M16s, shotguns, 9mm side arms, a couple of M60s, at least ten LAWS, ten Stingers, and boxes and boxes of 20mm rounds stacked to the overhead. There's enough small arms ammo to open our own Cabala's and I've examined the two 20s on the fantail. They need electrical power but that should be an easy job. We going to war with a small country or what? We got enough ammo to hold off an entire navy!"

"Good. We'll need it. I want to make sure you can still handle the main battery. When we go on the sticks, I want to fire a couple of rounds to test out the systems. You ready?"

He smiled put his hands together as if he was praying and said, "You want to make an old decrepit gunners mate happy? Just let me shoot. I be ready!" He did an about face and hurried out of CIC on his way to the magazine.

I asked Sparks to send a secure message to Gman. I handed him a message form I had prepared:

JB
  Approached on barge by a Richard Kopf.
  He said he was your rep.
  He requested to ride GL.
  Denied request.
Kopf dumped in water.
Kopf not aboard GL.
Did you send him?
If not we may have a security breach.
K.
Sparks said, "No sweat. I'll get this baby out right now."
I thanked him and went over to the WCP, took out the pubs, and

started to refresh my memory. It had been a long time since I operated a fire control system. I ran some basic tests on the Mk 92 system. All was in working order. I put the 'egg', (Combined Antenna System or CAS) through its paces. No surface or air targets showed on any display. The sea and sky around us was empty.

0930 4 April and everyone was up and about. Masters was on the bridge and Boats huffed into combat with a sour expression on his face, looked around, then spit out, "What dick head brought that fuckin' pink apron with crossed anchors on the front aboard? When I find the cross-eyed fucker, I'll have him holy-stonin' the superstructure! I'll be inspecting this bucket for anymore surprises if anyone needs me" He glared at me and quickly left combat.

Sparks could hardly contain himself and laughed out loud. It was contagious. I started laughing and managed to say, "Beats the shit out of me."

"Gman strikes." I thought to myself. *"I'll have to get even... Fuck no... Ahead!"*

Everyone was rearing to go. Most had eaten, showered, shaved, shit, and shined. José cleaned the galley, washed all the dishes, refreshed the coffee, and delivered some to Masters on the bridge. I checked with Masters via the headsets and asked him if he was ready to go foilborne.

"Not yet. Came back then he clarified with, "I would like to wait until we change course to 090 true in about an hour. That will be our final course correction before we make our run into the Fortress.

"Make it so." I agreed.

An hour was perfect. That gave me time to work out who would be where, doing what, 'before' we went on the sticks.

Boats would be on the bridge as Officer of the Deck, or Conning Officer on PHMs, José would be helmsman, and Masters would be on the bridge, give maneuvering orders and be acting "Captain." Greasey and Fritz would man the EOS, Sparks and I would be in combat. Preacher would man the gun and be ready to reload the ready service rings.

I couldn't help myself. I picked up the General Announcing

System, whistled the best bo'sun pipe imitation I could and said, "Now hear this. Now hear this, all hands 'flying stations' are:" I read the assignments I'd just finalized.

Masters called down from the bridge and asked if everyone was in place. I checked with Boats to make sure the deck was secure. He assured me it was. That left nothing to do but watch our Nav-Plot and wait for Masters to verify we reached the waypoint. Sparks and I were strapped in our chairs keeping an eye out for ships or aircraft.

I felt the ship make a 90 degree turn to port.

Boats came over the headsets with pre-flight orders, "Configure for flight."

José answered, "Configure for flight, Aye" And turned on the Automatic Control System (ACS).

So far so good. We were all functioning as a team like we never left this life. All of the commands and actions came flooding back. I am sure each one of us had in his mind a picture of every action and how the ship and crew would respond. Sparks was sportin' the biggest shit-eatin' grin I'd ever seen! The bridge team was in full swing now. I could hear the back and forth staccato of commands and acknowledgements.

José, "We have a green Ready for Flight illuminated."

Boats, "Very well. Set foilborne engine to 80%. All engines stop."

José, "Engines answer back foileborne engine to 80%. All engines stop."

Boats, "Very well. EOS Bridge. Transfer throttle control of hullborne engines from the Pilothouse to EOS. Should show transfer available." At this point José flipped the toggle switch for transferring hullborne engine control to EOS.

Greasey, "Show transfer available." After a few seconds, "EOS has throttle control."

Boats, "Very well. De-clutch port and starboard hullborne engines and secure after cool-down." Greasey repeated the command to confirm engineering got it.

Boats, using the General Announcing System announced, "All hands stand by for foilborne operations. I have secured the main deck. No one will be allowed on the main deck without my

93

permission." Addressing José he ordered, "Advance foilborne throttle to 100%."

I could feel the speed climbing, and the ship pounding through the waves. The ride would be bumpy until she hit thirty knots: Take off speed!

Boats, "Set depth to 2.2 meters, and raise the ship."

José, "Depth set 2.2 meters."

I felt the ship rise straight up knowing that the hull was now about eight feet above the water.

José, "Ship is foilborne. Time 1220."

Boats, "Very well. Left 3 degrees per second. Steady on course 090." After a few seconds, "Retard foilborne throttle to 95%." That gave **Goat Locker** a cruise speed of 50 knots.

We were flying! I checked for surface or air contacts and reported all clear.

I called the bridge, "Bridge, Combat: request permission to go hot with main battery. I intend to fire two rounds from WCP."

"Combat, bridge: Verify the area is clear of surface contacts and commence fire. We will be in international waters for approximately 45 minutes."

"Gun control, Combat: I have set target GPS coordinates into the computer, selected shore bombardment mode, entered High Explosive Point Detonate rounds into the FCS, and am ready to commence fire." I said over the headsets to Preacher.

"Combat, Gun control, ready when you are." He answered.

I made one final check, "Bridge, Combat: Is Otto pissing?"

Boats laughed and reported, "Aye, and makin' a fine mess of my deck!"

I assigned the gun to the target and saw it line up. I set salvo into the gun control and pushed the fire button on the WCP. There was an immediate response as two rounds fired. The recoil slightly jarred the ship and the gun's report was loud.

A few seconds later two distinct explosions could be heard and Preacher said, "Two rounds expended, bore clear, no casualties, magazine rotated into re-load position."

The main battery worked to perfection. With a little drilling and a few more live firings, we could handle a skirmish.

After five hours of foilborne operation, we were all tired and hungry. We could get up and use the head as long as the bridge wasn't maneuvering wildly around but flying on a relatively straight course. I requested that we resume hullborne operation in order to feed everyone and allow some rack time. The fortress was a little more than an hour out: we were within 15 miles. I could see the island on radar. Masters agreed and we followed procedures to return us to hullborne steaming. Boats and José came down from the bridge and headed for the galley. Masters stayed on the bridge with *Goat Locker* on autopilot and cruising at about 10 knots. Sparks said he would stay on watch and keep an eye on radar. I departed for the galley, but made my first stop the bridge to talk to Masters.

"How did we do, Bill?" I asked.

"Not bad for a bunch of old farts who don't do this all the time! I was really surprised how well it went. No fumbling for switches, no repeat of orders, no mistakes. I guess you old Chiefs know what you are doing." The left hand compliment was a welcome change from what officers, ex-officers, usually thought of us Chiefs…

"Thanks," I replied "Things come back; memories return. We can't move as quickly as we used to but we can get things done. Right now, we all need some chow. José put something together and made fresh coffee. I'll send a plate up for you. Next time we go on the sticks, let's change some stations around so everyone gets up to speed on the bridge. I would like Sparks and Preacher to stand at least one underway bridge watch. Preacher is a qualified watch stander but Sparks isn't. Might pose a problem later but I hope not."

"Sure." Was all Masters said.

"There is one more thing I need to talk to you about. There are two new 20mm guns on the fantail instead of Harpoon launchers. We only have to man them during a firefight. Any ideas?"

"Possibly but we will have to wait until we dock at the villa." I left the bridge with Masters deep in thought.

I made a beeline for the galley. When I got there, Greasey and José were in a hot Acey-Ducey game and Boats and Preacher were sitting, drinking coffee while telling sea-stories. I peeked into the galley to see what, if anything was cooking. A good sized spread was laid out ready to be served.

"Who did all this cooking?" I asked.

José said, "I had it all prepared before we went flying. I just had to heat it up. You guys hungry?"

"YES!" echoed off the bulkheads in one big voice.

I asked Boats if he would take some food and fresh coffee to the bridge for Masters. Preacher and Greasey did the same for Sparks and Fritz. I sat down, and started to eat; José took a seat opposite me.

He acted as if he had something to say, "What's on your mind José? Spit it out."

"I like cooking; this is a fine galley. I like the bridge too: did I do alright today?" He asked with a questioning look.

"You did fine. Masters said he was surprised there were no mistakes since we've all been away from this for so long. You cook as if you own a restaurant. The food is great! Don't worry."

"Something must be buggin' him." I thought.

I finished my burrito and returned to CIC. I checked the LN-66 repeater and noted we were about seven miles out from the island. A quick check of the message board showed no new traffic. No news meant no change in mission parameters. We would hear from Gman if the situation altered. I made a cursory inspection of the main deck, and stopped at the bow for some fresh air and to look around. Since we were hullborne, there wasn't much headwind. It was quite comfortable standing on the bow looking at the Island and mainland in the mist behind it. It felt like old times. I didn't stay long even though the prow cutting through the waves was hypnotizing. I needed to start preparing to enter port.

I'd just stepped into combat when Masters keyed the general announcing system and said, "Make all preparations to enter port and moor port side to."

Boats came from the galley on his way to the bow. As he exited, he yelled for Preacher and José to help man the mooring lines. It would be twenty minutes before we moored. I returned topside to observe. Masters placed **Goat Locker** right alongside the pier: slick as a whistle! No wonder they called him 'The Ship Handler'.

Several armed men were milling about on the pier but they displayed no aggression just intense interest in our arrival. No doubt, they were expecting us. Boats and his deck hands made short work of securing us to the pier. He lowered the port brow. I stood back out of the way and watched the activity. I felt the diesels shut down and Greasey came out on deck. Sparks shut off the LN-66. I'd have to shut down the Mk 92 system in a while.

I stuck my head into CIC and told Sparks to send this message to Gman. "Tweet... Moored." I hoped that would get him scratching his head. He deserved it. I considered it pay back for the birthday message.

"I waited for Masters to come down from the bridge. When he arrived, I said, "Looks like you haven't lost it!"

Masters said, "Thanks. All in a day's work. The men on the pier are part of the families' security force. There are about twenty permanent men here at the Fortress. They will guard the ship while we all go on up to the house for the night. We will rendezvous with *Scrap Dealer* tomorrow at noon. We have to be under way by 0900 at the latest. OK with you Kensey?"

"Sounds good to me. Can you set the security watch while I shut-down the Mk 92 and secure CIC?" I asked.

"Aye, aye" he said while departing *Goat Locker*. Masters was approached by a large man. The man wrapped his arms around him, bear hugged him, and I could see tears in his eyes. They chatted a few minutes and then Masters waved for us to join him on the pier. I looked around. The entire crew was standing on the deck waiting for instructions.

I yelled, "Wait a minute." I ran into CIC and secured the Mk 92 then went back out on deck.

I motioned Greasey over and asked him to secure the Ships Service Power units and generators.

He turned and hollered to Fritz to secure the equipment. Fritz popped to attention, clicked his heels together, and shot his arm out in a Nazi type salute and shouted, "Jawohl!"

Five minutes later Fritz returned and reported, "der Bigen mudderfukken machinens ist putten zu bet Herr MFWICEN!"

Everyone except Greasey was chuckling as we departed the ship single file down the brow. We followed Masters to a parked van that took us to a huge fortress style house. The Masters' 'villa' looked like an English twelfth century castle minus the moat. A large wall surrounded it with gun emplacements on corner turrets. This house was well defended. It would take a division of marines to successfully invade it.

As we approached the front door, a heavy set, elderly, Mexican woman came running out and grabbed and hugged Masters. She spoke to him in Spanish through her tears. She was obviously happy to see him. She retraced her steps and led us all into the house.

Masters said loud enough for us to hear, "Mamma Maria. It is so good to see you. As you can see I have brought the guests to the villa. Is everything in order?"

She took us all in her gaze and with a large, wide smile said, "Si. It is so good to see you and your friends. All has been prepared as you asked. Javier will take care of you while I go and see to dinner!" With that, she gave Masters another big hug, kissed him on the cheek and then departed to the interior of the villa.

Once inside, we were approached by Javier, who I assumed was the butler, with a large tray of ice-cold Dos Equis beer. With the much-appreciated refreshments in hand, Masters led us into a large room lined with bookshelves filled with hardbound books.

Chapter 16
The Fortress

"Welcome to my Father's library. Please sit where you want and enjoy the cervesa. I was informed dinner would be ready soon but until then enjoy." Masters said, and then he continued, "I spent a lot of time here in my youth between school and vacations. When I was growing up the family would fly down here and spend the entire summer fishing and enjoying the sun. This is where I learned to sail and handle boats. I could go from here to San Francisco, Los Angeles, San Diego, or south to Cabo. We had all kinds of sea craft, both sail and powered. My favorite was a three-masted schooner called *'Pure Joy'*. I used to sail her during summer break from high school down to the South Pacific and relive the old TV series *'Adventures in Paradise'*. My father had an old Navy Captain to tutor me in the fine art of sailing. Gramps had a salvaged WW II PT boat for a while and I ran that thing at full throttle all over this patch of Pacific. That naturally led me to the Academy and a career in the Navy. When I was in the Academy, Dad would fly me down in a private jet every leave. Right behind the house is an airfield and a hanger with at least one Lear jet. We didn't need a security force until the drug cartels started getting too big and rich. They looked to take over this island, but Dad drove them off and killed quite a few. From what I understand and remember, it was one hell of a fight! Now we have to have a permanent force, well armed and ready to fight to keep it. There is radar and sonar buoys all around so it is almost impossible to approach without being detected. We can all get a good night's sleep tonight."

He took a long pull on his beer. The guys sat there and listened, obviously interested in what he had to say.

"If you don't mind me asking, how did your family create the wealth?" I asked very tentatively so as not to offend Masters.

"No I don't mind at all. My grandfather was a contemporary of Joe Kennedy. Gramps was a very good bootlegger, gunrunner, and drug dealer before it was popular. Drugs were somewhat legal back then and morphine was usually the drug of choice. He was exceptional at turning a profit. During the Depression, he was making more money than Capone or Kennedy! By keeping a low profile, he was able to run his businesses without interference from the mob or the government. After Gramps died, my father converted most of the money into legitimate businesses. He invested vast sums in war material production during WW II, Korea, and Viet Nam. He was interested in high tech companies and invested heavily into computer companies. Dad had a knack for seeing the 'Next Big Thing' and was always in on the beginning and out before it collapsed or became commonplace. For instance, he was the main investor in *'Phoenix Software Associates'* and financed the Clean Room approach. Out of this, came Phoenix Bios and the ability to run and make IBM PC clones. That's one example and there are many, many more. Time and time again, flying low and keeping out of the public eye made his ventures profitable. Dad passed away a few years ago, and Mother lives the good life in the South of France. He was going to turn the business over to me as soon as I retired from the Navy, but as you know, I had a little problem. Instead, while I was in Leavenworth, my brother took over and I was disinherited. I was an embarrassment to the family and deserved it. I have no hard feelings at all. It was my own damn fault."

This was a long speech for Masters. It was rather revealing and I appreciated him telling us this story. For once, Greasey didn't make a comment, Boats drank his beer quietly, Fritz stared at the floor, and Preacher studied the bookcases. No one wanted to say anything. We were saved by the butler announcing dinner was ready. That broke the tension. We followed the butler down a long portrait lined hallway to the dining room. The table was heaped with food. When José saw it, he almost started to cry. Every food Mexico is famous for was on that table, along with many pitchers of cold beer.

"Help yourself and dig in!" Masters said.

He did not have to say it twice. Everyone grabbed plates and started selecting what they wanted.   We ate heartily and for the most part in silence. After dinner, we returned to the library and ended the evening with a snifter of fifty-year-old Napoleon brandy. During the general chatter, Masters asked me and José to accompany him to another room.

"Sure, but why?" I asked.

"I need José for translation. My Spanish is very rusty and I want to talk to two of the security forces while you are present. They have volunteered to go with us to help fight and man the 20mms." Masters said.

"You got me interested. OK with you, José?" He nodded yes and we rose to leave.

"You guys wait here, and if all goes well, I will bring back two volunteers for you to meet." I said. "Any comments?"

Greasey and Fritz waived a hand and Sparks shook his head.

Preacher nodded in the affirmative so hard I thought he would sprain his neck and said, "Bless you. Go for it!"

I knew he could use help loading the gun when we engaged shore targets. The three of us left the library and entered a door down the hall. We walked into a huge office containing a large desk made of a dark cocobolo. The desk alone probably cost more than my apartment! The wall behind the desk contained an outsized window framed by several file cabinets. A large, fully stocked bar was on the left and bookshelves lined the wall on the right. Two men dressed in security guard's lightweight blue uniforms sat in front of the desk.

"Kensey, Sanchez, I would like you to meet Manuel and Jorge Gonzales. These brothers have been with the family for over forty years. My father insisted that I have bodyguards. They have expressed a desire to accompany me like old times. They don't have any idea what we are going to do or where but they want to go and protect me. We played together as kids on the island and they accompanied me as crew members on many an excursion in the vast Pacific." As Masters said this, we moved into the office, he motioned for me to sit at the desk, and José moved to the opposite side of Masters.

I acknowledged Masters and said, "You two want to come with us, yes?"

"Si, Mister Kensey." The taller of the two said. "We want to help. I speak for my brother; we want to protect Mister Masters. I am sure he will pay us well and we can be of great help to you!" He spoke very good English and I wondered why Masters asked

José to be there.

"We are going to a place, fight the ship, and possibly get killed. Does that bother you at all?" I said in the sternest voice I could muster.

"We understand. We still want to go and be with Mister Masters." The tall one replied.

I glanced at José and he dipped his head which I took as affirmative, "Which one are you?" I asked the tall one.

"I am Jorge and I am the oldest, so I make the decisions. Can we go with Mister Masters?" He pleaded.

"If it is all right with the rest of the guys, I don't see why not. We sure could use the extra hands, especially on the 20mms and 76mm magazine. José, what do you think?"

"Fine with me." Was all he said.

I looked at Masters and he kept a blank face but his eyes were laughing and I could tell he was satisfied. I told José to take the two brothers and introduce them to the rest of the crew.

After they left with José, I said to Masters, "I know I can trust them and we need the extra hands. The foilborne operation today, was it today, seems like an eternity ago, demonstrated that we needed extra crewmembers. Bill thanks. I know you had a lot to do with recruiting the brothers and I am sure they will get up to speed fast."

"I know they will. They were my closest friends growing up on the island. Their father was a local fisherman on the mainland and when he died my dad brought the brothers and their mother here. She was the lady that greeted us when we arrived. Maria took care of me and my brother like a Nanny along with her two boys. My brother wasn't as close to Jorge and Manuel as I was partially because of all the time spent together at sea. That made it a lot easier to recruit them. Shall we join the others?"

We left the office and returned to the library. When we entered, the whole crew was sitting together and talking as if they were all old friends. Jorge and Manuel were made to feel like accepted members of the crew. Preacher was gesticulating and demonstrating as best he could how to load rounds in the magazine rings. I could tell that the two new guys had no idea what Preacher was trying to show them.

102

I walked over, put my hand on Jorge's shoulder, and told him, "Don't worry, plenty of time tomorrow to show you."

He smiled at me and resumed listening to Preacher. I checked my watch and said, "It is getting late, everyone hit the sack. Be ready for breakfast at 0700. We are underway at 0900."

"There are rooms made up for us. Toiletries, clean sheets, and towels are in the rooms. Put your soiled clothes outside your door and they will be laundered and returned by 0600." Masters said.

A butler appeared as if by magic and said, "Please follow." He led us, with the exception of Masters, upstairs and pointed to a long hallway.

"Your rooms are down this hall. Names are on the door. If you need anything, there is a pull chord inside the room, pull it to summon me."

We said OK and headed down the hall. On the first door we encountered, the nametag said **KENSEY** in bold letters. I opened the door and entered a very large and pleasing bedroom. The bedroom contained a double-sized bed, four drawer dresser, and nightstand with a lamp and alarm clock. The head was off to the left and on the right was a closet. *"Very comfortable indeed."* I thought. I undressed, put my soiled clothes in the hall and hit the rack, set the alarm for 0600 and I fell asleep immediately.

After breakfast, we departed the house and returned to the pier and *Goat Locker*. Nothing untoward had occurred during the night. She was as secure as when we left. I thanked the guards, told Greasey and Fritz to get power up and ready to get underway at 0900 on the dot. Several minutes later, we had lighting and ship's service power. I lit off the MK 92, loaded the computer, and ran self-checks. Sparks did the same for the LN-66. Sparks also lit off all the comms, booted up PCs and SatCom. After all was up and running, Sparks called me.

"Hey Kensey," he shouted across combat, "We have a message from Gman," and he handed me a piece of paper. The message read:

Goat Locker:
Regarding your ride-along: I did not send Richard Kopf.
Cartel in negotiation with pirates for release of yacht.
Need to proceed with most haste.

Believe package has not been compromised.
Yacht still at anchorage.
Will inform you of any changes.
JB.

That was all it said. Of course, that put more emphasis on us getting to the IO. I took the message up to the bridge and showed it to Boats and Masters. They both nodded and said very little. I left the bridge, stopped in the crew's mess then continued on to the magazine. I found Preacher showing Jorge and Manuel how to load projectiles into the outer rotating ring.

I eavesdropped and heard, "Mister Meechum, I see all of the rounds along the bulkhead, is that where I get the rounds to reload?" I left before Preacher answered because I knew it would be like a sermon. I stopped at the athwart ships passageway on my way to CIC. Boats went by to get the mooring lines in. As he passed, he yelled for Preacher and Sparks to get their asses out on deck to get the brow up and lines aboard.

Chapter 17
A Little Skirmish

0831: I was on the fantail watching us get underway. Boats had lines singled up and a security guard on the pier was ready to cast them off from the bollards. Masters finished his preps and just announced, "Cast off all mooring lines!" over the General Announcing System.

The last line was aboard and *Goat Locker's* stern slowly swung away from the pier. A security guard came running down the pier, wildly waving his arms, yelling something.

Masters, standing at the port bridge window, got on the bullhorn and yelled down to Boats. "We are going to moor back up to the pier." He maneuvered *Goat Locker* back alongside.

Boats scrambled on deck, uttering unflattering platitudes to no one particular but still in control. "José! Quit skylarking' and help with this fuckin' Chinese-Fire-Drill. Get that messenger secured to the mooring line and heave that monkey-fist on the pier so that guy standin' by the bollard can pull it over!"

Once secured to the pier, Boats lowered the brow. The security guard, speaking rapid fire Spanish, proceeded aboard before the brow was even secured.

"What's so urgent?" I asked him when he stepped aboard.

"Señor Masters por favor." He managed to say. He was out of breath and flustered.

I don't speak Spanish but I knew what he wanted. José was standing by the aft line. I motioned for him to come over and translate. Masters was already on his way down from the bridge. In a few seconds, Masters was standing conversing with the security guard in rapid Spanish.

The conversation was short and to the point even though its content was Greek to me...

Masters turned to me and said "Looks like we are going to have company. Our island radar picked up several small craft from the mainland heading this way. Our coastal watch seems to think that the boats are from the local drug cartel. They are moving too fast for fisherman or charter boats. He said there has been an increase in radio chatter since **Goat Locker** arrived. I think this might be a good time to either shit-and-git or stay and fight. If it were up to me Kensey, I would take **Goat Locker** out and swing north. Fly for a few miles, turn 180 degrees, and hit them on the flank... only going to take one or two hits from the 76mm to discourage them." I mulled everything over and said, "What if they are not armed? Do we have any proof they are druggies? Could they possibly be Mexican Coastal Authorities?"

"Not a chance. Mexico doesn't have an effective coast guard and certainly not down here. If they were official, our coastal watchers would have recognized the boats. It won't take much to find out if they are armed. Let's make a high-speed pass and see if they shoot at us. If they do, you and Preacher can take them out. Jorge and Manuel need training and Preacher loves to shoot." He said with a laugh.

I thought the whole thing over and came to a quick decision, "Masters we need to deal with this situation but we need to know if they are armed and hostile **before** we blow them out of the water. At any rate, we need to decide before we rendezvous with **Scrap Dealer**. We can't have armed boats harassing us during the loading operation. No need for stealth. They know we are here. We should see them on radar when you round the northern end of the island. We'll plot a CPA, (Closest Point of Approach), of about 300 yards and see what they do. I'll take care of CIC. You and Boats can handle the bridge; Sanchez can translate for Preacher. Let's get underway as fast as possible. If they are hostile we'll introduce them to Davy Jones."

"Thanks! General quarters and get this ship underway and flying!" He said and quickly returned to the bridge.

"Now hear this! Now hear this! The following is a test of the general alarm from the bridge." Erupted from the General Announcing System followed by, "**Bong! Bong! Bong**! All hands man your Battle Stations! All hands man your battle Stations."

That got everyone's attention . . .

Boats hurriedly issued orders to José and bellowed at the security guard on the pier to cast off lines. He started to pull up and stow the brow with the messenger still on it. Before the messenger could pick himself up from his tumble onto the dock

106

Boats had all the mooring lines aboard and *Goat Locker* was backing away from the pier. Boats scrambled to the bridge. José was on his way to the galley. I stopped him and told him to round up Manuel and Jorge and report to Preacher in the main battery rotating machinery room/magazine.

I took up station in CIC as *Goat Locker* moved out of the harbor. Sparks started checking message traffic and I lit off the MK 92 and ran self-checks. I felt the ship heel hard to starboard.

"This is not a drill! This is not a drill! General Quarters, General Quarters all hands man your battle stations. *BONG! BONG! BONG!"* Blared from the General Announcing System speakers.

We should have been forewarned by a trill from the Bo'sun's pipe. We didn't have one onboard. I reminded myself to remedy that!

We cleared the harbor and commenced flying north at 42 knots. Jorge and Manuel were frozen in place holding on for dear life. Their eyes bugged out and faces were pale. Preacher and José led them to the magazine, José calming them in Spanish all the way.

Masters flew several miles north of the island then turned east and followed the coastline. It wasn't long before we could see the formation of four small crafts on the LN-66 repeaters. They were heading toward the island's northern most point.

I tracked two surface targets with the 'egg' and reported to the bridge: "Bridge Combat. Locked on and tracking two fast moving surface targets bearing one-one-zero true, range 17,200 yards and closing!"

"Bridge Aye. If these targets are hostile, we will know soon enough. I intend to close within 300 yards at high speed."

"Bridge, Combat. Recommend you come starboard to 111 true. CPA will be 350 yards. Range to targets 15,700 yards and closing… Fast!"

"Combat, Bridge. Coming starboard to 111 true." I felt *Goat Locker* heel into a starboard bank.

"Gun Control, Combat. Report when ready." We didn't have much time but I was sure Preacher was on the ball.

"The gun, she be ready. Ain't so sure about this green crew but the gun be ready!" Preacher announced over the headsets.

"Combat, Bridge. Time check 0857:09."

Sparks answered, "Bridge, Combat. Chronometers compare." Target bears 001 relative. Target speed 18 knots. Time to CPA . . . Fuck! Seven minutes! We shifted slightly port. I guess Masters wanted to see the whites of their eyes!

Four Minutes later Masters reported two targets maneuvering, "Combat, Bridge. Two targets changed course. I can't believe they are attempting an intercept! Guess they can't see that big gun on the bow pointed at them.

Goat Locker didn't make a course correction. GPS showed our CPA cut down to 175 yards . . .

"Bridge, Combat. Reset HYCATS CPA! That alarm is driving us nuts."

"Bridge, Combat. We will pass well within small arms range!" I reported.

"Combat, Bridge. Aye." That was understated but I felt a small course correction to starboard.

This little course correction was followed shortly by some commotion on the bridge.

The General Announcing System squawked to life, "Incoming! Small arms fire from automatic weapons!" It was over before it started but whoever was shooting at a 42-knot target with rifles and scoring some hits was someone to be wary of.

"Combat, Bridge. These fuckers are definitely hostile!" Masters reported.

Goat Locker heeled over in a high-speed starboard turn and target range started opening. Minimum target range was 1500 yards. Mechanical cutouts on the gun prevent it from depressing enough to shoot at a target that is closer.

Target range opened to 10,000 yards. "Bridge, Combat. Target range 10,000 yards. Recommend course change to 010 True."

"Combat, Bridge. Aye. Weapons Free! Commence fire at 8000 yards when we settle out." *Goat Locker* changed course.

Gun control, Combat. Stand by for live fire"

"Combat, Gun control. Manned and Ready."

Five seconds passed, "Bridge, Combat commencing fire!"

I had a firing solution for two targets heading due east. I selected a salvo of four HEPD rounds, depressed the firing switch and the gun responded. Two rounds fired at each target.

108

Three and a half miles away four distinct balls of fire ruined someone's day. One target appeared dead in the water and the other couldn't be seen. I had a firing solution on the remaining two boats.

"Bridge, Combat. Expect to engage remaining targets in three... Two..."

Masters interrupted, "Cease fire! Cease fire!"

Combat, Gun control. Four rounds expended, bore clear, no causalities." Preacher sounded disappointed. . .

"Combat, Bridge. We have one target completely destroyed, one beat to shit but floating . . . barely, and two flying white flags. I am going hullborne."

Bridge, Combat. I'm securing combat operations. Preacher, Jorge, Manuel and I will arm ourselves and go topside.

Boats come on the General Announcing System and announced, "All hands secure from general quarters." I just had to get him a boatswain's pipe!

Three small craft, a collection of thirty to forty foot vessels, congregated near an oil slick and a spreading debris field of flotsam. On our approach, all activity stopped and thirty or forty men raised their hands in the air. It was quite a sight! Seas were running about six feet and it's a wonder no one fell overboard.

Jorge and Manuel were armed with M60s. Manuel sort of looked like Rambo with the bandoleer draped across his shoulders. Preacher and I carried M16s, in full auto, and Glock 19s around our waists. It was unlikely there was much fight left in the survivors. We were prepared if there was.

Masters left Boats in charge of the bridge and was soon standing at my side with José. "José is going to use the bullhorn and find out who these clowns are and what they want."

José haled them in Spanish, "¿Quién eres tú, ¿qué es lo que usted desea?"

The English response surprised me, "We work for Don Carlos. Why are you armed? What are you doing in our territory? What do you want?"

Sanchez looked at me. And I started slowly so he could keep up and translate. "Tend to your dead and wounded. Return to your Don Carlos with this message: Come after us or to Isla de Cedros again and you will all return home in body bags. Set course for home and don't look back!"

No one replied. The survivors crowded into two boats, and then set course for the mainland at about seven knots.

I turned to Masters and said, "Hell of a job! Do we need to scrape any of Don Carlos's paint off our side? Those Bozos should have raised the white flag to start with . . . I think they will stay away long enough for us to clear the area and rendezvous with *Scrap Dealer*."

"I want to notify The Fortress of what happened and have them be on alert. Can Sparks raise The Fortress on radio?" Masters calmly asked.

"Sure. I will ask him now. Get us on course to rendezvous with *Scrap Dealer* and I will notify you when Sparks has The Fortress on radio. We'll transfer the call to the bridge. Does the fortress have a secure frequency?" I asked.

Master's reply was a surprise. "No just contact them on VHF. They usually monitor Channels 18 and 79."

"Preacher, let's get these weapons stowed . . . unless you want to play quick draw or something!" I said on my way to the armory.

I stuck my head into CIC and relayed Masters' request to Sparks. When I got to the armory the Brothers were talking to Preacher in Spanish and gesticulating with their arms.

"You all did a fine job. I told you God was in this here magazine with us. He would guide your hands to re-load the gun and expel the casings!" Preacher didn't notice that Jorge or Manuel didn't understand a thing he said.

Preacher took my weapons with a scowl on his face. "I think you be a little skimpy on the firepower Skipper? It's gonna take a couple of hours for me and Manuel to swab the bore and probably the deck if Boats has a say in it. That's a whole lot of work for four measly rounds! And to add insult to injury I'll have to stuff a rag in the muzzle to keep the spray out. We didn't have time to remove the tampion!"

"If your pop gun wasn't so tight that all four rounds landed on top of one another we could have emptied the magazine before we hit one of those 35 footers! Would that be better?" I asked with a hint of sarcasm. Preacher looked serious . . . I don't think he knew

I was having him on.

"No." Then continued in his deep southern voice, "Thank You Kensey. And thank God for these two recruits. They done a fine job on the skirmish. All I had to do was point to what I wanted and they jumped like grasshoppers on a hot plate and did it. The gun firing kind of shook them up a bit. I don't think they expected such a loud bang. They cleaned up all the puke already! They a bit seasick."

I laughed and said," They will get over it. I started to leave then turned back to Preacher. "When we get to *Scrap Dealer* take a couple of shell casings to the machine shop and have them make a new tampion for that po….fine shooting gun of yours." With that, I returned to CIC.

Sparks was busy as usual. I didn't even have time to sit down before he handed me a message and said. "I got The Fortress on VHF and patched it up to Masters on the bridge. He filled them in on our action and told them to be on the alert. From the looks of it we will have to be on the double alert!" The Message Read:

Kensey

Much activity around 'chicken coop'.

Appears Bears and Muskrats para military taking up residence there.

Do not know what this signifies but be advised foreign interest a problem.

Take care, keep you informed.

JB

This was a new complication we didn't need but it wouldn't stop us. The General Announcing System startled me with the order to prepare to go foilborne in five minutes. I thought to myself, "I've got to get Boats a pipe before that fuckin' thing gives me a heart attack!" I decided to show Masters and the rest of the crew this message after rendezvous with *Scrap Dealer*.

That reminded me of something. I got Boats on the J-Dial, (ships internal telephone system). "I didn't even know this thing worked . . . what do you want? Er… Bridge."

"We got any 21 thread on board Boats?" I could still do fancywork and thought I'd make a nice lanyard in case I ran across a Bo'sun pipe.

"Fuck Kensey we got extra mooring lines, a three hundred yard spool of 3/8" braided, a spool of ½" braided, a spool of heave line, and 17, what the fuck are we gonna do with 17 . . .spools of shot line? I think I spotted a couple spools of jute but no 21 thread. And by the way, no towing hawser so make sure those snipes keeps my ship running. Why?" Boats sounded puzzled.

"Thought I'd do some fancy-work on your apron!" I quickly hung up and got back to business.

Chapter 18
Rendezvous

We resumed foileborne operations without a hitch and Masters set course for the rendezvous. By 1130 we made radio contact with *Scrap Dealer* and established the final meeting coordinates. The order from the bridge to go hullborne was issued a minute before noon. Once *Goat Locker* was riding the waves, I left CIC and went topside. *Scrap Dealer* was 1500 yards off our bow according to radar. You couldn't miss her... I felt the ship slow down to a walking pace as we made our approach. She was the weirdest looking ship I'd ever seen! She looked exactly like the heavy-lift barge that delivered *Goat Locker* except she had a bridge structure on the bow for seagoing operations.

Maneuvering *Goat Locker* into position over skids designed to secure her during transit was a difficult, precise, operation. First *Scrap Dealer* would fill her ballast tanks with water and submerge the deck. Next, Masters would carefully run *Goat Locker* over the submerged deck and hold it there while *Scrap Dealer's* crew securely tethered her. When *Goat Locker* was in the proper position, and secured by the lines, *Scrap Dealer* would pump her ballast tanks. Hopefully *Goat Locker* would settle onto the on-deck skids. Masters informed me the skids were originally built to support sea going tugs, Coast Guard Cutters, and various ships, about our size. We didn't have a shaft or propeller to worry about and that made it a little easier. We had to settle very gently on the skids to preclude damaging the hull. The entire operation would take several hours. The crew, so I was informed, was very good and had accomplished this type of operation many times.

Masters wanted me on the bridge to help get *Goat Locker* into position. I told Sparks to watch the radar closely; we did not want any surprises from good Ol' Don Carlos for the next several hours. These maneuvers were tricky enough without interference from pissed off druggies or the Mexican Navy. Aye, aye was all I heard and I proceeded to the bridge. Masters greeted me and said he was talking to *Scrap Dealer* on VHF. He said the plan was to position *Goat Locker* on a parallel course alongside *Scrap*

Dealer. This had to be done slowly and gently. There is no room for mistakes! We came along side *Scrap Dealer* and slowed to a knot or so to maintain steerage. I knew why I recruited an experienced ship handler. This was going to be dicey!

We sat there with engines idling barely maintaining steerage. I could see *Scrap Dealer* slowly sinking. Masters told me she would settle until her deck was about twelve feet under water. This would leave plenty of water between *Goat Locker* and the skids. *Goat Locker* only drew six feet of water when hullborne. I called down to the galley for some coffee. José answered and said a fresh pot was brewing and he would run some to the bridge when it was ready. Four cups of coffee later *Scrap Dealer* was at depth. Boats must have been bored; he rang four bells over the General Announcing System. *Scrap Dealer* informed us to prepare for lift.

Masters radioed back, "Affirmative. Ready to proceed." He called Fritz and told him to prepare to shut diesels down, de-clutch, and put them in cool down as fast as he could. Aye aye came back instantly.

Scrap Dealer, on bridge to bridge VHF, gave us a heads up, "Ready to position *Goat Locker* over deck."

Masters gently maneuvered *Goat Locker* over the deck placing our bow as close as he could to the bridge structure. Next, he threw the helm hard to starboard and lined us up with the stern structure. Lines shot on deck and Boats, Preacher, Greasey, and Sanchez grabbed them and secured them to deck cleats. At the same time, Masters cut power to zero and told Fritz to de-clutch and cool down the diesels. This evolution was very fast; there were no major problems. The ocean current started to push the *Goat Locker's* stern out of position. The lines tightened up and held her fast. I could see *Scrap Dealer* starting to pump water from the ballast tanks and slowly rise. *Scrap Dealer's* crew kept a watchful eye on the line-winches to keep *Goat Locker* in position. Two hours passed; the skids were very close to *Goat Locker's* hull. Using hydraulics, the loadmaster began moving the skids into their proper position. Ever so slowly, *Scrap Dealer* rose and *Goat Locker* settled onto the skids. Five hours from start to finish: I hoped we never had to do this in a hurry…

114

The crew secured *Goat Locker*, shut down all engines. Greasey connected shore-power cables to *Scrap Dealer* and shut our SSPUs down. Sparks secured CIC with the exception of SatCom and sent a scrambled message to JB informing him we were on *Scrap Dealer* and on our way.

"Man you did a great job. Have you done this before?" I asked Masters.

"Yes, several times, but never with a PHM. I did two cutters and a large sea-going tug. They are much harder to get on the skids because of the rudder and screw positions. I wouldn't say this was easy but it wasn't that difficult. It's time to go see the Captain, and introduce you and your crew. The next thirty days should be very interesting and comfortable as well." Masters said with the first big smile I'd seen.

We all gathered on the deck and waited for *Scrap Dealer's* crew to rig a ladder. We didn't have long to wait. Within five minutes, we were standing on the wet deck of *Scrap Dealer* admiring *Goat Locker's* hull.

"Man that took a while but no marks at all on the hull. She sits pretty on the skids." Greasey commented.

Boats did a thorough inspection of the now exposed hull. Debris or imperfections on the hull could cause major problems when flying.

He reported to me, "She is in excellent shape. Not a ding, mark, or scrape anywhere on the hull. There are a few bullet marks on the superstructure forward under the bridge from the AK-47 rounds those assholes shot at us. I didn't see any damage to the CAS or anything else. I'll fix those on the way over. When we arrive, *Goat Locker* will look squared away."

We followed Masters single file to the bridge. *Scrap Dealer's* Captain would be there to meet us. I had no preconceived notions about Captain Shaw. I knew he worked for Wilson Brothers: nothing else. The crew was well trained and efficient so I expected the Captain to be the same. We climbed several ladders and entered the bridge. Masters introduced us to a bearded man in his mid fifties wearing a Captain's uniform.

"Kensey, I would like you to meet Captain Jacob Shaw. He's the longest serving captain with Wilson Brothers Salvage and my old boss." Masters said with a great deal of pride.

He stood with casual ease but you knew instantly he was in charge. Captain Shaw was a powerful looking, muscular man in his mid 50's. He easily topped five-feet ten inches and carried a solid one-hundred-eighty pounds. If it wasn't for his full salt and pepper beard you would swear he was much younger. His merchant marine captain's uniform decorated with brass buttons and gold braid completed the picture. *"Captain Shaw knows his business!"* was my first impression.

"How do you do Captain. Your crew is very efficient and I am duly impressed." I said as I shook his hand.

"Welcome aboard **Scrap Dealer**. We will do everything in our power to make you comfortable and get you and your ship... **Goat Locker**... to your requested destination." He said with a large grin while pumping my hand with a very firm grip. He continued, "We have provisions for ninety days at sea. We have enough JP-5 for you to run as many training exercises as you deem necessary. However, Mr. Masters has informed me time is critical and it takes about eight hours to do a transfer, so keep that in mind. My crew is constructing a cover to camouflage **Goat Locker**. It won't totally conceal the fact that she is a ship but will hide your armament and that silly looking radar dome above the bridge." He was still smiling. "Ladders will be rigged so you will have free access to the ship for whatever work and onboard training you need to do. Shore power, fresh water, and CHT (Collection and Holding Tanks) are already rigged. If there is anything special you need, ask. We have a lot of talent aboard **Scrap Dealer** including: machine shops, welders, carpenters, and an exceptionally good cook! Food is damn good if I may say so myself." He finally let go of my hand.

"I feel welcome already, Captain. We are grateful for your support and, as you stated, time is important if not critical. I've made this transit many times in my life. I'm looking forward to the time aboard to finalize our plans, and put **Goat Locker** and my crew through their paces. Thanks again."

"I would like to introduce you to your steward, Winston Churchill. Please, his mother was enamored with the great Englishman. He will take care of you while you are onboard this

116

ship. He will now escort you to your quarters; dinner will be served in a few hours, so take it easy until then. I have set course due west at a speed of 25 knots. Fast for us but well within our range. Good day, Sir, see you at dinner."

We followed Winston Churchill off the bridge and down a few ladders. First, he showed us the lounge, and then our staterooms. Each stateroom was equipped with a private head, closet, nice double bed, desk, which doubled as a table, small sofa, and two chairs. This was more comfortable than my apartment. Winston informed me that I didn't have to clean it... He was in charge of the steward department and they did the housekeeping chores. Winston told me he had seven men working for him. Laundry and such would all be taken care of by his crew. I felt as if I was on a luxury liner. I thanked him and he left. After a few minutes, I went looking for Boats.

I found him inspecting his stateroom and asked, "Boats, when you can, could you make sure *Goat Locker* is... taken care of? I would feel a lot better if you inspected her and was on hand when she got covered up."

"Consider it done Kensey. I sure wouldn't want them to fuck up an antenna or radio mast. Besides, I want to get a few beers off the ship before she is secured tonight."

"Beers? What beers?" I asked dumbfounded.

"Oh, you didn't know. Gman stocked the forward Bo'sun Locker with about forty cases of San Magoo." Boats smiled at me.

"I'll be damned. Make sure you bring back enough for everybody, at least two cases." I said. I couldn't help but laugh.

I thanked Boats and went looking for Sparks. I found him in the passageway looking confused.

"What's up? You lost?" I asked him.

"Well, couldn't remember which way to go. I'm on my way to the radio room. I need to notify JB we are on *Scrap Dealer*, and to send all traffic to us encrypted. I brought a laptop off *Goat Locker* and it has decryption codes and software installed. *Scrap Dealer* will get the raw message, give it to me and I will decrypt it and get it to you." He rattled all this off before I could even ask.

"That will work and it would keep us from maintaining a radio watch on *Goat Locker*. But our HF and SatCom are up and running on shore power from *Scrap Dealer*. I think it would be easier to run our own comms. We need to think about security. . . Until we get this sorted, go that way and up." I said pointing the way. "When you finish, find me in the lounge."

I found the rest of the crewmembers and told them to be in the lounge at 1830. It was now 1740 and dinner was, if I remembered what the Captain said, at 2000. I returned to my stateroom, and spotted my suitcase sitting on the deck. That was a welcome site. I showered, shaved, and changed into clean clothes before going to the lounge and then on to supper.

Chapter 19
The Journey Starts

I entered the lounge at 1830 on the dot. The entire crew was assembled, drinking San Magoo, and chatting quietly with each other. I grabbed a brew found a chair, and sat facing them.

"Good evening. I thought this would be a good time to plan the next thirty days of activity and discuss a plan of action. We need to start planning our mission. No doubt we will get new and/or updated information while in transit. A plan is easy to change. Not having a good one is a disaster! First, we need to get the 20mms up and working. Fritz, Greasey, and Preacher take care of that. Preacher says you will have to rig up twelve-volt power. We need to train our newcomers, Jorge and Manuel, how to shoot them. Next, Sparks needs to get checked out on the bridge. Masters and Boats can do that. Boats, what was the result of your topside inspection, and are we secure on the skids in case of heavy weather?"

"Aye, *Scrap Dealer* crew has several stanchions in place and a lightweight cover on deck. By tomorrow morning, the only thing showing will be the main mast. The cover poses no problem, and the lines used to secure it are relatively small. They pose no danger to any topside equipment and I believe there is plenty of ventilation. We can work on the ship without fear of overheating. Kensey, I saw a bit of topside rust forward that needs tending to. Saltwater can corrode plastic. Chipping and painting, never fucking ceases." Boats lamented as he took another beer.

"Kensey," Masters said, "about training on *Goat Locker*. I don't think we should move it off the skids. I sure as hell don't want to puncture or damage that hull in the process of floating or recovery if I can avoid it."

"Yeah I agree," I said, "We will have to train while it is on the skids. Sure, we won't have absolute realism, but buttonology and commands can be practiced. Dry runs are better than nothing. I checked the ship as we left and all the guns can be fired with no danger to *Scrap Dealer*. We only need electrical power to run system checks and weapons training."

Greasey jumped up and said, "Well, fuck me to tears that gives Fritz and me a whole lot of time to get those engines running to perfection. I have a few ideas to get a bit more flying speed. Right before I retired from GE, my group was working on some simple changes to the LM-2500. If I'm going to be shot at, I want to be going as fast as I can. A moving target is a whole lot harder to hit. The faster the harder!"

"Jawohl, I agree. We're in good shape with the diesels. The only way to hurt them is to shoot 'em with the M16s! Kensey, I want to fire the 20mms if all right with you." Fritz said.

"Sure, no problem. All of us need to be checked out on the 20s" I responded. "Another thing comes to mind. We are confined here for the next thirty days or so. I want everyone to get as much rest as possible but don't overdo it. Work as much as you want on *Goat Locker*. I was surprised to find MRCs on board when I first saw the ship so let's get as much PMS accomplished as we can. A lot of it is redundant, but the more hands-on time we have with the equipment the more we'll remember its eccentricities. *Scrap Dealer* probably has the right kind of gearbox oils, greases, and cleaning solvents we will need. The gun mount, CAS and comm gear all need a good going over. Our lives will depend on those systems. Let's use this opportunity to get the ship in tiptop fighting shape. Any questions?" I polled each man by looking directly at him.

When I got to Jorge, he asked, "Mister Kensey, we don't know what you are talking about. What are my brother and me going to do?"

"Awe, forgot you two are the newbies, sorry. Well, MRC stands for Maintenance Requirement Card and PMS is Planned Maintenance System. It's a systematic, detailed, way of keeping the equipment in top running order." I looked at the others and asked "Ideas?"

"I will take care of these two," Boats volunteered. "I'll teach them how to use a chipping hammer and fuckin' paint brush. If they are real lucky *Scrap Dealer* will have a needle-gun I can teach them how to use."

"I could sure use some help in engineering," Greasey said.

"I'll work with you," José quipped. "I am probably the only

120

man, besides Fritz, that could stand to work with you."

"Yeah yeah," Greasey whined, "José, I gonna get you fuckin' greasy." He finished with a twinkle in his eye and a big grin.

"I be trainin' Jorge and Manuel on moving ammo and loading the gun. Praise the Lord, last time was pretty good but they need a little more speed." Preacher said.

Masters said, "Kensey, you, and I need to work on several attack plans. I have a general idea of where to position *Goat Locker* during the assault and how to approach the target area. I borrowed several duplicate charts from Captain Shaw so I have a good understanding of the area."

"Good point Bill. I have satellite photos that will help us develop plans 'A', 'B', and 'C'." With that said, I stood up "Time to join Captain Shaw for dinner. Bill, lead the way." We milled around a few moments until Masters opened the hatch. Winston was surprised when the hatch opened; he just arrived to lead us to dinner. We followed him to a large messing area. With the exception of Masters and me, we were told to sit anywhere available. Winston led us to the head of the table where we joined Captain Shaw for dinner.

The meal was served by stewards dressed in white jackets and black trousers. Small talk was the order of day. Dinner consisted of medium rare steak with all the trimmings. While eating, Captain Shaw removed a piece of paper from his inner coat pocket, and handed it to me. I looked at a bunch of gibberish.

"This came in after your man, Sparks I believe, left radio." Captain Shaw said.

"Excuse me a minute, please." I rose and went over to Sparks and handed him the paper. "Get this decrypted after you eat. Thanks." I returned to my meal.

"I thought you would like to know that we are steaming at 25 knots, weather is exceptionally good. The forecast is not so good so I imagine speed will be down around 15 knots. Radar has reported that no aircraft or ship is in the area. So far we have been totally free of prying eyes." Captain Shaw reported in a matter-of-fact voice.

"Thanks, Captain. I appreciate the information and would like to be kept abreast of any changes in sea state or weather. While we are talking, I would like to ask your permission to hold a live firing of our weapons. My crew and I really need the practice. I promise no harm to your ship."

"I find that acceptable. I see no problem. Make sure you check with the bridge before firing. I want to warn the crew and make sure no one is in the area."

"Aye, will do." I answered.

We finished our meal, thanked the Captain, and retired to our staterooms. Masters stayed behind and continued to swap sea stories with Captain Shaw. I trusted Bill not to let anything about our mission slip out during the conversation. I hadn't been in my stateroom twenty minutes when a light tap on the door summoned me.

Sparks handed me the message and said, "Here you go Kensey, it's from our government friend."

"Come on in, I might want to send a reply and you can take it with you." I moved to the desk sat down and started reading:

Goat Locker, be advised that more foreign armed soldiers arriving in chicken coop.

Have arranged for 250 rounds 76mm and 10000 rounds 20mm delivered to you at following coordinates: 10°34'13.94"S 72°28'52.47"E.

The ship carrying your supplies is a civilian contractor; name of ship is Great White Way Liberian flag.

Send message three days prior to rendezvous for exact time and date.

They know nothing except to deliver cargo.

No further instructions or news.

JB.

"No reply. Don't think it's necessary." Thanks Sparks, see you tomorrow.

I was tired and decided it was time to shower and hit the rack. More ammo is good but storage might be a problem. If we had to, we could store extra rounds in crews berthing. There were fifteen racks and José, Preacher, and the Gonzales Brothers were the only ones using the bunks. That left eleven racks and the deck space around them to store 76mm rounds. All this activity, both mental and physical, since Jim found me sipping beer at the Safe Haven

122

finally took its toll on this old body. A good night's sleep would clear that problem up. It took about twenty seconds before I was sound asleep.

I awoke early next morning and dressed. I rang for Winston to deliver some coffee. I was totally surprised when he delivered a pot of hot coffee, along with a full breakfast of eggs, bacon, hash browns, toast, and fresh fruit. I thanked him, and ate. After breakfast, my next stop was the bridge to get an update and check on our ship. *Goat Locker* was in what appeared to be two halves of a large tent. One half was over the front and the other half over the rear. The mast stuck up right in the middle like a beacon in the night. All that was visible was the main mast and the HF whip antenna. I could see that the tents were tied down securely to the superstructure and not touching *Goat Locker's* equipment. We could work on the ship with no interference from the tents and she was concealed from prying eyes. Access to the ladder up to the main deck was through a small gap between the two halves. I was impressed.

Boats strolled up and suggested we inspect the ship together. We climbed the ladder to the main deck and went forward to examine the small arms damage to the superstructure. There were several marks running in a somewhat slanted path from fore to aft. It looked like a snake trying to crawl up the deckhouse towards the bridge windows. The damage was superficial but a reminder that we were not Superman. Boats said a little paint would take care of the scars. He showed me the rust and that had to be taken care of. All in all, he said about five days work. I agreed and started for the fantail to check out the 20s.

Mounted on the port and starboard sides of the fantail, replacing the Harpoon missile launchers, were two MK16 Mod 4, 20mm rifles. I recognized them. The Riverine used them on PBRs, (Patrol Boat, River), during the Viet Nam war. Gman did good choosing these. They were readily available, inexpensive, and easy to install. No support machinery or electronic equipment was needed. One man manually operated train, elevation, and firing. They had a 12-volt firing circuit, and lots and lots of ammo available. Each gun used a single ammunition box containing 385-linked rounds. Stack the boxes close to the gun and a heavy wall of fire could be sustained for quite some time. Effective range is about a mile: plenty far enough to handle small boat attacks.

Boats took a deep breath, "Those things look mean," and expelled the air.

"Sure are mean. The good news is they are easy to operate, train, elevate, and fire. They only take one man to operate and can do a hell of a lot of damage. I sure as hell wouldn't want to be on the receiving end of these babies." I told Boats.

I was startled by the sudden appearance of Greasey who said, "Easy fuckin' peasy. Got a bunch of 12-volt batteries in aft engineering storage locker sitting on a pallet. Guess they are for these two monsters. No problem hooking them up."

Preacher just finished inspecting both guns, blessed them, then turned to us and said, "I used to take care of these on an old Tin Can in my youth. The good Lord gave me a keen eye and steel nerves. These beauties can take out any heathen attempting to attack the good ship *Goat Locker*. I will get these clean, fill the oil dispenser for the rounds, and lube the gears. When can we christen them?"

Greasey and Boats both started laughing and I said, "Roger that Preacher. Go ahead and get them up and running but protect them from the elements, please. We should be able to live-fire them in a few days. I'll bet everyone wants a crack at them!"

Boats and I left the fantail en route to CIC. Sparks was already there and had a radio torn down. It looked like he was troubleshooting one of our HF transmitters. I asked him "What's up?"

"This transmitter keeps dropping out. I'm replacing the controller board. Found several spare parts and boards in the electronic ready spares locker. These transmitters were always known for controller board failures. I can't believe our luck, Kensey. We have enough spares in there to keep all this shit working." Sparks said.

"Luck my ass. Gman had a lot to do with this I bet. He rode the PHMs and couldn't help hearing and seeing all the minor problems that we constantly encountered. I remember one incident in particular. We were chasing some scumbags. We intercepted them and were preparing to board. In those days, we had to radio squadron headquarters and request permission to do our job. Right at that moment the goddamn HF transmitter went down. We raced around in circles trying to raise squadron before the assholes got away. Luckily, we had a backup, but it was a real stink at the time. After that little incident, all the ships carried spares for radios and radars based on usage and failure rates. That worked fairly well. We never had another problem like that. Gman, I am sure, remembered this little incident and had spares put together by Boeing."

"Well, at any rate let me get this fuckin' radio working." Sparks said as he returned to his task.

I went over to the MK 92 and lit off the system, ran self-checks, and all was in order. While I was yakking with Sparks, Boats wondered off to do what Bo'sun mates do: chip, paint, swab, and take care of the ship.

I was just finishing up when I heard Sparks shout, "She is working again. All up and running, Kensey. Man that was fun. Been a long time since I got to rip a fuckin' radio apart and put it back together again. My lousy civilian job entailed nothing more than removing and replacing entire units. No real troubleshooting or thinking was allowed. I don't foresee any more problems. The LN-66 is running great, IFF checks out, and all the radios work now. Think I will go check radio on *Scrap Dealer* see if we have any new traffic. Kensey, I think we should transfer comms back to *Goat Locker* when we clear the Malacca Straits. Security is pretty good but the closer we get to our mission the more paranoid we need to be! Captain Shaw and his crew are probably above reproach but…"

"Yeah… Let's plan on making-it-so. Draw up a watch plan some time before we get to Singapore."

Sparks left and I was alone in CIC. I left CIC and made my way to crew berthing. I wanted to inspect the storeroom. I was anxious to see how Gman provisioned the ship. Gman stashed forty cases of San Magoo in the Bo'sun locker. I was curious about what else I might find. First, I checked the storeroom next to the crews mess. There was quite a bit of food crammed in there. Most of it was quick and easy to prepare. Originally, PHMs were not

125

equipped with microwave ovens, but there was one installed in our galley. Gman didn't miss a trick. The spare parts locker Sparks had mentioned was aft of the food storage. I was surprised to find replacement modules for the MK 92, CAS, MK 75 gun, LN-66, MK 12 AIMS IFF, and all the various radios. It looked like we were in damn good shape for electronic spares. My next stop was engineering to check on their spares.

I continued aft and ran into Fritz, "How's it going? Got those diesels perfect?" I asked.

"Jawohl Kensey, those babies are perfect. I did some tweaking and tuning and modifying. I think we can make sixteen knots hullborne now. That's an increase of about four knots. I know it doesn't sound like much, but four knots is four knots. Those extra knots may come in handy, you never know. Oh, by the way I think Greasey has been working on the LM-2500 and I think he may have really got that thing ready to push this baby past 50. Man, flying at 50 plus knots is going to be a trip."

"Thanks Fritz, I'll go check on Greasey. By the way, have you thoroughly checked out your storeroom? Any surprises from Gman?"

"No surprises but if Gman outfitted this ship he did a great job. Only problem is all that 20mm ammo stacked everywhere. Can hardly move for all them damn bullets."

I laughed and continued on to find Greasey. He wasn't in the engine room so I went topside then aft to the fantail by the 20mms. These were impressive guns! Gman had them mounted: one facing port and one facing starboard. They were positioned so each gun had a field of fire of about one hundred and forty degrees in azimuth. One worry was the lack of firing-cut-out-cams. I didn't want anyone shooting holes in the superstructure during the heat of battle! I was sure Preacher was on that little detail but I would remind him to have *Scrap Dealer* make some firing stops. That would do the trick. Greasey was running some wires from a small pallet of twelve-volt batteries to the starboard gun.

"How's it going, Greasey?" I asked.

"Oh hello Kensey, it's going pretty fuckin' good. Got the port gun wired and almost finished with the starboard gun. I kinda dry fired it to make sure it would work. Preacher filled the little lube

126

bottle for the rounds entering the breach and when I finish up here, all should be ready to go. Do I get to test fire one?"

"Sure, and thanks. What about the LM-2500, Fritz said you were doing some modifications to get a bit more speed on the foils. Did you?"

"Not done yet. Still have a few more things to do. Gman left me enough parts to do what I want. Should get about fifty-six knots. When I was working for GE on these, we detuned them for the navy so the snipe on the ship could keep them runnin'. If you tuned and tweaked them, changed a bit of software, you could get quite a bit more out of them, but the drawback is they fail quicker and need a rebuild sooner. However, I don't think we have to worry about that on *Goat Locker*. We're only doing this once... Right?"

"Yeah, only once. I don't mind you tweaking the turbine just make sure the damn thing works when we need it." I said, and headed for the bow.

Preacher had the bow roped off, and he was running checks on the gun. I passed through the crew's mess and then forward into the magazine. Preacher was standing at the Local Control Panel running tests.

"Joe, how's it going with that gun? Any problems?" I asked.

"God Bless, Kensey, and no. The gun be workin' fine. I did all of the basic PMS on her. New grease, new gearbox oil, serviced the magazine rings, and so on. She be ready when you are, I guarantee it." Preacher was smiling. He was in his element.

"Fine, thanks Joe. I checked out the 20mms and have a few... concerns. They have no firing-cut-outs. Positive stops should take care of anyone shooting holes in the superstructure. And while I'm thinking about it, see if *Scrap Dealer* can fabricate some armored ready-service ammo boxes on deck. I'd hate to have some yahoo set off a couple hundred 20mm rounds with a tracer! Other than those safety items they look ready to shoot. Greasey got the firing circuits wired and we should be able to test them tomorrow. Thanks for helping Greasey out."

"No problem, but the heathen needs help in more ways than one... Anything else, Kensey?"

"No, everything is fine. I think we have a good selection of what we need in the armory. The M60s, M16s, Stingers, and the LAWS make me feel a bit better armed. Those Stinger missiles give us the air coverage we need in case our pirates joined the twenty-first century and come at us with helos. As a bonus they will work well against heavily armed small craft inside Otto's minimum range. The 76mm isn't the greatest against air targets and I don't think we have any Able-Able Common, (Anti Aircraft Common), rounds anyway. It's a good thing we have those shoulder-launched missiles! See you at dinner." I said as I left. I have a little errand to run on *Scrap Dealer*.

Chapter 20
On Board *Scrap Dealer*

I left *Goat Locker* and set course for *Scrap Dealer's* machine shop. I wanted to get something special for Boats. After two weeks on *Scrap Dealer,* I knew my way around the ship and had no trouble finding the machine shop. Two crewmembers were working on something as I entered. They were welding quarter inch steel panels into a shield looking affair.

The taller of the two approached me as I entered the shop. He was wearing a large leather welding apron, and protective goggles pushed up on his forehead, "Hello Kensey. Right? Good to meet you. My name is Rogers and this here is my shop. Masters stopped by and asked us to fabricate some steel shielding to protect the 20mm gunners. Glad we could help. Now, what can I do for you?"

I was surprised but impressed that Masters caught something I missed. I should have thought of that long before he did. It was my job to take care of these details. I was glad that my crew had my back.

"Thanks Rogers, looks like those steel sheets will do the trick. Don't think they will stop anything major but will do fine against small arms fire! Is it feasible to manufacture some ready-service boxes for the 20mm rounds and weld them to the deck near the guns? They don't have to be too beefy but they should be able to deflect armor piercing small arms fire. Some of that quarter inch plate doubled up with an air space between layers would do the trick.

Rogers thought for a moment then replied, "That shouldn't be much trouble. I'll get with . . . ah Preacher?" I nodded, "For the dimensions."

"Thanks." I said, "And on a personal note: I was hoping you could do me a small favor. I need a Bo'sun pipe made for Boats Clark. You think you can make one with what you have onboard?"

"Bo'sun pipe, huh. Yeah, I could do that. I have a small supply of stainless steel tubing that will do nicely. I made several pipes in my days ridin' merchant marine ships. It'll take a couple of days is that all right? I can even get a nice lanyard made for it. We have a mate on here who loves to do that fancy line work."

"Excellent! Is there a carpenter on board who could make a nice box for the pipe?" I asked.

"Sure... several of us dabble in wood-work and a few, not me, are really good at it. I'll take care of that too. Give me a week and come on down and collect it."

"Thanks, Rogers. I really appreciate this. I will reward you and your mates handsomely. Thanks again." I said.

"That would be right nice, Kensey. Lookin' forward to that. I'll see you in a week." He said with a large smile on his face.

I left the machine shop and proceeded to the bridge. Captain Shaw was there and greeted me with a firm handshake. "What brings you to the bridge, Kensey?" He asked.

"I received a message with the coordinates for an at-sea rendezvous with a merchant ship... the *Great White Way*. They have some needed supplies for *Goat Locker*." I handed him a slip of paper with the coordinates printed on it.

"Ah, very well. I will have these plotted and determine time and date of arrival. I will let you know as soon as possible."

"Thanks Captain. I need at least three days lead time to notify my contact. I have a request: I want to test fire the 20mms tomorrow afternoon with your permission."

"Permission granted. I thought you might want to do some target practice. I talked to your gunners mate and my engineer, and we agreed that firing the big gun might not be such a good idea. The recoil could cause hull damage from the skids." Captain Shaw pointed out.

"Yes, I thought about that too. Tomorrow we will fire only the 20s. I think we will live-fire the 76mm after we are back afloat. I have been working on a plan that should satisfy our training requirements. When I get the details finalized I'll let you know how we'd like to proceed." I said.

I left the bridge and returned to my stateroom to get a little shuteye. I was weary after working a full day on *Goat Locker*. I examined every square inch of her interior and exterior. I didn't find anything amiss or any surprises. Age was starting to creep up on me and I was tired. Sparks caught up to me just as I opened my stateroom door.

Sparks looked just as tired. He'd been monitoring comms from *Goat Locker* and making sure radio and CIC gear was working to specifications. He sounded puzzled as he handed me a message transcript. "Skipper I've been monitoring MARS and amateur radio frequencies. I caught this earlier today." He said and handed me a transcript.

CQ, CQ, CQ, This is RAM568. I'm looking for my lost Goat Herd. Over.

CQ, CQ, CQ, This is EWE856. I have you 5x5. How's the weather in the high Sierra. Over.

It's a sight better than that blow bearing down on you in Darwin. Over.

I'll take a little rain and wind over snow any day. I got a CQ from KID685 in Cape Town. He's got a problem with his Goats too. What's with you goat ropers? Over.

You know how it is once these old goats get a wild hair up the butts. . . Over.

Roger that! EWE856, Out.

Catch ya later. Don't get blown away. RAM568, Out.

"What frequency was this on Sparks?"

"It was just above the 30 meter band at 4.052011 mega hertz!"

"Gman." We said simultaneously.

I started to write a reply then thought better of it. Instead, I told Sparks to monitor that frequency and the next time anyone was on the air to send out GL in Morris code and make it sound like atmospheric interference.

I was asleep less than two hours when Sparks knocked on my door woke me up. I arose, rubbed my eyes, and opened the door. Sparks was standing there with another message transcript in his hand. He wore an ominous expression and I could tell he was concerned. He handed the message to me. It read:

Goat Locker, be advised: local contact reports armed helos have arrived in chicken coop.

No intel on who owns or who is controlling them.

Will advise when new information forthcoming.

JB

"Thanks Sparks looks like one more thing to worry about. Good thing we have the Stingers! We have an UnRep of sorts in a few days. We'll pick up some AA rounds for the 76mm that might be handy too! I don't want things to fall apart before we have a chance to do our job. I'm sure we still have the upper hand and a very nasty surprise for our pirate friends."

"Kensey, you don't think this is a major problem?" Sparks asked with a lot of worry in his voice.

"No I don't. We have the element of surprise on our side and we have a lot of firepower. The pirates are thinking about an assault from maybe the Cartel, or even the terrorists, but they will not be prepared for anything like us. We are going to hit them so hard they will think the Seal Team Six just landed on their ass." I said.

Sparks was somewhat sarcastic in his reply, "Thanks Kensey. I might sleep a little better knowing that..."

"Sparks, rest easy. I really don't see a problem. Now get some rest, see you at dinner."

"OK, see you at dinner." He said and departed down the passageway.

So much for rack time... I got up and went to the lounge. It was close to 1600 so we had a good two hours before dinner. I was alone when I entered but not for long. Masters came in a few minutes later and asked Winston, who was right behind him, for a pot of black coffee and several cups.

"Kensey, how is it going? I see you inspected every inch of **Goat Locker** today. Any surprises. San Magoo? Single Malt?" Masters asked.

"Fine, couldn't be better. No surprises pleasant or unpleasant. By the way thanks for arranging for a little armor around the 20mms. I appreciate that. With everything else going on I hadn't considered it. I'm having the machine shop fabricate some ready-service lockers for the 20mm. If I have any more brain-farts let me know!" I said.

"Don't be hard on yourself Kensey, that's why every Captain has department heads. We take care of those '*little*' problems. We're all winging it on this mission. Everyone needs to step up. Any problem we can identify and fix '*before*' the shootin' starts puts us ahead of the power curve: and that's where we want to be!"

"Yeah, thanks anyway. Got some news to pass on to the entire crew. Looks like you're the next to know. Our target village gained a couple of armed helos. Gman didn't know whom they belong to. It is safe to bet they aren't a welcoming committee. . . We'll have to wait and see. Luckily, we have those Stingers! The Mk92 does a decent job on air threats and the 76mm can do a passable job on bogies. We have some AA rounds coming and that will help too. I really don't think they will be much of a problem as long as we know they are in the area. Maybe we can take them out before they become a threat but if we don't they become the number one priority. We don't want them tail-bitin' our ass on the way out!"

"Well... It's good to know they are there ahead of time. We will keep a good lookout for them." Masters said thoughtfully and then continued, "If I know those helos are coming I will have to do some radical maneuvering. Along with the 20mm scatter shields and ready-service lockers we better devise some safety harnesses for the gunners! I'd hate to lose anyone overboard when we fly out of there! I've flown out of firefights before. It ain't pretty but a flying PHM is hard to hit especially when maneuvering. If I know those helos are coming I will insure *Goat Locker* will out maneuver and evade any incoming ordinance. Done it before, can do it again."

"I bet you can Bill. Have you given the attack plan any thought?" I inquired to change the subject.

"Yes, that's about all I have been thinking of. How about you, Kensey? You formulated a good concise easily executed plan, I hope. Masters said with a smile and sat there patiently waiting for my answer.

He could continue to wait. At that moment the rest of the crew entered, lead by Boats. They began to shuffle and find their own place to sit. After it was calm, and everyone had some coffee, I told them about the helos. They all started asking questions at once and I held up my hand to stop the chaos.

"Take it easy. We have the weapons to handle a few helos. Hell, Preacher can take them out by himself."

"Good Lord protects me. I ain't worried in the least." He said

Jorge and Manuel started yammering in Spanish to José about

133

what I just said. José was quietly calming them down. I assumed he told them they would be well protected by all the firepower we carried.

"OK, everybody listen up," I started. "I have a plan. We need to talk it over and work out any bugs we can find. This is the time for feedback and your thoughts. First thing I want to address is training. I received permission to test the 20mms from Captain Shaw. We are going to do that tomorrow. Everyone should get a turn popping those puppies off. Now as far as the 76mm is concerned, we can't shoot it while sitting in the skids on *Scrap Dealer*. The recoil might cause damage to *Goat Locker's* hull. So, I figured, we would refloat about a thousand miles from the target area and train. We can return to *Scrap Dealer* at the end of a day and refuel. From that point on, we stay aboard *Goat Locker* until our mission is completed. When we are clear of firefights and reprisals, we will rendezvous with *Scrap Dealer* and she will transport us back to the good ol' USA. We have an upcoming UnRep with a civilian supply ship. Our friend in high places has arranged for a few more rounds of 76mm ammo for Preacher. Some of it will be AAC. Preacher, I want 15 or 20 rounds in the outer ring. We can use the spare HEPD for training. Masters said flairs might be handy to use as decoys for any IR rockets the helos might carry. Preacher, do you think star shells would be effective? We still have time to get a few if you think they would be of use."

All eyes turned to Preacher, "I love to light up the heavens. We might use a few just to spook the natives but I don't think they would be effective as decoys. We have a full load of chaff and flairs for the RBOC, which will do nicely. Better safe than sorry though. A pallet of star shells (White Phosphorus or Willie Peter) would be easy to store. They can be used to set up a smoke screen, which we might need when departing. We can strap 'em in the spare bunks."

Any questions or comments?" I asked when Preacher finished.

"I think we should extend the training out to about 1500 miles vice 1000. That would decrease the chance that we might be spotted." Masters said.

I agreed and said, "Sure. I want to reduce any chance of being spotted."

"I would like to get checked out on the bridge." Sparks said, and continued, "Never stood bridge watches on one of these PHMs. Looks like it would be fun."

"That could be arranged. I will leave that to Masters to decide when you can fly the ship. I do want everyone checked out, including myself. Jorge and Manuel are not required to fly." I said, and went on, "José, can you get the galley ready to support us for, say, three weeks living on board?"

"Si. I have checked and there are plenty of dry stores aboard. The head chef on *Scrap Dealer* said he would give me what I need in perishables right before we refloat *Goat Locker*. Should be plenty of veggies, meat, and fruit to last about a month. That will completely fill the storerooms, cold rooms, and freezer. To let you know Kensey, I found a very well stocked medical locker with enough supplies to take care of minor aches, pains, wounds, and accidents. We are well provisioned and what is not currently on board will be before we float her." José informed the group.

José outdid himself. He was a man of few words. The information he relayed was good news. I thanked him. *Goat Locker* was gearing up and almost on a war footing. Dinner was in ten minutes. I told everyone to be back in the lounge at 2100 to go over some fine details.

Dinner was, as usual, exceptionally good. *Scrap Dealer* was putting on some great meals for us. I know I was paying for the excellent treatment, but appreciated it just the same. Captain Shaw reaffirmed that we could hold live firing of the 20mms tomorrow and could hold the exercise around 1400, right after the noon meal. I told him we would be prepared. The Captain also informed us that we would transit the Malacca Strait day after tomorrow while it was dark. That would help us avoid prying eyes. We would have to keep *Goat Locker* covered until we were well clear of the Straits and far into the IO. Our next big event was the rendezvous with our supply ship: *Great White Way*. The Captain said that once in the IO, it would take about four days to get to the meeting and all was in ready for that to take place. *Scrap Dealer* had made radio contact with *Great White Way* and was on schedule. Good news and a good meal, who could complain?

When I got back to the lounge, Greasey and Fritz were playing

Acey-Ducey. Boats and Masters were playing Cribbage and Sparks was reading, if you want to call it that, he was engrossed in a two-month-old Playboy magazine. José and the Gonzales brothers were deep in discussion in Spanish. I had no idea what they were talking about but they seemed to be involved. There were lots of hand and arm gestures and they were a bit loud.

Boats got up and poured himself a cup of coffee, and out of the clear blue sky said, "We might be in for a bit of a gale in the next few days. We look secure on the skids but the low freeboard on *Scrap Dealer* has me a little worried. I'll get with the deck crew and see how they deal with heavy weather."

"That sounds like a plan Boats." I replied. "Sparks intercepted a Ham Operator out of Darwin who was talking about a bit of a blow down under." I was sure *Scrap Dealer* operated in heavy weather and high seas before. Nonetheless, I will talk to Captain Shaw about it tomorrow."

All plans to finish my novel were out the window. My taste in literature tends towards good old-fashioned hardboiled detective novels. They are hard to put down once started! Hammett and Chandler are my favorite authors. I was half way through "The Thin Man," for the third time, but it would have to wait. It was time to go over training and attack plans. We had about a week before *Goat Locker* was refloated.

I gave my dog-eared novel a longing look and said, "Let's get started."

Chapter 21
Firing the 20mms

"Acey Mahoney motherfucker!" Fritz blurted out, "And game!"

"Timely..." I said, "Tomorrow is a training day. We are going to hit it hard. Preacher, I want you to load, unload, and reload the rings. Jorge and Manuel, get a good night's sleep, you're going to need it! Boats did you get a chance to check the scatter-shield on the 20s?"

"Yeah. And they did a fine job and primed the shields and deck where they welded. They'll paint everything white and do touch up on the deck day after tomorrow. They're still fabricating the ready-service boxes but should have them done in a few days." Boats replied.

"Masters, the *Scrap Dealer* crew is phenomenal! I wish they were on the tenders I had to deal with in the Navy . . ." I couldn't heap enough praise on them. "Boats you'll have to get *Goat Locker* uncovered, probably just the stern, so we can play with the 20s." I said to get us back on the subject of training.

"I'll get that done by 0600. *Scrap Dealer* has a couple of empty fifty-gallon drums we can use as targets. I'll get them staged and ready to kick over the side." Boats volunteered.

"Good. Boats you and Sparks will be first up. Masters and I will be next, then José and Preacher and lastly the Gonzales Brothers. We have enough ammo for everyone to fire one full box. I want everyone to get used to shooting at a small targets. Those fifty-gallon drums should do the trick. Any questions, comments, or suggestions?" I asked.

"Before anyone could answer I decided to present Boats with a gift. "Oh Boats. I have something for you. A small token of my appreciation." I said as I removed a small rectangular wooden box from my pocket.

The box was made of mahogany and had "Boats Clark" carved in the lid. I handed the box to him and he gave me a funny little grin and accepted the gift. He opened it... I swear there was a small tear in the corner of his eye.

"I don't believe it. This is the finest pipe I ever saw. This lanyard is pretty damn nice too. Whoever made it really knows his shit. Thanks Kensey." Boats murmured. Everyone could tell he was choked up.

"Give it a try. Give us an 'All Hands'!" I insisted.

He gave me a serious look, put the pipe to his mouth, and split the evening with a shrill tune. We all automatically tuned into the General Announcing System for the coming message. He didn't miss a note.

"Sweepers would be more appropriate." Boats grumbled, "We don't want *Goat Locker* to become a pig pen!"

"Perfect, Boats. Use the pipe next time you're on the General Announcing System." I said.

Boats put the lanyard around his neck, adjusted it to lie flat, and put the pipe in his shirt pocket. I think he was about a foot taller when he returned to his seat. Masters walked over to him and shook his hand, muttering something under his breath that I didn't catch. By the look on Boats' face, it was a compliment.

"Since there are no questions about tomorrow; enjoy the rest of the evening. Hit the rack early and get some sleep. We will be busy." I said.

I turned to Masters and asked, "How do you want to stage *Goat Locker* for the assault on *High and Mighty*? I have some ideas but I really need your input since you'll be driving. My ideas may not work and I need to know now."

Masters looked thoughtful then said, "I checked the charts. I think the best approach is to fly in from about four hundred miles. Here are the coordinates of the waypoint. The attack should be around 0100. I will coordinate with *Scrap Dealer* for current weather conditions before we actually finalize the operation.

If you set known target coordinates into fire control, we can use 'shore-bombardment' and take them out as they come into range. I think that would create the most chaos and give us the time along side *High and Mighty* that we need. Do we have new satellite recon of the target area? If not I'll see if Sparks can get them for us. We will probably need Sat-Info for target ID anyway. Kensey, Those Helos bother me. What are the chances Gman can get his 'native guy' to give us the coordinates where they are parked."

I said, "Anything that flies is always priority number one. I'll see what I can do. Next, any ship anchored in the vicinity should be taken out. We can be certain they are not friendly. The only worry is if the pirates have other hostages and they are on board those boats . . . The photos we have were taken before we left the Western Pacific so they will not be current. That reminds me. . ." I turned to Sparks and said, "Sparks, send a message to our friend and request updated recon photos and any new info."

Sparks replied, "You got it. I will send it first thing in the morning."

Masters was right but I voiced my reservations. "If we destroy a 'Pirate captured' ship, whatever country it belongs to may consider us pirates and bring their Navy down on our asses. We don't need that! Target ID is highly desirable and the only person that can get that Intel is our friend in DC. We will definitely check with him just before we go-in! With that said, our lives are on the line here. Once we fire the first round consider us in a shoot-shoot-look environment!"

Masters was a bit surprised, thought about it for a moment, then said, "The best tactic, and what I envisioned, is to head directly at the target at flank speed. That gives *Goat Locker* the smallest profile possible." Masters addressed me directly, "Kensey, you know if they have anything bigger than small arms?"

"You can count on RPGs and we know they have heavy caliber machine guns. As a minimum we can expect armed and pissed off pirates with AK-47s and a multitude of semi and full auto assault rifles and side arms looking to fuck us up. If Preacher does his job, most buildings in the area should be burning rubble. It is my intention to be well away from there before anyone can mount an assault with small arms. Regardless, we need to guard against all eventualities." I answered. Before Masters could reply I continued, "We will fly straight in and do a complete 180 turn. When was the last time you 'crash-landed' a PHM?"

"We did a lot of that in the Keys. A few practice runs is all I need. The small arms we're likely to be up against bothers me though. Can we mount one of the M60s on the CAS deck amidships? We will be port-side-to *High and Mighty* and the 20s bear on the beach. Either Boats or I can man the 60. From that height we can control the entire pier area." Masters said.

"That's an excellent idea! Just don't go all John Wayne on us. Remember who can and who can't fly us out of there . . ." I reminded him.

"Preacher, Sparks, Boats, José, Jorge . . . Manuel, any questions?" I asked

"We can fill the rings with HEPD. If you unload through the muzzle in rapid-continuous-fire Jorge and Manuel can reload the rings and then man the 20s in time for the crash landing alongside *High and Mighty*. And the Lord willing, I can keep up with the reloading on the way out." Preacher volunteered.

"It sounds like you have a handle on it Preacher. We will have a few rounds of Willie Peter and Able-Able-Common for you to work into the mix. We might need to start some fires or light up someone's life." I said.

"Amen! Ain't nothin' like lighting up boxcars or bunkers with Willie Peter! Oh, I almost forgot Kensey. You can use those star shells to create a smoke screen if you fire them at a low trajectory. They don't make the greatest smoke but do fill the area with white hot smoke." Preacher said punctuated with interesting hand jesters and sound effects.

That seemed like the extent of our war-council so I picked up my book with all intentions of seeing whom Asta bit and how Nick and Nora were going to handle it. Before I could find my place Boats pulled up a chair and sat down.

"Nice thing you did for me, Kensey. I appreciate it." He said.

"You're welcome. You know, I've been wondering why you hooked up with Masters after you retired. I know it isn't any of my business but I'm curious." I said.

"Well Kensey, it isn't really a big deal. You know I was Command Master Chief for the squadron. I got there about six months after the "Custer Debacle." You had just been promoted to Master Chief and reassigned. The first CO I had anything to do with was Masters on the *Gemini*. One of his crew, a turbine mech, can't remember his name was busted in town for drugs. Local cops said he was trying to sell some coke to a few shipmates. Masters, for some reason, came directly to me and asked for my help. I still don't know why he did that but I promised I would look into the situation. Masters told me the kid was a damn fine sailor, one of

140

the best in the squadron and it didn't make any sense. I hustled my ass down to the police station to get to the bottom of it. The cops let me interview the kid in private. Shit, in ten minutes I knew something was wrong. This kid was married, with two curtain-climbers at home. He was scared shitless. He had just sewn on second class stripes and was looking forward to a long Navy career. Masters told me he was one squared away sailor and after interviewing him, I believed it. I got all the information the arresting officer would give me which wasn't a whole fuckin' lot. It seems that the cops got the proverbial anonymous phone tip that there was a sailor in a bar called "The Junket" trying to sell coke. Cops raided the place and the only person even remotely around that had any drugs was this kid. Sure wish I could remember his fuckin' name. Anyway, this kid had some prescription drugs on him so the cops busted him. I thought this was going 'waaaay' overboard but the Key West cops were really targeting the PHM squadron sailors. If they wore PHM ships patch, they were targeted. I won't cast aspersions against my predecessor, but he didn't do a fuckin' thing about it. I went back and reported directly to LCDR Masters and told him I thought it was a screw job of some sort. I couldn't put my finger on it but it sure smelled. Masters was pissed, grabbed me by the shoulder escorted me to his car. Our first stop was his apartment. He made some phone calls. I learned later they were to his family's high-powered attorneys. By the time we got to the police station, the kid was in the waiting room, ready to go. Masters and I took custody and returned to *Gemini*. This kid was definitely set up. He wasn't even in the bar, but at the convenience store next door. He was returning to his car when the cops grabbed him, searched him, and arrested him. Masters interviewed the kid for over an hour. Finally, Masters said I could return to my office. *Gemini* was getting underway the next morning and I was to visit this kid's wife to reassure her all would be fine and not to worry." He stopped to take a drink of coffee.

"Please continue, Boats. What was the outcome? What did Masters do?" I asked. I was enthralled and was genuinely interested.

After a short pause, "Well, Masters' attorneys hired some

private investigators to look into the case. Masters footed the entire bill out of his own pocket. Seems that the PHMs were too successful and the drug cartels wanted to discredit the squadron. Druggies decided to start framing the sailors by setting them up for drug busts. A couple of local cops were in on it. The thinking was that if enough sailors were implicated and discredited, it would be impossible to prosecute cartel people. Because Masters got involved and wouldn't let it go, the plan fell apart. Several of the local authorities were prosecuted and the second class turbine mech received a hell of a lot of false arrest money from Key West. Masters made sure the kid put most of the money in college trust funds for the kids. For Masters to go to all of that trouble and expense for a second class turbine mech proved to me he was one good person. Couple that together with his expert ship handling and he became number one in my book. When I retired, I knew he was ready for release. Used some old shipmates to keep track of him and tell me where he was. I figured if I could keep him out of any more trouble he would make something of himself. I've been with him now for about fifteen years making sure he stays out of trouble." He stopped and took a deep breath and gulped some coffee.

"Thanks for the story Boats. So far as I can tell, you have done your job. He hasn't been in any trouble on this job, that's for sure." I said.

"Yeah, he needs the fuckin' money to start his own company. He wants to run charter boats out of Cabo. Wants to use The Fortress as his home base. His brother will partner with him only if he 'buys in' with two years of running costs in advance. The way Masters figures it, about a million ought to get him started. I plan on throwin' in with him if I score enough cash. I have kids and grandkids that need an education, but after that, who knows?" He finished.

I could see Boats was running down and wanted to leave. He had talked enough and I had a better picture of Masters as well as Boats. I now knew why the two had come on this mission. The prospect of getting the money for independence was what they both wanted. Sort of like the rest of us.

Everyone except Sparks had left the ship's lounge and turned in

142

for the night. Tomorrow was going to be busy.

"You have something on your mind Sparks?" I asked.

Sparks handed me a folded, yellow TTY sheet. "Our HF goat herders were on the air. I think they know we read them OK but I don't think they transmitted anything from Gman." He let me read and digest the transcript.

CQ, CQ, CQ . . . this is RAM586. Over.

This is EWE856 I read you 3x2. We have sunspots or someone is walking all over us. Over.

I read you 1x3. Someone is walking over us. The static is too regular to be sunspots. Over.

You came in 5x5 for a moment but the static is back. Over Let's give it 5 and see if the static clears. RAM586 Out.

"Do you think they picked up on your Morris Code?" I Asked Sparks.

"I do. They came back up five minutes later right on the dot." Read on.

CQ, CQ, CQ This is RAM586. Over.

This is EWE 685. I read you 5x5. Static is gone. Over.

Perfect! I was hoping this old goat wasn't losing his hearing. Speaking of goats, neighbors found mine eating the bark off their prized peach tree. Over.

That's a shootin' offense isn't it? Over.

Close enough! It compromised our friendship. I'll have to be real careful when I'm on their property! Over.

Ya. Be careful. We don't want you crippled before the big party! That's it for me. EWE856 out.

Catch you next time around. RAM586 out.

"I'm with you. I think they know we are listening. I don't think they had anything to say other than be careful . . . Like we didn't think of that! Keep an ear on that freq. Some day they may have something useful to say. I'll catch you in the morning." I left in a cloud of doubt. What if Gman was sending us information . . . It could wait until tomorrow. I was off to bed!

The next morning, bright and early, the entire crew was busy going over *Goat Locker* to get her prepared to live fire the 20mms. The *Scrap Dealer's* crew had removed the aft covering exposing the fantail. Preacher, Jorge, and Manuel were staging boxes of ammo next to the two guns. I called the bridge via the sound powered phone line that Sparks had rigged from *Goat Locker* to the *Scrap Dealer's* bridge. I asked Captain Shaw for permission to fire the two 20mms. He reported that radar showed nobody anywhere near, and the crew of the *Scrap Dealer* was prepared. Permission was granted.

"Boats, toss one of those drums over the starboard side. Sparks, mount up." I yelled over the wind.

Soon the target was well aft of the ship. I called up to the bridge and requested a reduction in speed to 5 knots and a course change ninety degrees to starboard. *Scrap Dealer* slowed and rolled slightly as she came about. The oil drum came into sight about 150 yards away. I made sure Sparks was ready and wouldn't shoot holes in the superstructure then issued the order: "Commence firing!"

He was ready and eager! BOOM, BOOM, BOOM, BOOM reverberated across the deck. Waterspouts shot up all around the target but not one round hit it. Sparks emptied one box of ammo and clumsily loaded another. Preacher stepped in to assist and speed the process up. I noted that we would all drill on loading these beasts. Sparks resumed firing in long sustained bursts. Recoil pushed the muzzle up; you had to constantly force it back on the target. After two full boxes of ammo one hole could be seen in the target . . . *"We might need several live fire exercises."* I thought. I was up next. Boats took up the loudhailer, checked that everyone and everything was clear, and then gave the order to commence fire.

I consider myself an above average shot. I have a lot of practice shooting game with large caliber hunting rifles. This was **NOT** what I expected. The 20mm is a completely different animal. I had one hell of a time keeping it on target: mainly because of the damn noise it makes. *"Note to self. Get earplugs for whoever mans the 20s in action!"* I didn't do much better than Sparks, but our target had half a dozen more holes. After Masters proved he wasn't any better, Jose fired. By now the target was about three hundred yards off and still floating. It was getting pretty far aft and I had Boats kick the other drum over the port side. He found a pallet and kicked that over the side too. Greasey mounted up and whined

144

about the target being so far out. Boats told him he couldn't hit it if he was standing on it and to quit bitching and start firing. I requested *Scrap Dealer* come to all-stop. Even at that Greasey only managed to heat up the barrel and hit the ocean. Fritz and Preacher were no experts either . . .

Now it was the Gonzales Brothers turn. Manuel gave Preacher a questioning look. He strode over to the gun and showed Manuel how to load and fire. I imagined he would be lucky to hit the water! I was wrong. He showed us all how to handle a 20! With short bursts, he totally annihilated the target three hundred yards away!

I called the bridge and requested *Scrap Dealer* resume speed at seven knots and come one-hundred-eighty about. Jorge prepared to fire the port 20 when the second oil drum came into view. This would be more challenging. Even Greasey recognized that and quit carping about being cheated.

Jorge commenced firing at a small, bobbing, target about two hundred fifty yards off. He walked right onto the target and then proceeded to sink it outright! Manuel asked if he could shoot at the pallet. I didn't hesitate. I wanted to see if he too could hit a small, moving target.

He rapidly reloaded the 20 and commenced firing. Within twenty rounds he was on target! After forty more there wasn't anything left to shoot at . . . We had our 20mm gunners!

I told everyone to secure the guns and ammo. I looked up the *Scrap Dealer's* mate and asked if they would replace the cover over the stern of *Goat Locker*. I asked everyone to meet me in CIC.

Combat was crowded and uncomfortable. I decided to keep it short. "That exercise proved one thing; the youngsters are the better shooters!" I complimented Jorge and Manuel, "You two will man the 20mms when the time comes. Any comments or suggestions from the rest of you?"

"Yeah, we got any noise suppressing sound powered sets like they use on the helo decks? Those fuckers are loud! No offence Preacher." Greasey said in his growly, whiney voice.

"I think so. If not we'll get some from *Scrap Dealer* and mount them on the shield. Preacher, take these two sharpshooters and practice loading and unloading the 76mm. Anything else?" I asked. No one spoke up and I told them to carry on.

My next stop was *Scrap Dealer's* bridge. I wanted to inform Captain Shaw that we were finished with the live firing exercise and check on 'ear-muffs' for the gunners.

Chapter 22
Great White Way

I found Captain Shaw on the bridge studying several charts laid out on the navigation table. He looked up and nodded as I entered. "We have completed the live firing and are re-rigging the aft cover on *Goat Locker*. Thanks for letting us shoot the 20s. We have them dialed in but it did prove what poor shots we old men are! I had a hard time hitting the ocean, for Christ's sake. The two, *'young'* Gonzales boys did a fine job and totally wiped out the oil drums. Nothing is left floating to foul the shipping lanes." I reported to Captain Shaw.

"Yes, I watched. At one point I was worried one of you old farts might put some holes in my ship." He said with a laugh. He continued, "I have some news. I made radio contact with *Great White Way* and will make the rendezvous with them in about twelve hours. Now, this isn't the Navy and we can't do a side-by-side high-line transfer. We are going to use small boats to move the supplies from *Great White Way* to us. It will take several hours but I, and the Captain of *Great White Way*, have agreed that's the most efficient way to transfer the cargo. From what he told me, there are quite a few pallets containing, as he put it, 'high explosives'. The smoking lamp will be out. I know none of your crew smoke but some of mine do. It will take all hands to get this cargo on board and properly stowed on *Goat Locker*. It looks like the cargo has to be hand carried up those ladders unless you have a better idea."

I thought a few seconds then said, "I'll have Boats rig a block and tackle on a portable davit to lift the cargo from your main deck up to *Goat Locker's* fantail. Preacher will supervise stowing the… 'high explosive' cargo. I'll use my crew to do that. We may have to borrow some equipment from you. *Goat Locker* is pretty much in fighting trim and we don't have a lot of deck equipment. If that's satisfactory, Boats can coordinate it. If you or your crew, professional cargo handlers after all, have any suggestions let me or Boats know." I said with pure respect.

"That is quite acceptable. We have tons of portable equipment for moving cargo and salvage around on deck. My crew will get with Boats and have everything ready before we go alongside the *Great White Way*. Is there anything else?" Captain Shaw asked.

"Yes. I am curious." I replied, and then continued, "How did Masters come to hire *Scrap Dealer* for this... adventure? I've been meaning to ask, but it never seemed like the right time."

"He didn't tell you?" Captain Shaw seemed genuinely surprised. Well... He used to work for Wilson Brothers Salvage. He was 'the' best ship driver on the payroll. He could put a Heavy Lifter ship like *Scrap Dealer* in the exact spot needed: first time every time. All other Wilson Brothers captains were jealous of his skills. Me included. I have to say, I was jealous but respected his skills. He was well paid. He earned more money than some of the newer captains, but he was only a pilot. One day he ups and says he's off to Newport News to work for a small, locally owned, salvage company. They offered him Captain of a salvage barge. I knew he was chomping at the bit for his own command so I can understand why he left. The company was surprised as hell when he contacted us about this particular job.

Scrap Dealer was killing time in San Francisco waiting for the Feds to renew off shore oil drilling licenses. A lot of people are! We have contracts to carry oil-drilling platforms out to drill sites. This job dropped in out of the blue and it was a way for us to earn our keep. It costs a lot of money every day *Scrap Dealer* sits idle. Regrettably, the current Administration, in cahoots with California Greenies, is making it impossible for oil drilling to start anytime soon. That goes double for the Gulf! That freed us up to take on this mission. That about sums it up: and here we are..." Captain Shaw finished with a twinkle in his eye. I believe he enjoyed this type of sea adventure.

"It is fortunate for us you were available. Does transporting armed vessels half way around the world bother you?" I asked.

"No it doesn't. I have Masters' word that we won't be involved in anything illegal. I believe him! I follow the news and I certainly know where we are. My crew gossips and yours are 'very' proud of *Goat Locker* and her capabilities. They talk. I have a good idea you are flying the US flag even though your jack staff is empty. *Scrap Dealer* and her crew will render any assistance necessary.

I'm not thrilled about anyone shooting at us and I hope it never comes to that... But, half a million dollars makes a very persuasive argument!" Captain Shaw said with a sly smile.

"Captain it is our intention to keep you as far away from the shit as possible. We are definitely, and I repeat definitely, not on an official US sanctioned mission. Once we are back in the states look me up. I'll be in **The Safe Haven** on the Seattle waterfront. Buy me a San Magoo and I'll give you the 'Osgood' version of this adventure. And Captain, remember 4.052011 MHz if you find yourself sinking."

I thanked him and left the bridge. I needed to inform the crew about the upcoming UnRep and get Boats working on the block and tackle system. I was looking forward to getting the last of our supplies from Gman. I figured that *Great White Way* was supporting the Navy's effort in the IO. I imagined Gman added a few 'surprises' to accommodate our ever changing mission.

I found Boats after about twenty minutes. He was on *Goat Locker*, of all things, painting. Where he found white paint to cover up those bullet scars from our skirmish with Don Carlos's sorry Navy was beyond me.

I interrupted his painting, "Boats, got a small job for you. In about twelve hours, we're going to be receiving some supplies. I need you to rig up a block and tackle system to get the cargo from the deck of *Scrap Dealer* to the fantail of *Goat Locker*. The rest of us will be on deck to stow the cargo. Think you can do that?"

"Does a bear shit in the woods? Of course I can! Do I look like a Twidget?" He asked and touched the pocket where his new Bo'sun pipe was stashed.

My rack was calling.... My next stop would be my stateroom to take a little snooze before the UnRep. It was going to be a long night. I spotted Winston and asked him to wake me in a few hours. Sparks came down the passageway and stood by my side.

When I finished talking to Winston, Sparks handed me a torn sheet of TTY paper and said, "I just received this message from Gman on the secure sat link."

At first glance this was not good news.

Old Goat: more arrivals target area.
Al Qaida flooding area with insurgents.

Woman and children evacuated from village.
Rumor mill states Al Qaida to take over operations.
Cartel soldiers still keeping low profile but are there.
Pirates still in control but don't know for how long.
Will keep you informed with latest.
New photos coming in three days.
Native spook completely silent. May have lost that asset.
JB

"Geez Sparks. It only gets better and better . . . I'm going to get some shut-eye I suggest you do the same. Thanks for running this up to me." These messages from Gman increased the pressure to get this mission completed!

I still planned on a day, or maybe two, training after we refloated *Goat Locker*. I was not taking *Goat Locker* and her crew into combat unprepared! Period! The mission itself was difficult enough. Without training, it was impossible. Good thing I could sleep through a hurricane! I had enough on my mind to keep anyone awake.

I awoke refreshed and looking forward to one of *Scrap Dealer's* exceptional dinners. I wasn't disappointed and decided some downtime in the lounge was in order next. *Goat Locker's* crew wandered in one and two at a time. Greasey and José took up a grudge match Acey-Ducey game. Boats and Sparks started a Cribbage game. The rest of us read books or perused magazines. The well-worn issue of Playboy already made the rounds but the Gonzales Brothers thought it was pretty damn good. They moved over to a corner and thumbed through the pages occasionally stopping to read an article... Preacher was reading his Bible and mumbling to himself. Masters was snoozing in a lounge chair. We were all killing time and relaxing. We would be plenty busy in a few hours.

"Boats, did you get the hoist system rigged?" I asked across the room.

"Aye, aye Kensey. Baked a cake and did the fuckin' laundry too!" He answered very sarcastically.

"Glad to see you are puttin' that apron to use Boats. I'd hate to see it go to waste. Do you do windows?" I figured I'd break his concentration and help Sparks haul a little timber.

150

"Fifteen two, fifteen four, fifteen six, fifteen eight, a pair for ten and a pair for twelve and no fuckin' way Kensey! I can kick Twidget ass at cards and anything else. Don't forget it." Boats growled as he pegged ten.

"Fifteen two, fifteen four, fifteen six, fifteen eight, and a double run for sixteen . . . and the two you forgot Boats. Hope you fucked me as badly in the crib!" Sparks winked at me and picked up the crib.

I buried my nose in *"The Thin Man"* . . .

Right at 2100 a messenger from the bridge came down to the lounge and informed us we would be alongside *Great White Way* in an hour or less.

I thanked him and said to the crew, "Ok, let's go and man *Goat Locker*. Preacher, we are getting a lot of ammo I suspect and need you to determine the stowage. Boats can run the hoist and the rest of us can hump the cargo. Any questions?"

"Yeah. What's a 76mm projectile weigh? How much of that shit do we have to carry?" Greasey whined.

"'Bout sixteen pounds each." Preacher replied. "And be careful with it and pray you don't drop it!"

"Amen to that. Let's get this show on the road." I said on the way out of the lounge.

"We reassembled on *Goat Locker's* main deck and devised a strategy to stage, carry, and stow cargo. We could make out the running lights of a large ship. *Great White Way* changed course and a quarter hour later she was alongside paralleling our course. We had enough speed to maintain steerage but not much else.

Great White Way lowered half a dozen small boats into the water and used her cranes to lower pallets into them. They transited the three hundred or so feet separating us quite rapidly. *Scrap Dealer* used her salvage cranes to lift the pallets onto her main deck and set them beside *Goat Locker*. Once the pallets were rigged, Boats ran an electric hoist and lifted them to our deck. I unrigged the pallets, removed the Visqueen securing the cargo to the pallet and Boats sent the snatch-hook back for another load. After the first few pallets, we settled into a routine. We held our own against the pace set by *Scrap Dealer* and hauled the last pallet aboard by 0400.

By my count, we loaded 250 rounds of 76mm ammo, 10010 rounds of 20mm, and best of all 16 Stingers. The 20mm ammo was staged on the fantail and strapped down. Stingers were stacked in the armory. We had limited stowage and had to remove the Stingers from their shipping containers and send those back to *Great White Way*. The 76mm rounds were stacked anywhere Preacher could find: crews berthing, mess deck, and passageway. The magazine was filled to capacity, and both rings were filled. The ship would never pass a Navy safety inspection. Gman did well. We had enough ammo to take over a small nation!

We were tired. The work of hauling and stowing that much ammo wore us old guys out. On my way to my stateroom, I dragged myself to the bridge. Captain Shaw wasn't there but the Officer of the Deck was and I informed him that we completed the transfer and all the cargo was stowed. *Great White Way* was already starting to pull away and would soon be out of site. *Scrap Dealer* started to pick up speed and set course due east. Soon she would be at 27 knots. Two days from now we would be at our predetermined position to float *Goat Locker*. That operation would consume the better part another day. It was time to plan the next step...

Chapter 23
Planning the Attack

Everyone was up in time for lunch and it was excellent as usual. All of us, except "the kids" were complaining about being stiff and sore from last night's cargo handling. I asked Winston for a white board and requested to have it set up in the lounge. It would be easier to draw out the attack plan rather than trying to explain it.

Once we were all gathered in the lounge, I started, "I want to take this time to plan out the next few days. I gave Captain Shaw the coordinates for the refloat point. We scheduled the refloat for day after tomorrow. Masters, here is your copy with the coordinates. I want to refloat *Goat Locker* and as we discussed previously, practice flying. I have permission from Captain Shaw to rehearse some 'Crash Landings' using *Scrap Dealer* as a target." This would be interesting, exciting and had a chance of being disastrous! I wanted to make sure Masters was ready. "You got any objections or words of wisdom Bill?" I asked.

"Yes. I need a lot of practice for that maneuver. For you crewmembers that have never ridden a PHM, 'Crash Landing' is a technique we used in intercepting stubborn drug runners. We fly straight for them at full speed and just before we collide, the pilot throws the helm over hard and at the same time initiates hullborne operations. This has the effect of throwing a huge wall of water over the target and dampening their enthusiasm for further actions. It looks like a skier coming to a sudden stop and throwing up a wall of snow. It takes skill and patience to achieve a perfect 'Crash Landing'. Kensey, I '*will*' need to practice." Masters said.

"Ok then that's settled. We practice 'Crash Landings'. Once Bill perfects crash landings everyone else, except the Gonzales Brothers, must spend time flying *Goat Locker*. Jorge if you and Manuel are interested; spend a few watches on the bridge to see how things work. The more you know about ship's operations the better it is.

Scrap Dealer is our fuel station. We will fly and then return, refuel, and fly some more. We may get tired and worn out, but we will all be proficient. Everything we do tomorrow especially, crash landings and flying is 'mission critical'. Bill can rest while we fly. Preacher and I will take the first four hours followed by Sparks and Jose. Boats, feel free to take the helm any time. You've already flown quite a bit but if you want more practice now is the time." I said.

"Aye, aye, Kensey." Boats replied.

I'd sketched the initial attack plan on the white-board. I pointed to it and continued, "Now, this little point right here I named *Point Luck*. It is 400 miles from the target area. Masters provided the coordinates. *Scrap Dealer* will arrive at *Point Luck* at 1500. After topping off fuel, we will depart *Point Luck* and fly into the target area. It will take us about ten hours to reach our objective. We will board *High and Mighty*, get what we came all this way for, then fly back to *Point Luck*. Preacher, the latest intel from Gman says all the woman and children have been removed from the village. *'That doesn't make a bunch of sense . . . Why remove all the slave labor and free pussy?'* That means no one with our best interest at heart will be in the line of fire. You don't need to worry about lighting up the village. *Scrap Dealer* will wait at *Point Luck*. She will be submerged and waiting for our return. We have no time to spare, and we will be very low on fuel: our navigation has to be spot on! Once we are back on the skids and *Scrap Dealer's* deck isn't awash we will get the fuck out of Dodge! We will remain at battle stations and armed until we are well away from *Point Luck* and any chance of pursuit. The plan is to ride *Scrap Dealer* all the way back home. Any questions... anybody?" No one spoke up. "None? Good. I am expecting a real-time set of satellite recon photos. They will give us an accurate picture of our target and harbor conditions. If we have the room we will crash land on *High and Mighty*. Previous intel shows us we have the room so I won't discuss plan-B. Masters will maneuver us to 'Crash Land' *Goat Locker* port side to *High and Mighty*. Boats and I will board her, get what we need and return. We will carry side arms and M16s. José and Sparks will cover us from *Goat Locker* with the M60s. Jorge, Manuel, and Preacher will reload the 76mm then the Brothers will man the 20s. I know that leaves the radars untended but I see no other way. I want the bridge team armed with side

154

arms and M16s. Come to think of it, everyone should have a 9mm strapped around their waist. The more fire power we have on deck the better I like it."

"I got a suggestion." Fritz jumped up, clicked his heels together, and said, "I will cover the starboard side with an M60 and Sparks stays on radar. I should be able to make it from EOS to the starboard side main deck in less than a minute." With that said, he sat down at attention.

"Great idea, Fritz. Make it so. We'll have to stage the M60s and plenty of ammo before we make our run in. That leaves Greasey free. I don't think he knows what end the bullet comes out of anyway!" I said with a smile.

"Very funny Kensey. I know how to shoot that fuckin' puny gun. No worries." And then Greasey added something that I hadn't considered. "Once hullborne, I'm free so I can fuckin' help with the 20mms until Jorge and Manuel show up. I am right there and should be manned-up before you and Boats waddle across to the yacht. If you aren't worried about me shootin' you in the ass that is!"

"Never had any lead in my ass and sure don't want any now. Just watch where you point that 20! Now I know why I chose chiefs for this mission. Thanks, Greasey. I'll feel better with that 20 protecting our backs. Make it so." I said with a better feeling about our success.

"Kensey. It ain't over yet." Boats said. "I have a little surprise for you and the crew. I made three grappling hooks to use on the yacht. I also modified the brow. I added steel hooks to the end of the brow. When we get alongside the yacht just drop the brow. The steel hooks will secure *Goat Locker* to the yacht. It should hold long enough for us to get aboard, do our business, and return. *High and Mighty* is mostly wood and fiberglass so Masters only has to hit the throttle once we are back aboard the ship. The brow will rip out and fall in the water. Fuckin' easy."

"That solves that problem. Thanks Boats. Any more questions?" I asked. Watching their eyes, I knew it was a go and they were ready.

"Oh. One more thing before you go back to what you were doing. Preacher, make sure you reload the rings with VT Frag and

Able-Able Common rounds after we sink the *High and Mighty*. If we are attacked, it will be from the air. Sparks, send a message to Gman. I need those recon pictures asap."

"We still have to worry about pursuit from small craft; Zodiacs, if you remember, are tough and quick!" Preacher reminded me. "If we get them on radar VT Frag set for 30 foot burst height will send them straight to Hell before they get inside our main battery's minimum range. Gman sent 15 rounds of Willie Peter. We can use that to set up a nasty smoke screen so they can't see they're on their way! If I load all 15 you still have 68 rounds in the ready service rings for air defense." Preacher added.

"Load 10. I don't think they will be in any shape to pursue us on the way out but who ever thought half a dozen braves in rubber boats could make a Custer pin-cushion out of a PHM!" I replied.

"Will do, Kensey." He said then he handed me an official looking form. It was an Initial Velocity (IV) report and a complete inventory of ordinance: quantity and type. According to Preacher's inventory, we had available:

60 Rounds: AA Common
160 Rounds: VT Frag
15 Rounds: WP
285 Rounds: HEPD
520 Total Rounds of 76mm
10395 Rounds (27 containers): 20mm
20000 Rounds: M60
20000 Rounds: M16
100 Rounds: Shotgun, 12 gauge
91 Rounds: Shotgun, 12 gauge powder charge only
2000 Rounds: 9mm
26 FIM-92G Stingers
10 M72 LAWS
100 Flares: RBOC
300 Chaff Bundles: RBOC

"Thanks Preacher. I'll attach this to the WCC. I need to input the 76mm ammo information and IV into the computer. Running out of bullets doesn't appear to be a problem! Stowing it will be a challenge though." I said.

Masters approached the white board and examined it closely. "I think this is a damn fine plan of action. Distance is always a problem but four-hundred miles should be out of their range, especially if we sink their fuckin' mother ship. Returning to *Scrap Dealer* might be a little hairy if those damn helos get airborne. *Goat Locker* is hard to hit traveling at fifty knots but I'm still worried about those helos."

"We have the means to handle them. The Stingers and VT Frag from the 76mm should be sufficient to put a hurt on them, if not destroy them. We will scare the shit out of them! They will think twice before making a run on us." I said with more confidence than I felt.

"Confidence is a great tool. I sure hope we can pull this off." Masters said as he moved towards the door. "I'm headed up to the bridge to talk to Captain Shaw, if it is all right with you Kensey? I want to work out the practice details for crash landings with *Scrap Dealer*. Don't want any surprises. We will be at the refloat point soon enough."

"I think that is a good idea, Bill. If nothing else, it will make Captain Shaw feel as if we are including him in our decisions and prepare him for crash landings. Oh, and could you ask him to get the hoses prepared to refuel *Goat Locker* at sea? Thanks."

A few hours later Sparks came rushing in the lounge with a handful of papers. "Kensey. This just came in over the SatCom. Here is the latest and greatest." And he handed the sheaf to me.

I started to peruse all of the papers Sparks had given me. There were a few detailed satellite recon photos of the harbor and village. I studied them closely. They showed that the *High and Mighty* was at the same anchorage. Directly across the harbor, three good sized ships were at anchor. They looked like coastal or tramp steamers. They were definitely at anchor: neither showed a wake or stack smoke. The photos did not have enough detail to make out their names or who's flag flew from their sterns. I didn't spot any helos in the photos. That was a real disappointment and could cause us considerable grief! They must have moved or, hopefully, gone elsewhere. Those helos were a high priority and my number one concern. I couldn't get rid of the thought. *"Where did they go..."* Shit! I selected the next paper; it was a message from Gman:

Latest intel not good. More troops arriving.
Helos have been redeployed. No info about where.
No other hijacked ships in harbor. Sink all ships present.
Take care.
Mission is a GO. Inform me if conditions change.
JB.
Well, that settled the question concerning the other three ships. They go straight to the bottom. That problem was solved.

"Sparks, send a message to JB saying "Thanks. All conditions go." I said and handed the papers back to Sparks. "Make sure Masters, Boats, and Preacher see these and José if you see him. That's all."

Sparks left and I contemplated the next move: practice boarding procedure on *Scrap Dealer* or trust to luck. I decided I would rehearse the whole scenario as many times as I thought it necessary. With that decision made, I picked up my book and continued reading. There was very little to do until *Goat Locker* was refloated.

Chapter 24
The Storm

Captain Shaw's messenger woke me early. He informed me that a severe gale was coming our way and Captain Shaw thought we should float *Goat Locker* and ride out the storm at sea. I thanked him, showered, and dressed. I woke Boats and Masters for a quick conference before making a decision about refloating. Masters and I went to the bridge to get a better picture of what we were in for. Boats said he would wake the rest of the crew and start preps to refloat *Goat Locker*.

Captain Shaw greeted us and said, "Looks like a major blow headed right at us. I changed course a couple of hours ago to put us on the edge of the storm. If this gale tracks like it's supposed to we shouldn't be in too much trouble. Time is not on our side. We will start seeing sea-state four or five with twenty or more knots of wind in about six hours. I recommend we refloat *Goat Locker* now and get her underway. Ten to twelve hours from now, we could be in sea state eight with thirty footers and forty knots of wind. *Goat Locker* won't ride those skids well in seas like that! This storm covers several thousand square miles. It is huge… Currently it is tracking to the north and west of our position but it is moving at about thirty knots and could turn. We won't be able to go around it, but we can easily weather it by staying away from its center."

Masters looked worried. He had experience with heavy weather and *Scrap Dealer*. I could tell he was leaning toward refloating and getting under way to ride out the storm.

Captain Shaw continued, "We have an additional worry. Taking time to refloat *Goat Locker* will allow the storm to catch up with us. Trying to out-run the storm with *Goat Locker* is risky. If it changes course and catches us, we could lose *Goat Locker*!

"That cinches it!" I said more to myself than anyone in particular. "What say you Masters?"

"Refloat! *Goat Locker* can run on the sticks in sea states that would wreck a normal surface ship. It would also give Captain Shaw one less worry. We might lose a few days, but I know I can weather the storm with *Goat Locker* underway. I Guided *Gemini* through several hurricanes. This won't be any different." Masters said without emotion.

Boats had the crew up and grumbling. When he got to the bridge he just caught the tail end of the conversation. I asked him point blank, "What are your thoughts Boats?"

"I agree with Masters. I talked to a few of *Scrap Dealer's* crew. They are good at what they do but cannot guarantee *Goat Locker* won't be damaged riding this out on the skids. A Coast Guard cutter on the skids during a gale didn't fare so well! They almost lost it.

Captain Shaw interrupted, "The cutter sustained major hull damage. Luckily we were transporting her to the scrap yard!"

"We certainly can't afford major hull damage to *Goat Locker*." Boats finished Captain Shaw's thoughts.

"So be it. We refloat right now. Let's get going. Thanks Captain Shaw." I said as we left the bridge.

We assembled in CIC on *Goat Locker* then Masters immediately left for the bridge. I concentrated on immediate concerns. "Preacher, we have to get all the extra ammo secured for heavy weather. We don't want any 76mm rounds becoming missile-hazards when we start rolling around! That would fuck up everyone's day! José, secure the galley and make sure everything is stowed or securely tied down. Greasey and Fritz, you two do the same for engineering spaces. I don't want toolboxes or oilcans rolling around loose. This storm is big and powerful. It's going to take all of our skills to weather it without damage. Those extra rounds pose a very big danger because they are all live. Sparks, you, and I will take care of combat." I hesitated and then said, "OK. We have about four hours until we are at sea under our own power. Let's get to it."

"Boats it's going to be pretty hairy flying. We will be in the shit for at least six hours maybe more. I'd like you to get with Masters and set up a bridge watch schedule. If either of you need help with helm, José, Preacher, or I can help man the bridge. Two hours at a stretch will probably be enough!" With that said, Boats left combat to make sure topside was ship shape.

The next four hours were hectic. Preacher, Jorge, and Manuel

160

tied down every pallet of ammo. Preacher paid special attention the star shells. If one those shells were to detonate, *Goat Locker* would be lost. A white phosphorus fire cannot be put out with seawater and it burns right through aluminum... Boats was everywhere doing everything topside.

We were beat when Boats piped all hands followed by Masters on the General Announcing System, "We are now steaming under our own power. Prepare to go foilborne in five minutes."

I checked the radars and determined that a heading of 300 degrees true would take us around the storm. Radar showed the beast was huge and covered almost the entire scope.

I came up on headsets, "Bridge, Combat. I recommend course change to heading three-zero-zero degrees true. Three-zero-zero will put us in quartering seas and skirt the northern edge of the storm and keep us out of the heaviest seas."

"Combat, Bridge Aye." Masters replied.

"Bridge, Combat. Maintain this course as close as is safe for three hours. After that reverse course and return to *Scrap Dealer*."

"Bridge, Aye."

Goat Locker heeled over in a hard starboard turn and picked up speed. The orders to go foilborne followed shortly. I watched the ship's heading marker swing around to settle on 300 degrees true. Five or six minutes later, we were flying on the sticks at 45 knots. I planned following this course for three hours then return on the reciprocal course in following seas.

I compared our heading to the storm's radar track. It looked like there was no way we could completely escape, but on this course we would skirt around the worst of it. I could feel *Goat Locker* maneuvering to avoid deep troughs and severe rolls. Both Gonzales Brothers were puking their guts up and everyone felt the effects flying through heavy seas.

An hour passed and we were not getting beat up too badly. "Bridge, Combat. How you doing up there Masters?" I asked over the headsets.

"Combat, Bridge. I could use some coffee if José has any made."

"Bridge, Combat. I'll check the galley and bring some up if

161

José is on the ball." I said.

"Bridge aye."

I zigzagged to the galley. Walking on a rolling ship is better than hours on a *Nordic-Track*! José had a fresh pot brewed in the big urn. He made half a pot that was sloshing two-thirds of the way to the top. I filled two cups, put tops on them, and stumbled best I could up to the bridge. This reminded me of my very first typhoon.

I was stationed aboard the *USS Chicago*. We were two days out of Sasebo, Japan when we crossed the eye. We were constantly rolling thirty-five degrees or better. I was asleep, face down, spread eagle, arms out to both sides like chicken wings, and the bunk-strap latched to keep me in my rack. We rolled more than forty degrees around 0100 and a fifty-five gallon, galvanized shit-can, broke loose and skidded across the berthing compartment. It slammed into TJ's bottom rack covering him with a day's worth of trash. Perry jumped up to tackle the shit-can, lost his balance and ended up head first in it while careening to the other side of the compartment before smashing into the opposite bulkhead. Perry was out cold and the shit-can was now rolling through the compartment. Everyone was up chasing it. Three of us finally caught it, got it under control, and tied it down. I didn't need a repeat of that nightmare. *Goat Locker* was well secured!

When I got to the Pilothouse, Masters was strapped into the helm chair. I bear hugged the observer's chair and got Bill's attention, "Here you go, Bill. Fresh hot coffee straight from the galley in a Tommy-tippy cup for you. The sea is building up pretty good! It feels like we're taking twenty-degree rolls. We can't handle much more than that..."

Bill answered, "Thanks for the coffee. It is going to get a lot rougher in about an hour. I've been watching the inclinometer and *Goat Locker's* roll has steadily increased over this watch. It will get worse over the next few hours then start to calm. We can 'beat' into the weather until it gets too bad then 'run' back to *Scrap Dealer* in a following sea. The timing on that should be just about right."

I left the bridge feeling ill at ease. The image of a runaway shit-can filled my mind. I bounced off bulkheads all the way back

162

to combat. Once seated I keyed the General Announcing System and reminded everyone to double check all ammo and make doubly sure it was secured. I called Greasey and told him and Fritz to recheck everything that could become a missile hazard and make sure it was secured! We were in for some heavy seas!

It wasn't long before *Goat Locker* slowed and pitching and rolling increased. Masters was busy maneuvering to avoid the heavy stuff, but *Goat Locker* was taking a beating. I heard a crash and José yelling for all he was worth!

"Sparks, watch the radar I'm going to see what the fuck happened!" I yelled as I ran and stumbled to the galley with Preacher on my heels.

When I got there, José was in the passageway aft of the crew's head and in the hatch to crew's berthing. He was standing there like Atlas holding the world on his shoulders. I made my way over to him still not sure what happened. One look convinced me we were in deep shit! The bunk with all fifteen star shells secured to it was... loose. The weld holding the bunk to the bulkhead failed from the rolling, pitching, and bucking. José managed to wedge his body between the bulkhead and the falling bunk. The pallet and rounds were still secure but there was a lot of weight pressing against him. I grabbed one end of the bunk and lifted, just then, *Goat Locker* took another hard roll and the bunk crashed back into José. The WP rounds shifted a bit and I was pinned between the pallet and bulkhead. It caught me squarely in the chest and knocked the wind out of me. Preacher grasped the bunk, and was turning purple from the strain. I was gasping for breath and glanced at José. He was laughing or wheezing. I couldn't tell! One end of the bunk hung up on the ledger it sat on. Bunk, pallet, and fifteen rounds of WP were going to end up on the deck with the next heavy roll. Boats was off watch and racked out across the passageway. The commotion woke him. He crawled under the bunk between José and I then heaved up with his legs and feet. That reset the bunk on its ledger and allowed José and me to wedge ourselves between it and the bulkhead. Preacher was helping keep things stable while Boats lashed the bunk and pallet back into place.

José took one look at me and started laughing, "You looked

163

like a gold fish out of water!" He said through his laughter.

"Not funny. This fuckin' thing is heavy! If these shells hit the deck, you won't have anything to worry about. There wouldn't be enough left to feed the fish!"

José wrapped my bruised ribs and I wrapped his sprained wrist. If that was all the damage we sustained we would be lucky.

Masters called on the headset, "Combat, Bridge. We will have to maintain our course of 300 true. We will have to go hullborne to turn 180 in these seas. You only think we are rockin' and rollin' now!

"Combat, aye. Advise us when it is safe to reverse course and return to **Scrap Dealer**." I hoped we didn't have to stray too far from **Scrap Dealer** . . .

"Bridge, aye"

Most of us were exhausted after six hours of rolling and pitching. Doing anything besides snoozing in heavy weather wears you out. You constantly bob-and-weave to keep upright and walking on bulkheads takes practice and burns a lot of energy! We weren't rolling near as much now and the radar showed we were clear of the storm, but we would still feel the effects for some time.

Goat Locker was running smoothly on the sticks. I took stock of my crew and ship. The ship sustained very little topside damage, but the bunk in the crew's berthing was destroyed. A few pallets of ammo shifted and chipped paint off the bulkhead. I received two bruised ribs; José suffered a severely sprained wrist. Sparks had fallen in combat and banged up his knee. He could walk but with a pronounced limp and a lot of agony. We were lucky.

Masters called down on the headsets, "Combat, Bridge. Contact **Scrap Dealer** on HF and get her coordinates."

"Bridge, Combat aye." Sparks answered.

Sparks took several minutes to raise **Scrap Dealer**. He received the coordinates for a rendezvous and passed them to me. I plotted the course and it quickly became apparent that **Goat Locker** would be dangerously low on fuel at the rendezvous. Sparks passed my concerns but **Scrap Dealer** replied that was the nearest point possible. I told Sparks to repeat the coordinates back

164

for confirmation.

"Bridge, Combat. Recommend course change to 160 true. It looks like we'll be running on fumes when we get along side *Scrap Dealer*. Masters, this point plots to roughly 380 miles! *Scrap Dealer* must have turned to take the storm on her stern. We've been steaming away from each other for eight or nine hours! If we conserve fuel, we should make it."

"Combat, Bridge. We'll get there. I will run *Goat Locker* in fuel conserve mode. Speed at 35 knots. Get us there in about 11 hours. Seas are calm so we should make good time. I'm good for another four hours. Have Boats relieve me then. I will relieve Boats in seven hours. That puts me on the bridge at rendezvous. HYCATS is great when it comes to steaming and conserving fuel. Relax Kensey, we'll get there. And ask José to run a cup of coffee up here now and then."

I sure hoped we would make it back before running out of fuel... I set a watch bill for the rest of the trip. Sparks and I would swap off combat watch. Preacher and José would take care of the galley details and Fritz and Greasey would swap whenever they wanted. I asked Preacher to make a topside inspection of the weather decks and look for any storm damage.

An hour and a half later, Preacher reported topside sustained some minor damage but we had a real problem in one of the forward compartments. Some lifelines and a few static lines used to secure whips and the mast were gone, but could be easily replaced on *Scrap Dealer*. He said we were very lucky. If we had a full complement of crew and topside life vests, boats and so on, they would have been lost. The P250 pump survived but some of the hose and one educator were gone! The pump is secured aft of Otto on the main deck. Its purpose is to pump out flooded compartments and can be used to fight fires. We rode out the storm in a modified-Zebra watertight condition and should not have any compartments flooded.

I figured we must have taken on water forward. "Preacher what the fuck is the serious problem forward?"

"Good Lord Kensey! Keep your hair on. You ain't gonna like this. I know Boats ain't. One of those bulkhead walking rolls broke half dozen cases of . . . San Magoo loose and they made a

165

hell of a mess . . . I guess it's fitting that Boats should clean it up. José ran his apron up to him with the last cup of coffee."

"Oh . . . . Shit! Sacrificial San Magoo and we have to listen to Boats moan too?" I was relieved no ammo-stored topside was lost over the side.

"Combat, Bridge. I fuckin' heard that!"

Ten hours later Greasey started hollering over the headsets that *Goat Locker* was critically low on fuel and recommended we go hullborne to conserve what remained. Masters and I both agreed and *Goat Locker* came off the sticks without any problems. I was getting worried that we would soon go DIW (dead in the water) while waiting for *Scrap Dealer* to reach us. If we had to, we could shut down all engines and run the generators to maintain power for the radios. We would shut down all non-essential equipment but keep the bridge and comms working.

Greasey came up on the General Announcing System and asked to slow down to six knots to conserve fuel. Masters agreed and *Goat Locker* started to slow. Six knots caused us to wallow in the troughs but it had to be done.

After an hour I contemplated shutting down all of the equipment when Sparks yelled across CIC at me, "Contact dead ahead. It appears to be *Scrap Dealer*. Request we come up on VHF and establish comms."

"Do it Sparks. Bridge, Combat. We have radar contact with what we hope is *Scrap Dealer*. Contact bears 180 true, range 50,000 yards. We will patch you through when we establish VHF communications." I said to Masters over the headsets.

"Bridge aye." Came back.

"Bridge, EOS. Be advised we are shutting down starboard diesel to conserve fuel. You will be running on port diesel only. I am transferring all remaining fuel to port tanks." Fritz said over the General Announcing System.

The situation was worsening and speed would be down to three or four knots. I did not want to go DIW. That was inviting all sorts of trouble.

Sparks suddenly yelled, "Kensey, I got *Scrap Dealer* on channel 79! She will come and get us! Captain Shaw said we could refuel before we are back in the skids. *Goat Locker* will need both diesels to maneuver over the skids."

"Pass that to the bridge Sparks, and have them tune their bridge-to-bridge to channel 79." I said and breathed a heavy sigh of relief!

What seemed like days later, *Goat Locker* was nestled securely in the skids. *Goat Locker's* crew was exhausted. I left Boats in charge of securing everything topside and I went to see Captain Shaw.

We were close to the training refloat point. I hoped Captain Shaw would slow down and give us a rest. "Captain, could we screw around and waste a little time before refloating at the training point? My crew is exhausted and we old men need a couple days of rest."

"Funny, I was going to ask the same thing Kensey... *Scrap Dealer* sustained some damage in the storm and we need time to repair and rest too. I already set our speed to 12 knots. That will get us to the training refloat point in seventy-two hours. Will that do?"

"I replied, "Yes sir. That will do nicely. It will give us time to repair and rest too. I see one of your HF whips on the fantail took a beating. Sparks can give you a hand with that or any other comms or radar problems that may have come up. Don't hesitate to ask. Thanks for the extra 'recovery time'."

"Thanks for the offer Kensey. I may take you up on it. The coupler is full of seawater and we don't have the expertise to overhaul it. I really would like all comms up and running 100% before you depart on your mission. We took green water on the bridge right after transmitting our coordinates. I'm glad that fifty-footer didn't hit us five minutes earlier!" Captain Shaw replied.

"Yeah me too! We'd have been in deep kimchi if we couldn't find you. I'll have Sparks get with your comms guy, Captain." I said before making a beeline for my beautiful, comfortable, non-rolling, or pitching, stateroom.

Chapter 25
Refloat and Rehearsal

Winston woke me early with a fresh pot of coffee and breakfast fit for a king. Eggs, bacon, toast loaded with butter, pancakes covered in syrup, orange juice and best of all, fresh melon, grapes and strawberries. What more could I ask for? I thanked Winston and ate with gusto. After breakfast, I showered, shaved, and proceeded to the lounge. The rest of the crew trickled in and Captain Shaw arrived.

"We will be at refloat point in three hours. Dawn will be breaking so I suggest you pack and move aboard *Goat Locker*. The covers have been removed and she is looking pretty. I want to take this opportunity to thank each and every one of you. You are the first passengers *Scrap Dealer* has ever had that actually gave more than they received. The crew of *Scrap Dealer* wants to thank you for all of your teaching, help and advice they received this past month. Even the old First Mate wants to thank Boats for his help. The engine crew wants to thank Mr. Bishop and Mr. Schmidt for their help in organizing and making the engine shop run like a fine pocket watch. Mr. Sanchez, my cooks want to thank you for the great recipes and help you tendered to the galley. Mr. Meechum, there are several of my crew want to thank you for tending to their spiritual needs. As for Mr. Kensey and Mr. Masters, thank you for including us in this mission. I am looking forward to the return trip. I will leave you now to get on with your move to *Goat Locker*. Fair winds and following seas. Auf Wiedersehen." Captain Shaw had a slight tear in his eye as he quickly left the lounge and returned to his bridge.

We left the lounge in silence and headed to our staterooms to pack. After two hours, we were all ensconced aboard *Goat Locker*. Greasey and Fritz had the generators running and we were on our own power. I lit off the CAS to insure the radar was working and Sparks lit off the LN-66. Both were in tiptop shape. I carried out some daily tests and there were no problems. While I was testing, I felt *Goat Locker* move a little; that told me we were close to refloat. I called up to the bridge and asked Masters to report on our status. He said we would be afloat in about two more hours because *Scrap Dealer* needed to sink a few extra feet to compensate for the added weight of fuel and extra ammo. Captain Shaw wanted to insure we cleared the skids. That accounted for the extra time required to refloat *Goat Locker*.

Finally, after what seemed an eternity, a shrill, familiar sound came over the General Announcing System followed by "This is not a drill! This is not a drill! General quarters. General quarters. All hands man your battle stations. Set modified condition Zebra."

We were afloat and ready to fly. Boats entered CIC and said Masters was going to fly and practice alone on the bridge. I prepared CIC and the MK92 for flying. I wanted to be on the radar and make sure we were unobserved as we flew around the IO. Masters alone on the bridge meant he had no access to the radar displays so Sparks and I took over that job. After flying around for a few hours with no problems I felt *Goat Locker* go hullborne and slow to about five knots.

Masters called down via headsets and asked if Sparks wanted to come to the bridge and fly a little? I said sure and Sparks agreed. Sparks practically ran to the bridge. It took a while but we were flying with Sparks at the helm and Masters taking the instructor role. Sparks did an admiral job and was soon maneuvering and handling *Goat Locker* like a pro. An hour later, we went back hullborne and Preacher took over. We followed this routine for Boats and José. When it was my turn, Masters recommended we return to *Scrap Dealer*. He would then practice 'Crash Landings'. I agreed, took the helm, and set course to intercept *Scrap Dealer*. Two hours later *Scrap Dealer* appeared on the horizon. Masters suggested going hullborne and I agreed and made the transition from foilborne to hullborne steaming and then relinquished the controls to Masters.

Masters called *Scrap Dealer* on bridge-to-bridge and arranged for refueling. Masters skillfully put *Goat Locker* alongside and Boats made quick work of securing us to *Scrap Dealer* with mooring lines. *Scrap Dealer's* crew rigged large orange floats between us as camels. A large hose was transferred from *Scrap Dealer* to *Goat Locker* where Greasey, Fritz, and Boats took over

170

the refueling process. After trial and error, they developed an efficient procedure to refuel *Goat Locker*. Once refueled, we slowly pulled away from *Scrap Dealer*, and opened enough distance between us to start practicing crash landings.

Goat Locker went dead in the water and Masters asked for a meeting with Boats and me. On the bridge, Masters said, "Kensey, I am going to practice the sequence you and I worked out. Captain Shaw has prepared his crew and we are prepared. When we complete the maneuver, I recommend we practice the actual boarding. I'll inform Captain Shaw so a few guns pointed in his direction won't get him excited."

"Boats, you and I will grab M16s and side arms and see how long it takes us to get to the brow on the port side. Fritz will join José to cover us. Greasey will man one of the 20mms. Preacher will stay in the magazine with the Gonzales Brothers for a time approximating reloading one ring. He will turn the brothers loose and they will man the 20s. Greasey will return to EOS. That's about it. Let's give it a try." I continued, "Now let's get to the armory and stage weapons and ammo. We can modify staging and traffic patterns as we go through rehearsals."

Boats and I made our way to the armory and yelled at Preacher to join us. He handed out the weapons and ammo and we placed them where we could grab them quickly. At our age, that was required. We all returned to our stations and prepared mentally for the next several hours of hard work and constant tension. I felt *Goat Locker* get underway and in a few minutes we were flying. Masters took us out several miles before we heeled over executing a 180-degree turn. He kicked it up to full throttle and *Goat Locker* was heading, according to my radar, directly at *Scrap Dealer*. All our pulses started to race. Adrenalin was flowing… A wrong move now and all planning and preparation went up in smoke or worse, to the bottom of the IO!

A shrill sound filled our ears followed by Boats' voice, "Prepare to Crash Land. Landing party prepare for boarding."

I got myself ready. I nervously watched us close *Scrap Dealer* at fifty plus knots. Suddenly the ship heeled over, changed course 90 degrees, and went hullborne all in one motion. As soon as I could, I got up, grabbed my M16, and ran for the port brow. I met

Boats there and a few seconds later José joined us. Unfortunately, *Scrap Dealer* was still over a hundred yards away…

Masters stuck his head out the pilothouse window and said over the loud hailer, "That was perfect. You guys were ready to board within three minutes of going hullborne. Kensey, either you guys need to put on water wings or I need to get a bit closer. Now we know everything works let's try again."

I gave him the thumbs up and we returned to our GQ stations. As I entered CIC, Sparks said, "Skies all clear and no other ship except *Scrap Dealer* is in the area."

"Thanks Sparks." I replied.

A few minutes later, we were on our second outboard leg. We repeated the entire scenario a few more times getting closer to *Scrap Dealer* on each practice run. By the fifth crash landing, our modified gangplank could drop on the gunwales of the target, and we could scamper aboard. However, *Scrap Dealer's* gunwales were way too close to the water to practice the actual boarding. I decided to check with Masters on the bridge.

"I think you got it close enough this time. While we are here, let's call it quits for today, refuel *Goat Locker,* and get some rest. I want to stay hullborne so we can eat and sleep comfortably. Boats has a watch bill posted for helm and CIC. Call *Scrap Dealer* and set up the refueling. See you later and Bill, you did good." I said and returned to CIC.

Enroute I met Boats, "Kensey, I think we should stage the M60 and ammo on the CAS deck and starboard side and our M16s right by the brow. Getting these weapons through the ship with modified Zebra set is a bitch! If we have to button *Goat Locker* all the way up because of a fire fight on the way in we will never get these weapons to where we need them! The M16s are bad enough but the M60s are impossible… I can secure them with a nice strong but easily removed line. As a matter of fact I'll use some of those 17 fuckin' spools of shot line! Staging our pieces here will save at least thirty seconds and besides, I will feel a lot more comfortable knowing those babies will be close at hand." He said.

"Good thinkin' Boats," I said. "Make it so. Any other good ideas? By the way, your pipe sounds real good and you ain't lost the lip."

172

Thanks was all he said and continued aft to help with the refueling.

Chapter 26
Casualty

I entered CIC and Fritz was waiting for me. He jumped up out of his chair, clicked his heels together, and threw me his mock Nazi salute, "Kensey, we have a problem with the port diesel. It is not running very well. It requires a tear down to fix. I think it is in the valve train but I can repair it. Boats will help rig up a transfer system for me to get to *Scrap Dealer* if I need anything from them. It's going to be a long night but I have to fix this engine. If we stay hullborne the starboard engine will be sufficient to maintain 6 knots."

Shit. We didn't need this but it was bound to happen. So far the only casualty we had was a radio, and now a diesel engine. "Go ahead and start the repairs. Keep me informed." Fritz left and I called the bridge to inform Masters that he was running on one diesel and the best we could make was six knots. I asked him to inform *Scrap Dealer* that we had one diesel down and our speed was limited.

A few minutes later Masters called me and said Captain Shaw offered to send over his ace diesel mechanic to give Fritz a hand. I acknowledged and said I would ask Fritz. I called back to the engine room and talked to Fritz. He said any help was welcome. By all means, send him over with his tools. I relayed that info and fetched Boats. I asked him to rig a transfer system to get the crewman from *Scrap Dealer* to *Goat Locker*. He thought a few moments, said that could be done quite easily. There wasn't much I could do for now except stay out of the way and let Fritz and the mechanic from *Scrap Dealer* get-on-with-it. I could smell fresh coffee brewing in the galley. I needed to get with José and talk about a few modifications to the battle plan that I was considering, and this was an excellent opportunity.

"José, when this coffee finishes brewing would you run a pot down to Fritz and Greasey? We should be getting a visitor from *Scrap Dealer* in a half an hour or so. He may want some too. I expect them to pull an all-nighter fixing the diesel. Can you keep the coffee on for them?" I asked as I entered the galley stepping around ammo stowed and secured in every nook and cranny. "Sure, no problem-o. I'll keep them fed too." José answered. "I'm rethinking our plan of action. I may want you to man one of the M60s. You will be exposed on the port side CAS deck. You OK with that?" I asked while still thinking about what I needed. "You would be the first to see action. You'd have to cover me and Boats until the 20s get manned up. Come to think of it, I might want you on the bridge during the run in . . ." "I'm not really thrilled about being exposed like that! I guess I could set up in the prone position. Except for the muzzle flash I would be hard to spot . . . Yeah; I think I can do that." José replied. "I'll think about it and let you know. Good coffee! You stash some **Starbucks** for special occasions? I asked. "Nope; **Seattle's Best.**" José said as I poured another mug full, grabbed a sandwich, and left the galley.

I checked Boats' watch bill and my name wasn't on it. I thought that was considerate but not necessary. I penciled my name in over Boats for the mid-watch on the bridge. He would need his sleep. I finished my coffee and sandwich in CIC. There wasn't much to do before the mid-watch so I went to my stateroom and racked-out.

I wasn't asleep for more than an hour when there was a tap on the door. "Yes. What is it?"

"O' Lord, forgive me," Preacher announced, "That gun developed a slight problem in the outer ring. She quit moving. I got to tear it down and replace a gear that broke a couple of teeth. Take about six hours including unloading and reloading."

"Thanks Preacher, keep me informed." I answered and immediately went back to sleep.

Sparks woke me at 2330 for the mid-watch. I got up, dressed, and made my way to the bridge. On the way, I stopped for some coffee and sandwich. That would do me for mid-rats. I relieved Sparks on the bridge and asked for our status.

"Fuel is at ninety percent. Fresh water is at eighty percent. Fritz and the crewman from **Scrap Dealer** tore the diesel down, found the problem, and repaired it. They are now putting it all back together. We should be ready to give it a test run about dawn. Preacher's still working on the gun. I checked with him about an

176

hour ago and he said it should be up and reloaded within the next few hours. All hands are aboard. No new info from Gman. Nothing! Zilch! Nada! *Scrap Dealer* is about two thousand yards to port and holding station. *Goat Locker* is on autopilot and we are heading two-seven-zero at six knots." Sparks, standing at attention, gave his turn-over report with a smile. He finished with, "I stand relieved. Permission to strike below."

I gave him the standard reply, "I now have the con. Permission granted." And then said, "Before you go, I would like to ask if you think you are now qualified to stand bridge watches and fly *Goat Locker*."

Sparks thought a moment and then replied, "Well Kensey, I did get good lessons from Masters and Boats. They wrote down the sequence of orders and expected responses. I really think I can fly this thing but not in combat. I would feel more comfortable if someone else was executing all of the maneuvers."

"Thanks. I will keep that in mind." I said.

He left the bridge and I checked the magnetic compass against our heading. Everything was in order. I put on the sound powered headphones and said "EOS bridge; what is the status of the repairs?"

"Bridge, EOS; Fritz is almost done. He's putting the head on right now. We should be ready to test the diesel on your watch." Greasey reported.

"Bridge Aye. Thanks." That meant sometime in the next four hours the port engine would be back on line. I called Preacher and asked his progress on repairing the outer loader ring.

"The Good Lord done blessed us. She be up and ready to put a hurt on those pirates in about two hours." Preacher relayed over the headsets.

"Bridge, aye." And that was that. We would be battle ready within the next four hours. The remainder of the watch was uneventful. At 0230 Preacher requested permission to test the gun. He wanted to rotate the loader rings and slew the gun mount to make sure his repair was complete. I checked the fo'c'sle. It was all clear so I granted the request. The gun moved from port to starboard cut-outs and then to its' centerline stow position.

"Bridge, Gun mount; she be up and runnin'." Preacher reported.

"Bridge, aye." All I needed now was a report that the port diesel was repaired. It came in at 0340.

"EOS, Bridge; diesel is up and running." Fritz reported.

"Bridge aye. Fritz go and get some sleep. Tell your helper that we will transfer him to *Scrap Dealer* later this morning."

"EOS, aye." Came across the phones with the purr of the port diesel in the background.

Well that was that. *Goat Locker* was up and running again. The sea was flat and dawn was close at hand. The sky was just starting to show red streaks in the east. I would be relieved by José in about twenty minutes. José showed up right on the dot. We ran through the turn-over routine and then I stopped by my cabin. A few minutes later I went to the crews mess for some good coffee and breakfast. The time was going on 0500 when Boats entered.

"Morning Kensey, thanks for taking the mid-watch. I really needed the sleep." Boats greeted me and continued, "I will have *Goat Locker* ready for refueling by 0800. Masters is on the next watch and he will put us alongside *Scrap Dealer*. I'll rig the transfer sling to get our visitor back to his ship. Anything else you need?"

"That's fine Boats. It looks like we will be at *Point Luck* tomorrow about noon. We should be able to get everyone rested and fed prior to our run on the *High and Mighty*. I am anticipating updated recon photos and any last minute intel before we set the plan in motion." I said more to myself than Boats. I was fine-tuning the timeline and battle plan in my head.

I finished breakfast and decided to run tests on the Mk-92 system. Sparks was already in CIC completing checks on radar and navigation systems. "Sparks, send a SatCom message to Gman. Inform him that we will be at *Point Luck* tomorrow at 1200, Z+3. We will launch at 1500. We will run in for ten hours and return trip should take another ten hours. Request latest intel on our target area. Sign it *Goat Locker*... And be a little cryptic. Imagine someone is listening in."

"Aye. I'd like to test the long-haul link. I'll see if I can raise KID in Cape Town or Ewe in Darwin. Any thoughts on an appropriate message?" Sparks asked. "I'll give you a few to think about it." He said and went over to the SatCom and waited.

178

Testing HF was a good plan. I had the message ready, "Sparks, refer to us as GLB, Goat Locker Boat, and give us the numbers 666. Send *'The beast is on the hunt'*. That should do it.

"I'll get to it in an hour or so. I take it you don't want me to copy Preacher on our call sign . . ." Sparks said.

"Hummm; didn't think of that." I replied, "But there aren't any sacred cows on this ship! Let me know if they are still out there listening." With that said, I started my fire control system testing.

The testing went well. Everything was as it should be. CAS was working, computer was fine, and all the displays were up. The only radar target on the scope was *Scrap Dealer* and it was almost at minimum range. We would be refueling soon and transferring our visitor. I grabbed some coffee and settled in my cabin for a short nap.

I barely had time to get one shoe off before Sparks knocked on the door and entered. "I transmitted, *'The beast is on the hunt'*. I received, from RAM in Darwin, 'beware the Ides of March.' Is Jim telling us to watch our backs? RAM didn't transmit anything else . . ."

I thought about it for a moment before answering. "I think we should consider the possibility that Jim has a leak. It would be a good idea to let everyone know what's up and tell them to be extra vigilant. Jim, and by default, everyone working with him knows what the target is and, more or less, what we look like and our firepower capabilities. I've been thinking about how we are going in and this makes my 'spidy-senses' tingle! We need another pow-wow before we start our assault . . ." Sparks did an about face and left to spread the word. I took off my left shoe, drained the last of *Seattle's Best*, and lay back thinking I probably wouldn't get much sleep!

Chapter 27
Point Luck

The refueling and transfer went off without a hitch. I decided we should remain hullborne and cruise alongside **Scrap Dealer** until we reached **Point Luck**. We would top off fuel and make any last minute repairs before starting our mission. That would afford the crew some rest and down time. We all needed it. A month at sea and working all night was catching up. Getting old sucks! I could do this for weeks on end thirty years ago... We don't have the stamina we used to. I would have to keep that in mind...

Sparks yelled across CIC, "Low flying aircraft bearing 300 degrees true, range twenty miles and closing."

I called up to the bridge and relayed the information. Six minutes later, the plane passed well in front of us and continued on, not changing course, or speed. I started to breathe easier but a fly-over could not be a coincidence. I lit off the Mk-92 and brought 'the egg' to radiate.

Sparks yelled, "Bogie is returning. Bearing 120 true, range 22,500 yards, speed 200 knots. I called the bridge and said pass GQ, break away from **Scrap Dealer**, go foilborne. We have an aircraft in the area and it may be hostile! I ran to the armory and grabbed a Stinger, and rushed to the CAS deck. I heard the shrill note of the Bo'sun pipe followed by "General quarters, general quarters. All hands man your battle stations!" I felt **Goat Locker** go foilborne and swing away from the target.

Once up on the deck I spotted a large single engine plane three or four miles off the starboard bow. If the sun didn't glint off the cockpit, I probably wouldn't have spotted it. It was painted black and it was descending rapidly to sea level. Either the pilot was lost and looking for help or he was a long way from home looking for us.

Goat Locker was doing evasive zigzag maneuvers. It was easier to keep my balance on the mechanical bull at **Gillies**! The plane had no markings and it was going to buzz us or line up for a strafing run... I just convinced myself it was a barnstorming display when I saw little bursts of flames coming from under the fuselage and a line of small water spouts coming right at us. The fool was shooting at us! He was shooting at a fast maneuvering target but he still managed to zing a few rounds off the fantail just aft of the 20s! The pilot was no dummy. He turned for another run well inside the main battery's minimum range. He lined up amidships; I aimed the Stinger, put the target in my sight, heard the tone go steady indicating target lock, and launched. The missile left the tube with a trail of smoke and a whoosh! It impacted the plane aft of the engine in a fiery ball. The sound of the explosion reached us as the plane cart wheeled into the water and completely broke apart. If it wasn't for the floating debris you wouldn't know a plane was ever here….

I came down from the CAS deck and stuck my head into the pilothouse as I passed. "Masters, go hullborne and steer to that debris and oil slick. We have to look for survivors." I continued down to CIC and grabbed Preacher, "Come with me out on deck help search for survivors." Boats was in the crew's mess and I motioned for him to join us.

There wasn't much to see. The sea was calm and we should see something: floating debris, oil, something… Boats suddenly yelled "Two points of the starboard bow! Something yellow is bobbing in the water. I'll go out on the bow and check."

As we maneuvered closer it became clear we were looking at the pilot wearing a yellow, inflatable life jacket. I called for José to join us on deck. The pilot, quite dead, was not African but a Middle Eastern man. I asked Boats to retrieve the body. When the body was laid out on deck, José examined him and informed us that the pilot was dead before he hit the water. I rifled his pockets looking for information. I found a telegram in his shirt pocket. It was written in English: **Armed vessel heading your search area. Intercept soonest and dispose.**

Shit! That cinched it! Gman had a leak in his organization. Someone got wind of our operation. That could be the only explanation. I had to let Gman know. Since there wasn't a description of **Goat Locker** or **Scrap Dealer**, I assumed that whoever leaked was not in Gman's inner circle but an analyst or someone privy to our message traffic. The fact that they knew where to look for us four-hundred miles from nowhere spoke

182

volumes.

"Keep searching, I need Sparks to send an immediate massage to Gman." I said and went straight to CIC.

"Sparks, we need to send a back-channel message to Gman right fuckin' now! I assume our secure SatCom isn't all that secure. Someone knew where to look for us and that information was never passed over HF. Put your thinking cap on; we need to let Gman know he is compromised... Hell the whole mission may be! First, get this message out on SatCom:

Goat Locker attacked by single aircraft.

Aircraft destroyed.

Pilot carried telegram warning of armed vessel. Ordered to destroy vessel.

Mission compromised.

Terminating exercise.

Send that right now."

"Aye aye." Sparks said. "Are you really considering fuckin' quittin'?" He asked before lighting off the SatCom.

"Fuck no! But I sure want whoever is listening in to think so! That plane had to fly two hours to get here. He couldn't have been searching long. I doubt he had any long-haul comms aboard. I don't think he will be missed for a few more hours. We still have time to get to *Point Luck*, refuel, and get on our way!" I said more to convince myself than Sparks.

I went to the bridge and asked Masters to raise *Scrap Dealer* on the bridge to bridge. I wanted to get to *Point Luck* as soon as we could and refuel. There wouldn't be a lot of time to fiddle around. I needed it done quickly. Masters contacted *Scrap Dealer* and I returned to CIC.

"Sparks, keep an extra close eye on radar from now on. I don't want any more surprises." I said. "Let's get on the HF and talk about our surprise party. Get on a headset. I'll have you in the right ear and MARS in the left. If you think of something... talk to me. We need to be 'cute' but get as much information to Gman as we can." Sparks gave me the OK and I keyed the mike:

"CQ, CQ, CQ. This is GLB 666. Over."

"GLB 666, this is EWE 856. Over."

"Someone put our party address out on *Facebook*. One of

the Hell's Angels from across the street got the date wrong and showed up on our doorstep today. Bummer! Over."

"Does Uncle Jim know? Over."

"No. I'm fixin' to call him on the cell and see if his friend, Dick Head, had anything to do with it. He tried to crash our party once before. Over."

"You may not be able to reach him. He is flying in for the shindig with a couple cases of champagne and may be in the air. Over."

(Sparks was in my right ear and I repeated what he was saying.)

"Oh. That sounds good. We should be cool. A few gatecrashers won't bother us that much. If you can reach Uncle Jim, tell him we are still good to go. Mom and Pop are probably still in the dark. Over, and out."

"EWE 856. Out." We would see what we would see . . .

I checked our position and we were still about twenty hullborne steaming hours from *Point Luck*, ten if we ran at flank speed. Nothing I could do about it. We just had to sweat it out.

Gman was half way around the world. I didn't expect a quick answer to our message, but I was wrong. Less than an hour later Sparks came over to the MK 92 where I was sitting and handed me new messages. I said thanks and started to thumb through them. To my delight, there were new recon photos of the target area that clearly revealed the three coastal steamers and the yacht. The coordinates were accurate enough to input into the computer for shore bombardment. I could also engage the steamers in shore mode. But what was important was the message:

Thanks.

More Al Qaida involvement.

Still no sign of helos.

Use best judgement.

Champagne on ice. JB.

That was that. Gman got our back channel message. We would continue come hell or high water. I started working out coordinates to input in the MK 92 computer and our firing plan. Two hours passed quickly. I told Sparks I would be on the bridge for the 1600 to 2000 watch if he needed me. I was preoccupied the entire four hours. The watch passed quickly. When Preacher

184

relieved me I had a pad full of notes and an assault plan worked out. I quickly went over the few changes I made since our practice runs then returned to CIC. Masters, Boats, and Greasey were in CIC rehashing today's action with Sparks. I asked Boats to pipe all hands and announce a general meeting in CIC. Several minutes later Fritz, Jorge, and Manuel crowded in to combat followed by José.

"This will be quick. We practiced the assault and have the timing down. I want to make two small changes. Boats, I want you to take the first bridge watch then get some rest. At T-1 hour, I want you in CIC with me. José I want you on the bridge at T-1 hour. As soon as we crash land, you will man the port side M60 on the CAS deck and neutralize any one on the yacht or pier. I started the mission clock at 2000. It was set to T-26 hours. If there aren't any questions, in the words of a great strategist and my favorite sleuth: 'The game is afoot!'" No questions were asked and CIC emptied with everyone deep in thought about what they would be required to do twenty-five hours from now . . . I brought everyone up to speed about the latest developments and assured the crew that we would carry out the mission.

After my watch, I ate and hit the rack. Tomorrow we would arrive at *Point Luck* and refuel. The mission was a go and the tension was starting to mount.

Several watches later, we arrived at *Point Luck*. We refueled and arranged to meet *Scrap Dealer* in just over 20 hours. Captain Shaw wanted to open the range from *Point Luck* to make sure *Scrap Dealer* was out of harm's way as much as possible. We were as ready as we could get!

I turned to Masters and said, "Get her on the foils. Let's get this show on the road! We have about ten hours to T-zero. We will rotate bridge watches. I want Boats, Preacher, José, and myself to stand watches. You get some rest. One hour out, T-60 minutes, you will take over and Boats, Sparks, and I will be in CIC. Preacher, Manuel, and Jorge will man the 76mm. José will back you up on the bridge and man the port M60 right after you crash land on the *High and Mighty*. The last thing we do before we start flying is pre-stage ammo, small arms, M60s, Stingers and LAWS, and arm the 20s. Let's do it!"

Chapter 28
The Run In

T-9, (pronounced Tee-minus-nine), hours-thirty minutes: we were flying. This was not a practice run. Boats was on the first bridge watch. He would be on the helm for five hours then get some rest before boarding **High and Mighty** with me. Masters would be on the bridge for the final assault and our withdrawal from the harbor. Sparks was keeping an eye on comms and the LN-66. I had the egg operating and was monitoring the radar displays. Air and surface were clear of contacts. We didn't need any surprises! Greasey and Fritz worked out the engineering watch bill so they could both get some rest. José was busy in the galley. I was confident we wouldn't starve before returning to **Scrap Dealer**. Masters was pacing. It was obvious he was not following my advice to take a nap. I just asked him to see if José had fresh coffee made when Preacher broke in on the head set."Bridge, Gun control. Phone check." Boats answered immediately, "Bridge aye. I hear you loud and clear. That was followed by, "Combat, Gun control. Phone Check." Sparks answered up, "Combat reads you loud and clear." Preacher came back, "Combat can we do some radical maneuvers for about ten minutes? The good Lord wants to see iffen' we can load the outer ring while flying and maneuvering."

Masters, listening on the speaker system weighed in. "That's something the Navy would never let us do! I hope we don't have to do that for real . . ."

I thought about it. Preacher would be loading before we crashed. The odds we would be maneuvering on the way in were good! This practice was dangerous, but probably necessary . . ."Gun control, Combat. Give us about ten minutes to prepare everyone. And Preacher, please tell me you have a few dummy rounds to play with . . ."

"That's a negative combat. We be real careful! We be loadin' as soon as **Goat Locker** starts rockin' and rollin.'"

"Combat, aye. EOS make sure engineering is prepared. Bridge, commence maneuvers ten minutes from my mark . . . . **Mark!**" I ould you warn José in the galley? Hold off ᴊfter the maneuvers!" With that done, I turned ρarks. I wanted to gather all the information in ᴊafe. I returned to CIC just in time. Boats piped ᴊr the General Announcing System followed by preρ ᴊnaneuver. I put both fingers in my ears: probably not an effeᴄᴛᴊve defense against a mishap in the magazine! We rocked, rolled, did everything but crash for seven minutes. Preacher came up on the phones, "Good Lord! That be impossible . . . We loaded ten rounds . . . dropped two. Jorge be chuckin' them over the side right now! Manuel's getting' a scratch seen to by José. You're good to go. Both rings be loaded and ready."

"Combat, aye . . ." There wasn't much else to say.

I retrieved all of the photos and documents from the safe in CIC and my cabin. We were foilborne, not maneuvering, making 50 knots in flat calm seas. Masters returned with fresh coffee. We examined, for the hundredth time recon photos. I placed them side by side with the earliest on the left and the latest on the right. We looked for any change in position or hint of movement from the various ships at anchor. Three cargo ships were in the same place but the **High and Mighty** moved. She appeared to be about two-hundred yards closer to the beach and pier complex. Masters noticed the movement. We agreed the crash landing was still a go but the pirates could react a little faster and ***Goat Locker*** would be just inside small arms range.

I concentrated on a close examination of the surrounding area. I was looking for those damn helos! I spotted a new clearing in the second photo. It wasn't in the first photo, and appeared camouflaged in the last! I jotted down the coordinates and decided to lob a few HE shells in there. I didn't see the helos, but it could be an ammo or fuel dump. Somebody went to a lot of trouble to clear the area then conceal it.

It was time for me to try and sleep. I asked Sparks to wake me in two hours, left combat, and stopped in the galley to check on José, Preacher, and the Gonzales Brothers. Manuel sported a three-inch gash in his left arm sutured with three butterfly bandages made from duct-tape. José tried to hide his smile and I knew damn well he had proper sutures. He was helping Preacher and the Gonzales Brothers stage ammo. Jorge and Manuel seemed to have their flying-sea-legs and Manuel, left sleeve rolled up, seemed quite proud of his battle dressing. I suggested everyone get some sleep or at least rest. We would be very busy in a little over eight hours.

My last stop on the way to my cabin was the bridge. Boats and Masters were going over strategies to accommodate the *High and Mighty's* movement. Boats said draft depth might be a problem but didn't think so. I hadn't thought of that but couldn't worry about it now. I went into my cabin and hit the rack.

Two seconds later… Sparks woke me. I showered and went to CIC. As I entered, José handed me a cup of hot coffee and a sandwich. We were T-five hours and ten minutes. I would be looking for another sandwich in a few hours. Boats called down via headsets and said Masters was taking the bridge, and he would get some sleep. He said he would be in combat on or before T-one hour.

I had plenty of time to kill. I checked and rechecked my shore-bombardment coordinates and went over my firing plan. The effective range of the 76mm gun is about 20000 yards. I could effectively engage targets at T-ten minutes. As soon as I started engaging targets with the 76mm our element of surprise was gone. I would open fire at T-five minutes, ten-thousand yards from crash landing. I would fire fifteen rounds of VT Frag at the three anchored ships taking out their comms and radar. Sixty-five rounds of HEPD fired at preselected targets would follow. All would be fired in rapid-continuous at eighty rounds per minute. We would be traveling at 50 knots and would get one hell of a lot of ordnance on targets before boarding the *High and Mighty*. I quietly prepared for whatever would happened. I put the combination to *High and Mighty's* secret compartment in my shirt pocket and buttoned it. I scanned the ammo inventory, noticed Preacher had adjusted 76mm by two, and placed current

IV computations on the WCC. I checked and updated the information. I noted the magazine temperature increased 4 degrees.

I scanned the check sheet for small arms, Stinger, LAWS, 20mm ammo placement, and RBOC launcher loads. There were four sets of initials and check marks next to each item. I wasn't the only one feeling a bit paranoid! T-four hours and nineteen minutes . . . I was as ready as I would ever be.

Chapter 29
The Attack

At T-50 minutes *Goat Locker* was making 55 knots at Fritz's 'improved' flank speed. Boats was sitting next to me at the WCC. The harbor and three cargo ships displayed nicely on radar. I could make out the pier but ground clutter obscured most everything else. Range to the pier read eighty-thousand yards, forty miles. I adjusted the time to T-40 minutes and asked Boats to pipe all-hands and announce general quarters.

Boats keyed the General Announcing System mike, piped all-hands, and announced, "This is not a drill, this is not a drill. General Quarters! General quarters; all hands man your battle stations!"

We set modified condition zebra two hours earlier and everyone was already on station. It took less than ten seconds before the first manned-and-ready report came in. "Combat, Bridge. Manned and ready." All other stations reported and received an acknowledgment within one minute. That had to be a record of some sort!

At T-30 minutes range to the pier read sixty-thousand yards. If it wasn't for the whine of the LM-2500 you could hear a clock tick. Everyone was keyed up and excited. I went over my firing plan one more time and asked Boats to announce T-20 minutes when it came around.

I made a last minute safety check with the gun crew. "Gun control, Combat. Make sure all fifteen VT Frag rounds are cycled into the inner ring. I'll be firing them first. I will give you a heads up when we go weapons-free. We will engage all targets in rapid-continuous-fire at eighty rounds per minute. Stand clear of the rotating rings! I expect to open fire at T-5 minutes if we are not discovered before then. Your crew will not have much time to reload."

"Gun control, aye. Could we have ten seconds of silent prayer for *Goat Locker* and a successful mission?"

"Combat aye." I wondered where the Southern drawl got off to . . .

Boats keyed the General Announcing System mike and piped all-hands." T-20 minutes. All systems go. Range to target . . . thirty-eight thousand yards."

Most of the ground clutter was gone and I could see **High and Mighty** and some movement near the clearing. I thought, *"Those must be large vehicles, probably earth movers. The range isn't closing. I don't think anyone sees us yet. If they do they don't know what to make of us . . ."*

I double-checked to ensure fire control was in shore mode and all coordinates were in the system. I think I only breathed twice when Boats interrupted my concentration, "You want me to announce T-10 minutes?" I was startled but answered up, "Negative." I came up on interphone. "All stations combat, T-10 minutes! Bridge, when I go weapons free engage HYCATS, and close your eyes. I don't want you blinded by muzzle flash! Gun control; make sure *'everyone'* is clear of rotating machinery!"

"Bridge, aye."

"Gun control, aye."

"Combat, Bridge." José was speaking but I could hear Masters in the background. "Inner harbor quiet. Intermittent lights north of pier. Cargo ships at anchor. No apparent signs of alarm."

"Combat, aye" José confirmed what radar was showing.

T-6 minutes. Luck could carry us only so far! "All stations, combat. Weapons Free! Gun control; stand clear of all rotating machinery!" I started the pre-programmed shore bombardment routine and my stopwatch.

Goat Locker shuddered and shook as the first 15 VT Frag rounds streaked toward three unsuspecting vessels in twelve-seconds. I watched relative bearing of the main battery as it started its firing sweep from 270 degrees. I hoped José and Masters, on the bridge, had earplugs in as well as eyes closed. It was noisy in combat. It sounded like firing the M60 without ear protection! One minute and four seconds later main battery returned to "stow" position.

"Combat, gun control. 79 rounds expended, bore clear no causalities." Before I could acknowledge José broke in.

"Holy shit!!!! My ears are ringin' and the place is a . . .a . . . inferno! Motherfucker! The jungle just erupted!
192

I issued the conversation stopping command, "Silence on the line!" *Goat Locker* was nine thousand-four-hundred yards from *High and Mighty* and a lot of things needed attention. Masters wasn't talking; he didn't have time. *Goat Locker* jinked right then banked into a starboard turn. We were lining up to crash land. WCC showed main battery being reloaded.

"Bridge, Combat. Report" I needed to know if any organized opposition was mounting.

José took a deep breath and started his report. "Three ships are afire and appear to be listing. The shoreline from the ships to the pier is ablaze. The pier appears to be intact but burning in several places. The concrete structures are burning here and there. The clearing behind the pier is . . . Son-of-a-bitch! Exploding and burning like a motherfucker!

"Combat, aye"

Sparks yelled over the phones, "LN-66 shows surface targets near the beach. Bearing two-four-five degrees true! It looks like they got some small boats in the water. They're moving too slow to interfere with 'Crash Landing'."

"Bridge, aye. Recommend we engage them with port 20. Get ready and hold on!" Masters yelled over the headsets. I clicked my stopwatch off. It read five minutes-forty three seconds… Boats looked at me, gave a wink, and said, "We're on. I hope Preacher put in a good word for us."

"Amen." I replied as I grabbed my chair with both hands and waited. *Goat Locker* heeled over on the starboard side and plowed to a stop.

Masters executed a perfect 'Crash Landing'. I jumped up and grabbed an M16. Boats had the CIC hatch un-dogged. I followed him at a dead run to the port side mid-ships brow. We could hear the rat-a-tat-tat of an M60 and the pop-pop-pop of an M16 as we ran. Masters was covering us from the bridge and José was on station on the CAS deck. I heard a few rounds twang off the superstructure but opposition was light. We were slowly drifting away from *High and Mighty*.

The port 20 erupted into action and I could see waterspouts stream into a group of small boats. I saw three reduced to kindling before Boats cut the restraints on the grappling hook-brow. It

193

banged over **High and Mighty's** port gunwale and stuck fast. I heard the starboard 20 explode into action. Preacher must have the inner ring loaded and released one of the Gonzales brothers.

We had kicked a hornets' nest and I could hear them buzzing all around us! M60 fire was almost continuous. I figured Fritz must be on station. I threw one grappling hook and Boats grabbed the other and threw it over. Both hit home, dug in and Boats and I tied them off. We were securely fixed to the yacht.

Boats and I scrambled across the brow. Boats stopped abruptly and I ran into him knocking him to his knees. Wood splinters filled the air around us as the coachwork disintegrated in a hail of M60 rounds. I spun around raised my M16 over my head, waved it around and fired off half a dozen rounds. José looked right at me and nodded. We nearly bit-the-dust and I was sure anyone in the salon fared worse.

We ran aft on **High and Mighty's** port side to the salon door. I couldn't hear shit! **Goat Locker's** port 20 was furiously engaged and continuously firing. There were almost no small arms bullets ricocheting of **Goat Locker** now. José, Greasy, and Fritz must be doing their jobs.

Chapter 30
High and Mighty

Half way to the cockpit two men popped out from behind the cabin. Boats fired from the hip and plowed a furrow of splintered deck and coachwork all about them! One went down and the other dropped to the deck, rolled around while firing a nine or ten millimeter handgun. I felt a tug and sting in my right thigh. I shouldered my M16, fired a short burst and he quit moving. Boats flattened himself against the cabin wall and crab-walked toward the cockpit. I followed suit ignoring a trickle of blood and hoping my wedding-tackle was OK! I could see muzzle flashes from *Goat Locker's* port bridge window; Masters was covering our ass and spotting targets. José was firing short bursts, both 20s were roaring, and it sounded like Fritz on the starboard M60 was firing continuously. Boats, then I, dropped into the cockpit. We flattened ourselves either side of the salon door.

A heavy machine gun started a steady barrap, barrap, from the buildings north of the pier. I could see the muzzle flashes and a trial of tracers walk into *Goat Locker's* port side just forward of the 76mm then aft up to the bridge. Boats emptied his M16 magazine into the salon door, dropped it, un-holstered his 9mil, jacked a round into the chamber then kicked the splintered door open and started down the ladder with me close behind. I caught a streak of light in my peripheral vision as I followed him into the main salon. I tapped Boats on the shoulder. He stopped; I passed him, handed him my M16, un-holstered my 9mil, and took the lead.

The salon was torn up pretty good from José's merciless pounding with the M60. Not much survived including two men crumpled in a heap against the starboard bulkhead. Ambient light was good but I brought my tactical flashlight up in my left hand. We went forward to the port side hatch leading down to the second deck berthing spaces and Captain's cabin. I cautiously descended the ladder, plastered myself against the bulkhead, and covered the forward staterooms and the aft Captain's cabin then motioned for Boats to join me. He was half way down the ladder when the forward most stateroom door burst open I clicked my tactical flashlight on and saw the new comer was stunned by the light. I double tapped his body and fired another bullet at his head. Boats slid in beside me as the second forward stateroom door opened and a man peaked around the door firing wildly. I emptied my magazine through the door, ejected it, and rammed another home. The door slammed against the bulkhead propelled by the dead weight of another martyr on his way to ecstasy with seventy-two virgins.

I motioned for Boats to position himself behind the ladder and cover me. Before moving I said, "Boats, the location, and how to open the safe is in my breast pocket." I didn't hesitate. I slid aft along the port bulkhead to the Captains' cabin. I slowly turned the doorknob, nodded at Boats then flung the door wide open. A torrent of bullets rushed out followed by two men. One looked directly at me as he took his first, and last, step. He fell back against his partner propelled by M16 rounds fired in full auto. They appeared quite dead but I double-tapped both as I passed them and entered the Captain's cabin.

Boats shouted, "Kensey if you don't need me in there I'll keep the dogs off you from here!" I gave him thumbs-up and said. "Thanks Boats. Keep a sharp eye!"

I removed the instructions from my shirt pocket. I was sweating and shaking but forced myself to concentrate on the task at hand.

The instructions weren't complicated. According to Gman, they *'must'* be followed exactly. Step 1: grasp the light fixture on the starboard side of the bunk's headboard. Pull it straight out as far as you can and tweak it right and left until you feel it engage an indent. I did as it said and the indent was quite evident.

Step 2: Turn the whole fixture clockwise 90 degrees. No more; no less. I did that and felt more than heard a definite 'click'.

"We got company coming." Boats yelled. I heard his M16 rattle off in full automatic. "I don't think they want to come back!" He choked from cordite and stale air.

Step 3: Turn the fixture back to starting position then turn 90 degrees clockwise again. Repeat procedure like a ratchet until compartment opens. I did just that several times. I was getting worried! I didn't see or hear anything opening... I was really starting to sweat. I thought *"This had better work or all of this is for nothing!"* The numbers were off. Boats and I had been here too long! "Fuck it!" I said to myself and turned to leave. A piece of mahogany wainscoting along the forward bulkhead was sticking slightly out. I moved to my right, grabbed it firmly, and pulled... It slowly opened revealing a solid steel lined compartment between the hull frames. Two briefcases were hidden there.

I grabbed them and hurried out of the cabin. A huge explosion knocked me down. "What the fuck was that?" I yelled at Boats.

"Fuckin' concussion grenade I hope! Think it did more damage to those assholes than it did us. Let's get the fuck out of here!" Boats yelled as he started for the hatch and upper salon.

Boats sprayed the passageway with the M16, slammed in another banana clip, and started up the ladder. We cautiously entered the salon and started to make our way aft to the cockpit. We hesitated at the ladder. I could hear both 20mms and both M60s firing continuously.

We popped out on deck and saw bodies lying everywhere. José and Masters were busy indeed! Lucky for us.... We crouched low and scrambled back to the brow. *Goat Locker's* amidships hatch was open and I stumbled through. I figured Boats would trample me but he wasn't there!

Boats was lying on the quarterdeck, grasping his left thigh, and yelling something about mother fuckin' mother fuckers!

Sparks was prone in the passageway with an M16! I yelled, "Boats is hit. Give me a hand and let's get him inside!"

High and Mighty's aft mast and rigging disintegrated in an ear splitting explosion and massive ball of orange and yellow fire. Another explosion off our starboard side pushed the brow into her coachwork and she groaned as *Goat Locker* rode up and down against her port side.

"What the fuck was that!" Sparks yelled.

"Artillery!" I yelled back.

We half carried half drug boats into CIC. *Goat Locker* shook under the impact of another explosion. We were already moving and zigzagging out of the harbor. Half of *High and Mighty's* port gunwales and all her lifelines came with us. I scrambled back up to the quarterdeck and cut the grappling hook lines free with my *Ka-bar*. Everyone was awake now! Small arms, and heavy machine gun fire whined and buzzed all around! A smoke trail followed by a loud explosion up forward convinced me to dog the hatch and get to combat!

"Get us the fuck out of here!" Sparks yelled over the headsets.

CAS displays were blank! The egg was off line. I mentally counted five muffled explosions, some port, some starboard, and some aft while I checked all circuit breakers and threw every battleshort switch I could remember. I cycled the egg to ready and held my breath . . .

Goat Locker settled out and EOS reported, "We're flying!" One of the 20s was still firing, but soon stopped. After all the noise and chaos, the silence was eerie. . . Radar displays were back up and I felt a whole lot better.

Blood was oozing from a bullet wound in my right thigh and my left arm was riddled with wood and fiberglass splinters. I quickly checked my leg wound. I had a nasty bruise and a gouge. I applied a battle dressing and keyed the General Announcing System, "All stations, Combat. Report!"

"Combat, Bridge. Minimul damage. Broken glass but no damage to equipment! José took some shrapnel and has a nasty wound. He's sewing it up right now." Masters reported.

"I have a bullet wound in my left arm. Not serious but it sure as fuck hurts!" Greasey reported.

"Ja you can always use your other hand, but that furrow across your ass is gonna take some fixin!" Fritz chimed in.

"Combat, Gun control. Both rings loaded with a mix of AA-Common, HEPD, WP, and VT Frag. Jorge and Manuel are both wounded but not serious. More scratches than real wounds." Preacher reported.

"Bridge, Combat. Is José in any state to come down here and see to Boats? He looks pretty
bad . . ."

"Bridge, aye. He's on his way down now." Masters replied.

José hobbled in to combat and immediately examined Boats. "It looks worse than it is." Was his assessment. "He will be fine. I

198

gave him some morphine for the pain. Those steel-jacketed bullets punch neat little holes. The bullet went clean through the fleshy part of his thigh. Missed bone and arteries. He is one fuckin' lucky fellow!" José said.

"Lucky fellow my ass! It hurts like hell!" Boats yelled at José.

I thought we'd be well into the morning watch. . . We were at T+21 minutes! Range to the pier was ten-thousand yards and rapidly increasing. We had one last task to do before bugging out.

"Bridge, Combat. Come about to heading two-seven-zero!"

"Bridge, aye."

"Gun control, Combat. Keep the 20s manned and Weapons free!"

I felt the ship heel over and reverse course. I checked the radar and set in firing coordinates for the beach and the yacht. There wouldn't be any surprise this time . . . We settled out on heading two-seven-zero. Range to the pier was ninety-three-hundred yards.

Sparks reported seeing moving targets near the pier. I sent four rounds of HEPD into *High and Mighty* and ten more into the pier. Three explosions reverberated through the hull. Masters reported, "We've been bracketed!" and started evasive maneuvers. I selected HEPD and lit up the shoreline either side of the pier. Two explosions rocked *Goat Locker*. Range to the only moving target, five-thousand-six hundred yards. An ear-splitting explosion shook *Goat Locker* and both CAS displays went dead! I switched to LN-66 video, spotted a large moving target, and fired thirty rounds of VT-Frag at it. I could hear the muffled sounds of HE rounds landing all around us, one after another. They were getting further and further away. I selected HEPD and AA Common and saturated the block buildings north of the pier. Range to shore line three-thousand-three hundred yards. I heard explosions in the water all around us. They were getting louder and louder. I showed three WP rounds ready to fire and the magazine door open. Preacher must be scrambling to reload.

"Bridge, Combat. Can you verify *High and Mighty* is destroyed?"

"Negative! Everything is blazing and it can't see shit in this wind tunnel!" Masters reported.

We were paralleling the shore on a heading of zero-one-zero true. *Goat Locker* was bracketed close enough to make her shudder. A loud metallic clang followed and *Goat Locker* shook like a wet dog then settled down.

"Bridge, Combat. Come about and run by the pier. We need to verify *High and Mighty* is destroyed!"

I selected the three WP rounds and fired at the only target still moving while Masters in a high-pitched excited voice reported, "I think we took a round through the fo'c'sle! Steering is a bit weird but I still have good control. Let's get the fuck out of here!"

We banked into a port turn and settled on a SSE course. I could clearly see a large target one thousand yards dead off the stern on the LN-66. Rounds were landing all around us then suddenly stopped.

"Uh . . . combat, port and starboard 20. Uh . . . we fired two LAWS at a big motorized cannon that was firing at us . . . Uh. Over . . ."

"Port and Starboard 20s, combat. You got em! Lay below and help Preacher reload!" I needed Preacher to make a damage control assessment up forward.

"Gun control, Combat. Jorge and Manuel will be there shortly to finish loading. Make sure I have WP in the mix. I need you to go forward and report on damage."

"Combat, Bridge. We just ran by the end of the pier. All that's left is burning oil and some scrap wood! A group of small boats just came out from behind the freighters! Recommend course change to zero-nine-zero!"

"Combat, aye!"

"Combat this is Preacher. We got one jagged hole in the fo'c'sle amidships and another port side just above the water line. Boats lost some more gear and we got about six inches of water on the deck. I stuffed Greasey's mattress in the hole and its keepin' the water out. It be a miracle none of this ordnance got touched off! Praise the Lord! Amen . . ."

We were in dead calm seas and Masters had slowed us to forty knots. Radar showed a group of small, high-speed targets pacing us four thousand yards astern. Sharks waiting for us to go dead in the water!

200

"Gun control, Combat. Cycle ten star shells to the inner ring."
Following us was about to become difficult.

"Si . . . aye" Jorge answered up.

"Bridge, Combat. Come starboard ninety degrees." *Goat Locker* banked into a starboard turn.

"Bridge, Combat. Engage HYCATS. Weapons free!"

"Gun control, Combat. Stand clear of rotating machinery!" I selected 10 star shell rounds laid the main battery just forward of the small armada and mashed the firing key. A fog bank appeared four thousand yards off our starboard quarter and the sharks were engulfed in a cloud of white-hot phosphorous smoke. If they survived that, they deserved to follow us all the way to *Scrap Dealer*!

"Combat, Gun control." Preacher was back on station. "Ten rounds expended. Bore clear no casualties. Inner ring loaded with VT Frag and AA Common. Loading outer with HEPD"

" Combat, Aye. Bridge, Combat. Resume course and speed."

José entered Combat to check on Boats and me. He was pale and looked worn out. Speckles of blood colored his t-shirt where his stitches were. He didn't waste any time and got right to a medical status report:

"Greasy ain't gonna sit for a while and I put his left arm in a sling. Fritz has a bunch of small wounds and couple of bruised, if not, cracked ribs. Jorge and Manuel are covered in shrapnel wounds, they look ugly but are minor, and I had to tape two of Jorge's fingers together. I think they are broken. Masters' entire left side looks like hamburger from flying glass. Most of the bridge windows are missing and he put duct tape over his left eye. It has a little blood in it and it is watering but I think he will be OK. He has at least one cracked or broken rib. I taped him up. If you think we are out of the soup I'll relieve him on the bridge as soon as I sew you up and make sure Boats is OK.

"Sew me up? I just got a nick, duct tape pulled all the wood, and fiberglass splinters out of my arm. I think relieving Masters is more important!" I wasn't all that convincing . . .

José closed my wound with six big, ugly, jagged, stitches that he said would give me bragging room then tended to Boats. He was sitting up in the corner with a silly grin on his face. José removed the battle dressing, said it was the last one he had and rebound his leg with a pink apron.

I checked the clock. Forty-one minutes ago, I opened fire on the **High and Mighty** . . .

Chapter 31
Defend the Ship

0128. T+1 hour 28 minutes: Goat Locker was flying in a relatively straight-line, conserving fuel, at forty knots. I stepped out of CIC and scanned the seas with my binoculars. It was dark with a crescent moon and a few scattered clouds. There was a distinct orange glow due west: the burning aftermath of our attack. I walked to the fantail.

Boats would be pissed! It was gouged, dented, and scraped from shrapnel and bullet trails. It looked like the port 20 scatter shield was never painted! Starboard was in better shape but how the Gonzales Brothers survived at all was a miracle. The turbine exhaust funnel was dinged, dented, and in places holed. It took the brunt of the artillery barrage and probably saved Jorge and Manuel... I picked up three or four pieces of shrapnel lodged against the bulkhead and put them in my pocket. Thank God for the scatter shields and ready service boxes for the ammo . . . I took a few steps aft, turned, and surveyed the upper superstructure. The egg was cracked and part of the mast along the starboard yard-arm, SatCom, TacAn, weather birds, and NIXI were . . . gone! Our HF whip was still there but seemed raked back a little more than usual. I knew the LN-66 was still operating; its survival was another welcome miracle. Most of the bridge windows were blown out and Old Glory, at least part of the stars and one scraggly ribbon of white and red, was flying from a make shift halyard attached to the mast's aft brace. I couldn't spot the ensign halyard so it probably went with the top of the mast and starboard yard...

I heard Sparks yelling over the General Announcing System, radar contact. I ran back to CIC and checked the radar repeater. I saw clear seas with the harbor forty-seven miles astern. Sparks said, "Sorry Kensey. Hope that run didn't get your leg to bleeding again."

"Yeah. José says we don't have any more battle dressings . . . Ha! What did you see? What am I looking for?" I asked.

"Look dead aft. Something pops up then disappears. Probably

just the radar acting up. I hope it doesn't crap out on us . . . There, two-six-eight true! See it Kensey?"

"Yeah . . . fuck me to tears . . . Bridge, Combat disengage HYCATS and come starboard ninety degrees. I think we found those helos! Sparks sound general quarters and pass the word for Masters to report to the bridge. Gun control you still on the line? Prepare for air action starboard!"

"Si. You shittin' me Kensey? Preacher's with Boats. I get him. Gun ready to shoot!" Jorge replied.

We didn't have a real good defense strategy and very few crew to spare. I turned to Sparks, "Grab José and Manuel. Send them to the CAS deck and break out Stingers. You get to the fantail and set up a Stinger. Boats had shielded them pretty good. The Stingers on the CAS deck were tucked up against the deckhouse under a deck plate steel shed he welded in place. The same affair sandwiched between the turbine exhaust funnel and bulkhead saved the fantail Stingers and LAWS. I'll engage the bogies with 76mm until I empty the magazine then try to join you. It's up to luck after that!"

Goat Locker banked starboard and I heard the LM-2500 wind up to flank speed. José was on the ball. Fritz must be in EOS. It would be hard for Greasey to strap in with his ass all shot up. What a time to smile . . ."*I couldn't get the image of how José managed to stitch and bandage Greasey's ample ass out of my mind!*" Three bogies vectoring in off the starboard bow at twenty two thousand yards jolted me back to reality. They had to be right on the deck . . .

"Bridge, Combat. Weapons free. Air action starboard! Gun control. Stand clear of all rotating machinery." I placed the Mk-92 in surface mode, 120 rounds per minute, selected, VT-Frag and AA- common with sixty foot burst heights synced it with radars' decreasing range and mashed the firing button.

Forty-five seconds later Preacher reported. "Forty rounds expended. Bore clear. No casualities. Cycling all HE rounds to inner ring!"

I selected AA mode and two distinct targets at thirteen thousand yards heading aft and mashed the firing key. Masters and José on the bridge would be getting one hell of a Fourth-of-July display!

204

Thirty seconds passed and Preacher reported. "Combat, gun control, 31 rounds expended. Bore foul. We have a hang fire!" He was going to be busy . . .

"Bridge, Combat. Start evasive maneuvers. Bogie 'Alpha' at bearing three-zero-four true, twelve-thousand yards at 160 knots. Bogie 'Bravo' at bearing two-two-three true, eleven-thousand-six-hundred yards at 180 knots! Switching RBOC control to the bridge. You got it! Combat off line!"

"Combat, Bridge. Aye Skipper" I ripped off the headsets and ran for the fantail . . .

Masters keyed the General Announcing System and warned all hands topside to brace for high-speed maneuvers.

Boats had rigged foul weather lifelines before leaving *Point Luck* so we could traverse weather decks while flying. It was still tough going. Sparks was strapped into the port 20 with one Stinger slung over his shoulder and the other at ready resting on the top of the scatter shield. I grabbed the last two Stingers from their shelter, strapped myself into the starboard twenty, and readied my weapon.

I saw two flashes of light off the starboard side at a relative bearing of about zero-seven-zero, the starboard RBOC popped four times, followed by the port launcher, and a trail of light left from the CAS deck. I couldn't see anything flying but did see the RBOC chaff rounds explode and the flares light off followed by two streaks of light heading at us and slightly aft. I was searching where I thought the helo would be, got a steady tone on the Stinger, and pulled the trigger. A ball of light and thunderclap erupted a hundred yards off the fantail and I saw a splash fifty or sixty feet in front of me. Just before *Goat Locker* heaved up on her starboard side then crashed, I saw a ball of fire close to the water five or six hundred yards off the starboard quarter.

A line of tracers walked across the deck from behind me. I ducked under the scatter shield in time to miss the exhaust as Sparks fired a Stinger. More tracers danced around the deck then traversed up and forward. I felt more than saw two Stingers leave the port side CAS deck then heard the helo pass close overhead. We were dead-in-the-water with two Stinger missiles between us and a nasty adversary on the loose! Sparks unstrapped from the

20, casually walked to the port life line, searched with the end of the Stinger, looked behind him to make sure I was out of the way then sent his last missile on its way.

I followed his missile exhaust with the end of my Stinger and yelled at Sparks to get the fuck out of the way. The doppler tone went solid and I fired the last Stinger. A bright orange explosion lit the skyline followed a few seconds later by another.

I grabbed the sound powered phones, "Bridge, Fantail" I wasn't sure we even had communications anymore.

"Bridge, Aye." Came the welcome response

"Bridge, Fantail. Two bogies splashed. We are in good shape back here with no injuries. Are there any causalities up there?"

"Negative but Jorge is a bit singed. We still have radar and the gun and magazine is buttoned down for another nine minutes before Preacher can extract the hang fire. He's on the CAS deck reloading RBOC. Fritz is trying to find out why the LM-2500 shut down and Greasey staggered below and will have diesels on line. We should be underway momentarily." Masters finished with, "The more miles we can put between us and that glow to the West the better I like it!"

"Amen! Fantail off line" The diesels rumbled to life . . .

Sparks was still standing at the lifeline looking out to sea. I walked up behind him and put my hand on his shoulder. He was shaking. "Jesus Kensey . . . I thought we were going to die!" he blurted out.

"Me too . . . I think we're shakin' in sync. It's the adrenalin rush. We need to contact Gman. Check out comms. We lost SatCom and the HF antenna is a bit beat up. If we can communicate come get me. I'm going to check with Masters and Preacher then I'll be in CIC." With that, I left for the CAS deck and bridge.

Preacher was just loading the last RBOC tube. Jorge and Manuel were watching and learning. Jorge's flak jacket was scorched and I could see patches of whitie-tightie where his coveralls were burned.

Preacher finished up, wiped the launcher down, and handed me his prized purple cloth. "Nice shootin', Twidget! Hang this here cannon-cocker badge out your back pocket. You earned it. I got one for Sparks too."

206

"Thanks." Was all I could manage . . ."Preacher, how much trouble is that hang fire gonna give us?" I asked to change the subject.

"Not much. I'll be shuttin' down the salt water-cooling come ten minutes from now and ifn' Otto be cool I'll extract the round. You want it for a souvenir? Preacher asked nonchalantly.

"Hell no! I want to live long enough to show this gunners mate merit badge off! Chuck it over the side . . ." I replied and started for the bridge.

Even at ten-knots, the bridge was breezy. José and Masters just finished checking helm and engine controls and José said, "I'll take the next three hours if you'll relieve me at 0500."

I asked José about the status of the LM-2500 and wings. "Fritz said some mumbo-jumbo about hydraulic controls and compressed air and he should have it up and running soon. He already checked both wings and the hydraulics and controls are sound. We should be flying within forty-five minutes. Masters didn't have anything to add so I asked him to accompany me to my cabin. It was time to see what was in the two briefcases from the *High and Mighty*.

Chapter 32
The Prize

Masters followed me to the Captain's cabin. I fumbled with the Sergeant Greenleaf on the file cabinet; it opened on the third try. I removed the two briefcases retrieved from *High and Mighty* and handed them to Masters. "A little light aren't they? I hope there is some money left in the operating fund or we're doing this job for free . . ." he commented.

"They '*are*' a bit light . . ." I replied as Masters set the briefcases on the desk. On a whim, I thumbed the latch release buttons, "Bet we'll have to saw these apart." I said as both latches popped up. "I'll be damned! Don Carlos was either too arrogant to think anyone would mess with his stuff or stupid . . ."

The briefcase contained papers and three compact discs. I set my laptop on top of the remaining briefcase, woke it up, and slipped in the CD. A window opened and I clicked on the documents folder. Spreadsheets with names, dates, cash amounts, what information was passed, what task were accomplished, and by who, filled the screen.

"I think Gman will be happy. Maybe we'll hold a disc or two as ransom." I joked. If the papers and other two discs contained the same kind of data, Congress and the Administration were going to look a whole lot different in a few months! I pulled several blank CDs out of the top desk drawer and copied all the disks and handed them to Masters and said, "Keep these until I tell you to destroy them . . ."

"Ah . . . Sure, but why?" Masters asked looking surprised.

"Insurance." I didn't need to say more. I put the original CDs back in the briefcase, closed it, and set it on the bunk. "Let's see what this one has in it." I said as I thumbed the catches. It was locked. I pried around the edges with my *Ka-bar* but nothing budged. I knew Boats would have my ass if I broke the blade so I used my, ever-present, tweaker to break the latches free. This briefcase had a foam-rubber insert cut into compartments. The largest, about half the briefcase, contained a stack of Somaliland Schillings, a stack of Columbian Pesos, and a stack of greenbacks with a ten-thousand dollar band around it. Several smaller cutouts contained: one tube of twenty-five Krugerrands, one tube of 25 Maple Leafs, and one tube of fifty Half-Eagles. "Here's a bit of a payday in funny-money and gold." I said as I picked up the last object in the brief case: a thumb drive.

"Not much of a payday, but better than nothing!" Masters uttered.

I slipped the thumb-drive into my laptop and waited until *Windows* recognized it and asked me if I wanted to open or explore. I opted for *'open.'* I was greeted with, "Welcome to Bank of the Cayman Islands" and username and password boxes. "We might have to wait a while before we see what's on this drive . . ." I told Masters. I emptied the briefcase then handed it and my *Ka-bar* to him and said, "see if you can find a password anywhere in here."

Masters carefully removed and inspected the foam while I tried several back door schemes to open files on the thumb-drive. He carefully ripped all the linings out and disassembled everything possible. "No luck Kensey" he reported.

I handed Masters the stack of Somaliland Schillings and told him to go through them one at a time while I did the same with the Columbian Pesos.

Ten minutes passed in absolute silence. Sparks rapped on the cabin door entered and said, "HF is up. What's up here?"

I handed him the bundle of green-backs and said, "Payday"

"No shit! This is it . . ." He replied with genuine disappointment.

"Looks like it." I said, but you need to look at all those bills. We are looking for a username and password to open banking information on this thumb drive.

Masters and I finished, re-bundled the bills, tossed them onto the bunk, and had Sparks give us each a bundle of hundreds to look through. The third bill I looked at was a ten-spot!

"Hey! I got something here." I said and held the bill up for examination. I looked it over carefully then handed it to Masters. He held it up to the high-intensity desk lamp and smiled. Copy this down Kensey. "MiErdaAvaNumeroUno. No fuckin' way . . . That can't be his user name!" Masters laughed.

"What's so funny?" Sparks asked.

"That user name roughly translates to: Shit Bird Number One! Here Kensey, copy this down" Masters started rattling off numbers, letters, and symbols: **13#aZ38%&dQ9ps@16981ZA @69.** If I'm not mistaken that's the password.

I entered the username and password. The little blue ***Windows*** *'working'* doughnut came up and the hard drive light flashed off and on for several seconds. *'Access to the internet required'* popped up and flashed until I clicked on the *'cancel'* button.

"That's about all we can do until we get to ***Scrap Dealer*** and get on the internet." I said. I put everything back in the file cabinet and secured it with the hated Sergeant Greenleaf. "Sparks let's get a message off to Gman."

Sparks, Masters, and I went forward to the communications room. Sparks handed me the mike, checked the frequency, and gave me a thumbs-up.

I keyed the mike, **"CQ,CQ,CQ, This is Gulf-Lima-Bravo 666, over."**

"GLB 666 this is KID 685. How's the party? Over." Came right back over the speakers.

"Party's over. Over." Sparks gave me a sour look but Masters held up his hand before Sparks could say anything.

"Sorry I missed it but I couldn't get away. Over"

I was thinking in overdrive. I urged Sparks and Masters to come up with a reply using hand gestures. Both gave me the Polish salute and I started hesitantly. **"We . . . Won the door prize . . . but may be too drunk to drive home. I'd call a taxi but can't find my cell phone. Over."**

"I'll contact Uncle Jim and see if he can pick you up. Over."

"Thanks. GLB 666 Out."

"KID 685, out." And that was that. . . The ball was in Gman's court now. Masters started to leave; the speaker squawked to life. **"George-Lucifer-Betty, this is Rickshaw. What is your ETA? Over."**

Masters stopped, turned, and said, "That has to be Captain Shaw on Scrap Dealer!"

Sparks gave me a skeptical look and asked, "Does Captain Shaw have our back-channel freq?   We've been on the air a while we could be tracked!"

I said, "Yes, and good point. We'll shut down transmitters and listen only from now on." I keyed the mike and transmitted, **"Rickshaw, half a day and break out the sewing kit. Out."**

We weren't all that secure and José, on the bridge, had been monitoring radar and the tactical situation by himself too long. I needed to get CIC manned and make plans to meet *Scrap Dealer*. I told Sparks to patch HF into CIC and get some rest. José was going to be relieved at 0500 and I figured that would be good for me too.

"CQ, CQ, CQ, This is EWE 856 blared from the speakers." Sparks gestured to the mike and I shook my head.

"Gulf-Lima-Bravo, make best speed to Diego Garcia. Champagne on arrival." Dead air followed.

Chapter 33
Return to *Scrap Dealer*

Fifteen knots wasn't moving us from hostile territory fast enough. Preacher cleared the hang-fire at 0310 and reported both rings loaded with a combination of Able-Able Common, VT-Frag and HEPD. We were running dark, and silent, and I only allowed two or three active sweeps from the LN-66 every fifteen minutes. It was unlikely anyone would search for us until daylight but I couldn't count on that.

José called and said there was egg, bacon, and cheese breakfast burritos and fresh brewed, hot, *Seattle's Best* available in the galley. I asked him to make up three boxes of battle-rats, bring me one, and deliver one to Sparks and one to the bridge. I told him to remain on the bridge as a lookout. Sparks didn't get so much as a cat-nap, but neither did anyone else and we needed eyes on deck at least until we were seventy or eighty mile out to sea. I needed to set a watch.

"Gun control, CIC. I hate to do this to you guys but . . . There's food and hot coffee in the galley. Eat, then move six Stingers to the CAS deck, and the remaining Stingers to the fantail. Send Jorge or Manuel to the fantail and the other to the CAS Deck. Make sure they have binoculars! Sparks or I will be up on the CAS deck in a few." We were still in hot water without eyes, ears, or running shoes!

"Jeez Kensey . . . Where's Honest Abe when you need him? My boys are beat up and worn out!" Preacher wasn't one for bitchin' and moanin' but was sure good at it when he did.

"Twenty five hours away with the entire Confederate Army looking to destroy him . . . Good burrito! Make sure you guys get some. It may be your last if we don't get a move on it!" Masters put his two cents worth in.

"Be about ten minutes more." Fritz chimed in. Our phone discipline was gone to hell but I didn't think it was worth mentioning.

I did my 0315 radar sweep and returned the LN-66 to dummy-load. I didn't see any contacts, but really wished the egg was working so I could see what was happening above. It was another fifty miles to our turning point . . . Three and a quarter-hours at this rate!

Captain Shaw requested to move **Point Luck** one-hundred-fifty miles south after we were attacked. I'd consented and asked him to consider moving between one-hundred and one-hundred-fifty miles west in case we ran into trouble and had to return on diesels. I really hoped he did just that! We planned on running due east after the attack then turn northeast at pre-determined coordinates to make finding us more difficult.

Masters reported a flooding alarm in the Bo'sun locker and hullborne steering was a bit weird. Once we were back on the sticks, the flooded space would drain. It was a nuisance but not much of a real problem.

"CIC and Bridge, EOS. It looks like we are good to fly." The LM-2500 wound up and Masters and Fritz started the flying checklist. We were flying at 0330! I asked Fritz if we had enough fuel to maintain flank speed for five hours. He said we could do six but would have to break out the oars in eight.

Sparks staggered into CIC, cup of steaming coffee in one hand, and burrito in the other. "What the fuck Kensey? Can't a guy get some sleep around here?" He grumbled.

"We need to get some eyes on the sky at least until we change course. We aren't all that far from the hornet's nest we kicked! You want to take CIC or a couple of hours on the CAS deck?" I answered probably sounding as annoyed as I looked.

"I'll take two here then relieve you." Sparks answered.

"Bridge, CIC see if you can get some sound powered communications on the CAS deck. X-43J2 or 10-JP1 circuits should still be working. We are going to maintain lookouts there and on the fantail until we reach **Scrap Dealer**. You guys got foul weather gear and eye goggles up there?"

"Bridge, aye. I hope we don't get a head wind!" José answered up.

I gave Sparks the standard watch relief routine and told him we could probably use radar in another half hour. Even if someone saw the radar, they wouldn't identify us as a surface target. We

214

were moving too fast!

It was breezy, chilly, and noisy on the CAS Deck. Jorge was huddled against the deckhouse, binoculars dangling from their strap. He touched his sound powered phones then pointed to a pair on the starboard side. I put them on and ran a phone check. Bridge, CIC, EOS and Gun control all answered up.

"Manuel, phone check."

"Si signore Kensey." Good! Comms were working.

"Listen up." I started. "Manuel you are fantail. Jorge you are port lookout and I am starboard lookout. Attack from the air is still possible. You must keep your eyes moving. Scan the entire horizon high then low, take a break then do it again. If you see, or *think* you see, '*anything*' report it using a relative bearing and elevation angle. Every second or third sweep use your binoculars. Anyone who can get eyes on a reported contact do so. Any questions?" There were none.

"All lookouts, CIC. Report."   I thought Sparks may be exacting some revenge . . .

"CIC, Starboard lookout. No contact."

"CIC Fantail. No contact."

"CIC, Port lookout. No contact."

Two hours and thirteen minutes until sunrise: this was going to be one worn out crew . . . *Goat Locker* banked starboard and settled on her northeast leg. It was starting to lighten up. That improved our chances of spotting an attacker. If Captain Shaw stuck to the original plan we were about six hours from *Scrap Dealer.*

Red streaked the eastern sky. Preacher had relieved each lookout for a coffee and piss break. It was my turn. I was glad for the diversion. The adrenaline was gone and I was bone tired. I stopped in CIC to see if Sparks had picked up any new HF radio messages. He said no but he had some chatter at regular intervals by the same two guys. Sparks said he had no idea what language they were speaking but one sounded like he was transmitting from a plane. I thought, *"This might be a search plane and I hope they are south and west!"* Whoever was searching for us would be widening their search pattern. I stopped on the bridge with a couple of sandwiches and coffee for José and Masters. Carrying on a conversation was nearly impossible so I resumed my starboard lookout.

"Bridge, CIC. I have a contact at bearing two-seven-zero true, range 18 miles. He is closing at 120 knots. I recommend coming to course zero-nine-zero. Let's see what he does."

"Bridge, aye! All lookouts keep your eyes peeled starboard!"

If this was a plane, the pilot made a basic error. Our air search capabilities were gone with CAS. As long as he flew on the deck the LN-66 would track him and feed information to fire control.

"Bridge, CIC this yahoo changed course and is headed right at us. Range ten-thousand yards and closing fast!" The general-quarters alarm sounded and the main battery slewed. Starboard RBOC spit four times and the main battery came to life at sixty rounds per minute. Flares and exploding ordnance lit up the skyline. A twin line of waterspouts ran in at us. *Goat Locker* banked hard port making it hard to keep standing. I scooted downhill on by butt to the Stinger storage, grabbed and readied a launcher. I searched port and aft until the tone went steady, yelled at Jorge to hit the deck and I pulled the trigger. A streak of fire left the fantail a few heartbeats later followed by the 76 mm re-engaging. A ball of fire erupted about two thousand yards off the port side closely followed by another and exploding AA common and VT Frag.

"Hot damn, Kensey! Shootin' my gun be more fun than loading or fixin' it!" Preacher probably wouldn't let me forget he shot his gun using my fire control system . . .

"You can teach an old dog new tricks, but he's still an *'old'* dog and Manuel and I splashed that bogie!" I retorted.

"Silence on the line! There may be others out there!" That was Greasey being a wise-ass but he had a point.

It was 0530. We could assume it would take an hour or so to mount another effective search for us. We already destroyed two planes and three helos. The dirt-balls ashore couldn't have many more attack aircraft . . .

"All hands, starboard lookout. Let's secure lookouts for the time being. We'll reassess in an hour. José if you are up to it a hot breakfast would be very welcome!" I set my sound powered phones down and made my way to CIC . . .

Preacher was sitting in my chair with his feet up on the WCP. "Glad you could make it Kensey. Had a little trouble with an airplane but The Good Lord done took care of it!"

"Get your feet off my WCP." I said while laughing. "Good shooting Preacher. Better reload those rings, and RBOC launchers we may need to use them."

Preacher got up, walked over to me, and gave me a hug. Under his breath, he said only loud enough for me to hear, "I be scared shitless but I got it to work!"

That was the first and only time I heard Preacher swear. He had a certain swagger to his step as he left CIC on his way to reload the gun. I was certain José would hear all about it when Preacher passed through the mess decks.

Chapter 34
Back on the Skids

The sun was up and another brilliant, hot day was in the making. We hadn't seen or heard a thing for two and a half hours. Last night's events were two-hundred-fifty miles in our wake. I thought we should see *Scrap Dealer* on radar in another two or three hours if all went according to plan. We were traveling along the same line in opposite directions. If Captain Shaw was steaming at thirty knots, we had a closing speed of eighty-five knots! If he stopped at *Point Luck,* we would be very low on fuel when we got there.

"CIC, EOS. I recommend we reduce speed to forty knots to conserve fuel. We are at fifteen percent. That leaves us two and a half hours at flank speed."

"EOS, CIC. Make it so." I figured fuel would be low but fifteen percent was cutting it close!

Everyone was winding down and resting. Masters and José were switching watches on the bridge every hour. Boats and Greasey were in their racks. Fritz was manning EOS. Sparks and I were in CIC with very little to do. Preacher dragged a mattress into the magazine and was racked out there. Jorge and Manuel were switching lookout watches every hour on the CAS deck.

0930 rolled around; Fritz called and said we were at seven percent fuel. I reduced speed to thirty-five knots and started rethinking the HF radio silence.

Sparks broke the silence. "Kensey we either have another low flyer or *Scrap Dealer!*"

"Let's hope it's *Scrap Dealer.*" I said as I pressed the salvo alarm to wake Preacher.

"Bridge, CIC. We may have company dead off our bow about thirty-six miles. It may be *Scrap Dealer.* See if you can raise her on VHF. Use all the helm and speed you need. I'm going to general quarters! CAS deck lookout, remain on station, and make sure you have a Stinger or two handy!" Before I could sound the general alarm, the sweet sound of all-hands trilled from the speakers. Sparks must have patched a squawk box into the

General Announcing System from the officer's stateroom. Boats could barely get around the corner to the mess deck let alone negotiate ladders and passageways!

"Combat, CAS lookout. I am manned and ready Skipper" Sparks reached over and keyed the general alarm and flatly stated. "Here we go again . . . Kensey."

The LM-2500 whined into flank. I selected a mix of VT Frag and AA common and set burst height to sixty feet. Sparks and I kept our eyes glued to the radar repeaters. Our contact showed about every third sweep. I really wished I had the egg up and running!

Ten minutes went by in a blink. We were painting the target with every other radar sweep. Closing speed was 60 knots. *Point Luck* and *Scrap Dealer* should be another hour and a half away.

"Combat, Bridge. You might want to aim the main battery elsewhere otherwise Captain Shaw may take his ball and leave . . . I have him on channel 79."

"Combat, Aye! Gun control, unload one round, well away from *Scrap Dealer*, and stow the mount."

"Gun control, Aye!" Otto spat out a round. "Combat, Gun control. One round expended. Bore clear. No causalities." I acknowledged and told Sparks he had CIC. I wanted to be on the bridge when we came along side *Scrap Dealer*. As I walked out the hatch I heard Sparks on the phones to Boats.

"Boatswain Mate of the Watch pipe secure from general quarters, and pass the word for all hands to prepare to come alongside *Scrap Dealer*!"

I stopped in the galley, picked up two cups of coffee and made my way to the bridge. Masters reported *Scrap Dealer* fifteen miles ahead and submerged. That was good news. We could get on the skids and vamoose!

We flew to within five hundred yards of *Scrap Dealer* then went hullborne. With Boats out of action, Preacher was running the deck. Masters slowly maneuvered *Goat Locker* into position over the skids. *Scrap Dealer's* crew shot lines aboard the bow and stern. Preacher and José secured them to the deck cleats. *Goat Locker* was tethered in position and *Scrap Dealer* was slowly rising.

220

The general quarters alarm suddenly blared from the topside speakers. "This is not a drill! This is not a drill! All hands man your battle stations."

I grabbed a set of sound powered phones, put them on, and picked up a Stinger. "Combat, Kensey. What's going on?"

"Captain Shaw reports a fast moving radar contact coming in at 090 relative. The only thing we have clear to fire is the starboard 20 and Stinger on the fantail and whatever you can see on the CAS Deck." Preacher sprinted out onto the CAS deck. Readied one Stinger and slung another over his left shoulder.

Preacher and I scanned the horizon but couldn't see much against the high bright sky. I saw a line of tracers then heard the rat-a-tat-tat of machine guns. Bullets whined and ricocheted off our fantail and *Scrap Dealer's* aft superstructure. They were after the 20s on the fantail. Preacher and I both saw the plane as tracers walked up the turbine exhaust and onto the CAS Deck. Both of us fired at the same time. I saw Preacher spin around and slam into the deckhouse as the all black
plane flew directly over us. He seemed close enough to touch! Preacher didn't appear to be bleeding so I concentrated on the plane. He only went out about five hundred yards then turned, and climbed a bit. I had him locked on his outbound leg. I pulled the trigger just before he completed his turn to make another strafing run. My missile smashed directly into his propeller. The plane disintegrated in a ball of flame and falling pieces.

I spun around to help Preacher. He was sitting propped against the deckhouse staring at half a Stinger launcher held in both hands. "The Lord wants I should build him a fine house. I can see he aims to be sure I get it done . . . I be keepin' this to remind me so. Amen." I was speechless. I really thought we would be conducting a burial at sea.

All I could say was, "Damn Preacher! You keep tearing up Gman's toys he ain't gonna let you play anymore . . ." I handed him my purple rag. "Here! Just in case you need to clean out your skivvies!"

"CIC, Kensey. Another pilot just screwed the pooch! Preacher is banged up a bit more but he's ok. Do you or *Scrap Dealer* see anything else out there?"

"It looks clear Kensey. Why don't these assholes send more than one at a time?"

"Don't look a gift horse in the mouth Sparks! I'm glad they attack piecemeal. It's a lot easier to shoot them down one-at-a-time!

"Boatswain Mate of the Watch, pipe secure from general quarters."

"Aye Kensey, and could you tell me what damage this latest dickhead did to my boat!"

"We took some fifty-cal on the fantail, turbine exhaust, and CAS deck. Preacher put a fine dent in the deckhouse and we burned up a bunch more CAS deck paint. There's enough work to keep a deck-ape happy for a long time. I'll stop by with a better report and a cold San Magoo in a bit" Boats wasn't gonna be pleased when he could see the damage himself. Just for starters, there wasn't much of the fo'c'sle that didn't have a 76mm horseshoe on it!

"Thanks Kensey. I'll be waiting."

Chapter 35
Aftermath

I was weary. I was feeling my age. My leg throbbed, I'd torn several of José's stitches loose, and I had a million little aches, pains, scratches, and bruises. I was especially worried about Boats and Greasey. They would have to wait until we arrived at Diego Garcia before seeing a real doctor or surgeon. José's doctoring kept us moving but he was slowing down from a nasty shrapnel wound and other cuts, contusions, and abrasions. Fritz and Masters were taped up for fractured or broken ribs and the Gonzales Brothers were pretty beat up but didn't show it. Preacher was limping and rubbing his ribs so I imagined he was hurt more than he let on. Sparks was in pretty good shape but like me was scraped, bruised, and bleeding from two or three small shrapnel wounds. A San Magoo and a toast to making it this far was in order!

I stopped at the bridge and asked Masters if he wanted to take a break and down an icy San Magoo with Boats and me. There was little to do for the next hour or so until we started settling into the skids. *Scrap Dealer's* crew had things well in hand. He declined and said he would oversee the operation from the CAS deck close to the remaining Stingers! I stopped in CIC and told Sparks to secure the watch and join Boats and me in officer country. Sparks said everyone except Masters was already on the mess deck.

Sparks and I entered the mess decks. I poked my head into the galley where José was making sandwiches and said, "Break out the San Magoo but keep a couple on ice for Masters." José popped the top on eight, handed them to me, opened eight more, and then followed me out onto the mess deck. José and I distributed the bottles. Before I could raise mine and propose a toast. Boats raised his and said, "To the Skipper!" I stood there silent and a bit emotional while everyone took a deep pull on the icy brew.

I raised my bottle and said, "To the best damn crew of over the hill motherfuckers ever assembled!" One at a time empties were slammed down on tables until I slammed the last one down. I picked up another bottle of foamy, cold San Magoo, raised it and said, "To Captain Shaw, *Scrap Dealer,* and her crew!" Bottles slammed down on tables. When the last one banged down I said, "Gentlemen, well done."

"We're well done all right." Greasey whined. "My goddamn arm and ass hurts! Boats can only walk about one-hundred feet a day, Masters wears that duct tape eye patch like Captain Jack Sparrow and is still picking glass out of . . . everywhere, and Preacher, Jorge, Manuel, Fritz and you are all limping, bruised, and bleeding all over the place. On top of that, it looks like payday will be a little light! Well done is right . . ."

"Alles ist gut. We be goin' home in einen piece!" Fritz said as he popped to attention and clicked his heels together.

"Greasey, quit your bitchin'. You will be in a stateroom soon enough. I'm sure *Scrap Dealer* has some medication for pain aboard. We will know about pay day soon enough and besides the retainer was more than you've made in years." I said.

"Jesus H. Christ! I didn't crawl out of my comfortable rack to listen to everyone bitch. Lighten up Greasey. I'm sorry I couldn't get to my GQ station." Boats scowled.

Preacher tapped half a Stinger launcher on the table for attention. "It be a miracle anyone of us survived. Let us be thankful for that."

"Amen" I said. "Some of us are required on deck and we still need to keep any eye out for hostiles in the area. Let's get back to work until we are on the skids and well away from here." With that said, I turned and went topside. The sooner we were underway, the better I liked it!

Preacher followed me out to the main deck under the guise of handling lines. *Scrap Dealer's* crew was doing all the work under the watchful eye of Masters. "Preacher, you OK?" I asked.

"No. I'm angry that God and I didn't get a chance to use Otto against that airplane." He handed me his prized purple rag. "Thanks for letting me borrow this. We do make a good team. You did good Kensey. I sure am thankful to the Good Lord and Gman for puttin' all those Stingers and LAWS on board. Saved our hides from those airplanes! I thought for sure I was gonna shake hands with St. Peter today . . . Specially after two misses!" He handed me several flattened, fragmented, and burned 50 cal rounds. "Picked these up off the CAS deck. Thought you might like a souvenir." I was getting quite a collection of mementos and was glad my name wasn't on any of them . . .

"We do, do good work . . . Check with Masters and see if he needs help. I have to man CIC and check for radio traffic." With that said I returned to CIC.

For the next two hours, Sparks and I made CIC shipshape. We checked every nook and cranny. We put all publications and papers back in order. We had sound powered communications with *Scrap Dealer's* bridge and I spent a good ten minutes briefing Captain Shaw on the highlights of our adventure. He set course for Diego Garcia and said we would be secured and up to speed within forty-five minutes. I told him we couldn't thank him enough for moving closer to the action and we all looked forward to a good night's sleep aboard *Scrap Dealer*!

1230: I made the last entry in my log book: We are ready to depart *Goat Locker*. She is already being covered with tarps. All systems are secured. Two crewmen came aboard to help Boats navigate the ladders and passageways. Captain Shaw and I are the last two aboard. He and I will make a quick tour of *Goat Locker* then depart.

Captain Shaw and I climbed down the ladder and went forward along *Goat Locker's* port side. I hadn't paid much attention to the hole in our side since it was above the water line all the time we were flying. We had a ragged hole about eight inches in diameter with jagged edges. It looked like the exit wounds on beer cans I shot with a .22 as a kid. Seawater, beer foam, and paint oozed out making one hell of a mess on *Scrap Dealer's* deck. The salvage crew was moving cutting and welding gear into place and I imagined *Goat Locker* would be sea worthy in short order.

"I apologize for the mess Captain. I'll have my crew help clean up. Boats isn't going to be happy. We lost all our San Magoo and all his paint!" I was a bit mesmerized thinking about what our port side would look like if that round had detonated . . .

"Don't worry about it Kensey. You said the party got rough. That appears to be an understatement. I'll catch up to you in the lounge. I have a few things to attend to."

I entered the lounge and was greeted with a spread of

sandwiches, coffee, sodas, and a huge sheet cake that said "Welcome Back *Goat Locker*." The crew, with the exception of Boats, was already eating, drinking, and unwinding. We weren't completely out of the woods, but we could certainly see the edge of it.

I made a plate of . . . everything, grabbed an ice cold Pepsi, and said. "Thanks guys. You all did a superb job! I'm happy as hell to be here in one piece, more or less, and I know I wouldn't be without each and every one of you. All I can really say is . . . thanks!" I got a unanimous thumbs-up and continued. "When Boats and I boarded the *High and Mighty* what happened? Greasey did you have any trouble hittin' the water with the 20?"

"You're a real comedian Kensey. As soon as *Goat Locker* went hullborne, I ran to the fantail and manned the port 20. A shit-load of small boats launched from the pier area and beach. Those coastal freighters were burning like hell! I could see them starting to list. A lot of boats were silhouetted by the flames. I fired at the closest to us. The 20 fucked em' up bad! Any of those dickheads who survived will think twice before snatching another ship!" Greasey took a gulp of Coke and continued, "The assholes still afloat tucked under the pier and started shootin' at me! Bullets were hittin' the steel we welded up and the bulkhead behind me. That reminds me, Boats got a lot of work to do to fix those marks up! Anyway, I kept firing. Goddamn bullet grazed my left arm but I stayed on the gun. I must have hit a couple more boats because the firing at me kinda slacked off. I was bleeding pretty good when Jorge showed up. He manned the starboard 20. We were still getting lots of small arms fire then the tracers started coming in. You could see them when they ricocheted or flew overhead. Looked like fireflies on steroids... I hate those fuckers! I felt an awful burning pain! I thought maybe Jorge lit off a Stinger and singed my ass! A few minutes later Manuel showed up and relived me. By the way, Kensey, we owe them a '*big*' bonus. They really tore up those small boats. They shot directly at the pirates, not just the boats they were in. I never saw a human explode into pieces like that before. Don't want to see it again, and don't ever want to step in front of a 20mm round!"

Sparks piped up, "I realized you and Boats didn't have any
226

'close' support and nothing was happening in CIC. I grabbed an M16 and as many clips as I could carry and went to the athwart ships passageway. Shit was flying around in there until Fritz got the starboard M60 into action so I went prone. I knew no one was guarding the brow. I laid there in case a raghead tried to sneak on board *Goat Locker*. Shit, only two got by José and Masters. They were belly crawling down *High and Mighty's* port side. All I could see was the top of their heads. That was enough! After a lifetime, you came from aft crossed the brow and about stepped on me. I saw Boats get hit and thought he was a goner until he started yelling about mother fuckin' motherfuckers! Sure was glad I was in position to help carry him aboard."

"Glad you were there too, Sparks! I couldn't carry him by myself and Fritz was still engaged on the starboard side." I said.

"Ja, I was still busy on the other side and couldn't help . . . I manned the M60 on the starboard side. Small boats were coming toward us and firing AK-47s. The M60 made mincemeat of them! It was the most fun I've had in years! I saw a fuckin' raghead hiding behind the bow of a small boat and shootin' at us. I put a few rounds where I thought his head was. I saw his legs shoot up as he went down for the count. The M60 shoots right through boats. Surprised him I expect, but that doesn't matter now; he's dead! Masters shouted down the sound powered phones that some motherfuckers were shootin' out the bridge windows. José couldn't get on him and Otto was useless. I grabbed a LAWS and ran forward. Tracers were bouncin' round everywhere! I saw a halftrack with a big machine gun tearing up *Goat Locker*. I pointed the LAWS; I put the red laser dot right on the middle of it and pulled the trigger. It was beautiful! Streak of light, puff of smoke, big explosion and the halftrack went up in a ball of flame. Three-hundred-sixty new virgins needed. I yelled up to the bridge to let Masters know he could get back to covering you and Boats. I go back to the M60 and start firing at muzzle flashes along the waterfront. The 20 was doing a good job! It looked like those rounds knocked a bulkhead down and shot some assholes behind it. Impressive!" That was the most Fritz ever said at one time . . . probably in his whole life.

José took up where Fritz left off, "I unstrapped before we

crashed and held on for dear life. I hauled ass aft, went prone on the CAS deck with the M60, and started hosing down the schooner. That big machine gun sure chews up wood and fiberglass I tell ya! Some boats were raising hell with small arms until Greasey hammered them with the 20. I swept the *High and Mighty* from fore to aft! I didn't think anyone could survive. I saw movement amidships and started walking rounds into it. I about shit when you, Kensey, started firing up in the air! After that, I concentrated on a few small boats that got under the pier and a group of assholes shootin' at us from the end of it. Masters took out a few until the tracers started whizzin' by me. Some looked like sparklers after they bounced off the mast then the deck! It sucks when you can see the near misses! Both of us had to keep our heads down! A little while after the halftrack exploded, I saw some movement on *High and Mighty's* starboard side. They must have thrown a grenade into the salon. I could hear Masters firing the M-16 so I just hosed everything from the bow to stern. I saw one guy back peddling all the way aft and over the stern. It looked like he was swatting at bees . . . Right after that you and Boats came back aboard and all hell broke loose topside. I had to leave my position and get back inside! I wedged myself in a passageway but left the watertight door open. Manuel, Jorge, and Fritz were still firing when Masters got us the hell out of there . . ."

I was about to thank the Gonzales Brothers when Captain Shaw entered the Lounge. "I am happy to see you all made it back in one piece, more or less. I thought *Goat Locker* was beat up but Boats looks worse, and the rest of you don't look all that good either! We helped Boats to his stateroom and he is sleeping quietly." Captain Shaw handed me a message form and continued, "This came in over SatCom a few minutes ago. It looks like a Navy doctor will be boarding us tomorrow afternoon. Do any of you know Lieutenant Commander Madison?"

I didn't and was skeptical and still a bit paranoid. The message appeared legit. The date time group looked correct but I didn't request medical assistance and I was certain Captain Shaw didn't either. The message was short and to the point:

SS Scrap Dealer
Naval Attaché Diego Garcia.

228

Subject: Medical Request
CH-47 with one passenger, LCDR Phillip Madison MD
depart DG 3may2011 0800 local.
Arrive your coordinate's 1400 local. HIFR not required.
Jim Billings en route DG

"Captain I have no idea if this is legit or not . . . I suspect it is. Jim Billings is a close ally. I expect him in Diego Garcia but not many others do. I think we should take a few precautions though. I'd like to place M60s on the fore and aft superstructures along with the remaining Stingers and arm both 20mms on *Goat Locker*. Masters, Sparks, Preacher, and I will be on deck with M16s and side arms and I can arm any of your crew you like. None of this is probably necessary but *Scrap Dealer* and your crew has been in the line of fire twice already, I apologize for that . . ., and I don't think we should drop our guard now."

"Thanks Kensey I appreciate that. Station your men as you suggested. I'll arm my crew and have them stationed here and there . . . . We will be in Diego Garcia in about three and a half days. I was going to suggest you get some rest and enjoy the ride but I see that may be tough to do. Are you going to send a reply?"

"I don't think so Captain. I think it is still important for *Goat Locker* to maintain radio silence. I assume you are still monitoring the HF back-channel . . ." I paused and waited for an answer.

"That is affirmative. If anything comes in on that frequency I'll get you immediately."

"Thanks Captain. I don't think we can do anything until that Navy Hook shows up tomorrow afternoon."

Small talk and exaggerated, I thought, accounts of near misses gave way to yawns and a desire for a hot shower and long night's sleep. Masters, Sparks, Preacher, and I were the last to leave. I asked Preacher to see to getting M60s and Stingers in place tomorrow. He yawned, nodded and left. I told Masters and Sparks I'd retrieve the data and banking information from *Goat Locker* tomorrow and asked if they wanted to accompany me. Both declined, bid their good nights, and left. I finished my Pepsi, looked around the empty lounge, and said to no one in particular, "*Well . . . that's that.*" Bed and a hot shower were on my mind. I stopped at Boat's stateroom door and knocked gently. I heard loud snoring and moved down the passageway to Greasey's door. I knocked, and then peeked in. Greasey was spread-eagle on his bunk sound asleep. I figured he and Boats would be ok. My next stop was hot shower then bed!

0630 rolled around too soon. It took ten minutes to get all the bits and pieces moving in the right direction. My leg was the biggest of the million or so aches and pains! If a person did this for a living, he would have to be in better shape . . . and thirty years younger. I stopped at the lounge for a cup of coffee. Winston and Preacher were the only ones up and about. Preacher said he was letting Jorge and Manuel sleep in and he and a few *Scrap Dealer* crew had placed the M60s, loaded the 20mms, and staged two Stingers. Winston said breakfast would be ready at 0800. I thanked him, told Preacher to take it easy, and that I was going to *Goat Locker* to retrieve some items from the Captain's cabin.

I spotted Boats on a pair of crutches examining the port side patch. He was grimacing and mumbling to himself.

"Morning Boats! What the fuck are you doing out of bed?" I asked.

"Just checking to see what kind of work needs doing. This patch looks good. It may take a month to clean the mess inside though! What I can see of the topside spaces look like shit. I have the guys rigging a sling so I can get aboard later. I hope Gman bought a new PHM guarantee if he plans on keeping her . . . You know why Otto's all scorched? We have a fire on the fo'c'sle?" Boats would have a million more questions once he got a good look at all the damage topside!

"At least one RPG round found us. You'll have to ask Masters about the rest. I was very busy in combat during the artillery attack. Breakfast is at 0800. Get off that leg I'll see you there."

"Aye Skipper. Breakfast and propping this leg up sounds good." Boats wobbled toward the lounge and I ascended the ladder to *Goat Locker*.

The ghostly silence aboard was eerie after the noise and confusion of the past day. Topside really did look like shit! This was one tough little ship indeed . . . She wasn't ready for the bone yard but would need work if she was ever going to be used again.

230

I made my way to the Captain's cabin and wrestled with the Sergeant Greenleaf. It opened on the second try and I removed the two briefcases and returned to my stateroom on *Scrap Dealer*. I had one more thing to do before seeing what the Bank of Cayman Islands could do for us.

I pocketed the pieces of shrapnel and expended machine gun rounds and the tube of Krugerrands. I sought out Rogers and found him in the Machine shop. I showed him the items and asked if he could make eight medals. I told him the Krugerrands he didn't use were his to distribute to the crew. I asked him to check the internet and model the medals after the US military's Purple Heart. I wanted it inscribed with each man's name and *Goat Locker* on one side and *'Pirates Beware'* on the other. Rogers said he could do it but it would take a while. I thanked him, checked my watch, and made my way to the lounge and breakfast.

I had a few hours to kill before the helo arrived. I used it to connect my laptop to the internet. I inserted the thumb drive, waited for the username and password prompt, and then input them. I was worried; nothing happened. I brought up the Windows control panel to make sure I was on the internet. I was. The 'blue screen of death' appeared... The screen blinked then suddenly displayed The Bank of The Caymans logo and a button pulsating in the corner. I left clicked on it and the screen displayed account information. Account numbers were listed down the left and the amounts on the right. I did a quick calculation and was pleased! The grand total was thirty two million four hundred and seventy thousand dollars and sixty-nine cents! Three menu selections were displayed at the bottom of the screen: Exit, create a new account, transfer funds. I selected create new account. A new screen opened. It took me through the process of creating an account in my name, choosing a username and password, and transferring funds into it. I created a new account and then selected transfer funds. The program asked for: account to transfer from. I entered Don Carlos's first account number and pressed enter. A few seconds later, it was completed. I repeated the process for all of the accounts. When that was finished, the program asked: Make it permanent? I selected yes. There was a delay as the blue doughnut whorled around and around... And around… I was beginning to worry again. Two lifetimes later, the screen blinked and a new one opened. It was a welcome sight! Transaction complete followed by a receipt number. A bold message blinked at the bottom of the window: "Mr. Goat Locker. Your account number is 121218975643-L. The L signifies a locked account. It may only be opened with the password you supplied. This is a secure account. Thank you for doing business with The Bank of the Caymans.

I removed the thumb drive and then reinserted it. The screen came up with the same logo. It asked for username and password. I typed in the information I used when creating the account and a screen opened displaying one account number on the left and on the right: $32,570,000.69. Shit… I was a 100 grand off on my initial guess-timate.

I made an image of the thumb drive on the laptop, removed the drive, and put it back in the briefcase. I put the briefcase in the secure file cabinet. The prize was certainly worth the risk! All we had to do now was get home to enjoy it.

I had $32,570,000.69 to divide among the eight-crew members. Masters and I had already said that after the split, we would pay the Gonzales Brothers as we saw fit. That gave each of us $4,071,250.08. That was good news I could pass on to the crew. Greasey might not even bitch…

Chapter 36
Doctor in the House

Boats must be feeling better. Three bells sounded over the ships speakers. First things first.

At 1340 I found Captain Shaw on the bridge. I asked him if he would have some of his crew do a quick walk around on the fo'c'sle and check for anything that could get into the helo's jet intake. I told him the Navy called it a FOD-Walk-Down. (Foreign Object and Debris) The fo'c'sle was the only place clear enough to transfer the doctor to *Scrap Dealer.*

The shrill tone of all-hands sounded over topside speakers followed by, "All hands man your flight quarters stations" Boats was really feeling better . . . Captain Shaw gave me a questioning look. I just shrugged my shoulders and told him you couldn't keep a good boatswain mate down. The distinct sound of an approaching dual rotor helo ended the conversation.

Masters, Sparks, and Preacher were already stationed on the fo'c'sle ready to assist or repel. I joined them and took cover behind a gypsy head. A helo swooped in, nose down doing a hundred knots or better. It banked circled the ship, flared and approached the fo'c'sle nose up and hovered. I was looking up at a gunner with both hands on a fifty-caliber machine gun. I still had my M16 slung over my shoulder but I was sure he could see José on the bridge wing with an M60 and a Stinger.

First, a pair of kaki clad legs then a man wearing a Mae West and cranial descended from the other side of the helo and glided to the deck. Preacher grabbed him, unhooked the harness, and led him to me. Next to come was a large black doctor's bag and overnight bag then the helo backed off, reeled up the transfer cable, circled the ship once more and departed.

"Bob Kensey." I yelled over the downdraft of the departing chopper. "You must be Commander Phillip Madison." I said as I stuck out my hand and shook his. "Sure am glad to see you! Follow me. We'll take care of your bags. I'll introduce you to Captain Shaw on the bridge then take you to the lounge. I'm sure Winston will be there. He's the ships steward. He'll fix you up with a place to sleep." We gathered near the bags and I introduced LCDR Madison to Masters, Preacher and Sparks, and said he would be seeing them shortly. The boatswain pipe followed by, "All hands secure from flight quarters," sounded as LCDR Madison and I entered the bridge. Phillip gave me a quizzical look and I said it was just Boats trying to make himself feel useful and perhaps the good doctor could give him something to calm him down?

Captain Shaw introduced himself and said to me, "I rather like the heads up the pipe gives us. I wouldn't mind if Boats keeps it up. Welcome to *Scrap Dealer* Commander Madison."

"Phillip. Please. Happy to be here. Once I see to *Goat Locker's* crew, I'd be happy to attend to any medical problems you or your crew may be experiencing. Were you expecting trouble?"

"You never know in these waters. If you gentlemen will excuse me, I have company business to attend to. If I don't catch up to you sooner, evening meal is at 1900 this evening."

Captain Shaw departed and I took Phillip to the lounge. Winston was there with coffee and sandwiches. Phillip said he would make house calls starting with me as soon as he had a bite to eat and freshened up a bit. Winston led him off to his stateroom.

Fifteen minutes later Dr. Madison knocked on my door. He properly dressed my wound checked my ribs; started me on a Z-pack of antibiotics and said. "Jeez those are the ugliest sutures I've ever seen! It will take plastic surgery to fix the scar unless you want me to cut the wound apart and resuture it now."

"No thanks! It hurts bad enough as is. And besides, it gives me something to brag about. Can I ask you how you know Jim Billings?" All I knew was we had a Navy looking doctor aboard who arrived in an armed Navy helicopter.

"Gman said for me to break out my *'sewing kit'* and to expect a cool if not hostile reception. I am assigned to Jim Billings' department. I'm the doctor they need for 'the special people they arrest or detain'. I am supposedly on thirty days leave. Oh, I almost forgot… Jim said the smoked Chinooks were the best he ever had."

Well, that settled that. He was legit! I stuck out my hand and said, "Welcome aboard doctor. Damn glad to make your
234

acquaintance! After you've seen to my gunner, I'll have him gather up the ordnance and stow it. I'll get the word out that Gman sent you."

"Thanks Bob who do you want me to see next?"

"Greasey, and then Boats. After you see the guys would you have them come see me?" I asked as Dr. Madison left my stateroom.

Chapter 37
Payout

I heard Greasey bellowing and cussing up a blue streak. He usually just whined. I thought I'd better see what the problem was. When I entered his stateroom Greasey was spread eagle on the bunk yelling and swearing. The doctor was sitting in a chair trying to stifle laughter. "Did the same guy sew Mr. Greasey up? He did a marvelous job. I don't dare mess with these sutures."

"Bullshit! Take those fuckers out! Every last one of 'em!" Greasey was beside himself.

"I think the lips on one cheek and heart on the other is rather nice. Hobble your rosy ass over to my stateroom when you are finished." I laughed. "I have something that will take the sting out. Sweet Cheeks!"

"Ah . . . yes Mr. Sweet Cheeks, I'll be finished here in a minute or two." The doctor wasn't trying to hide laughter now.

"Fuck you Doc . . .and you too Kensey!" followed me out the door.

Five minutes later Greasey stormed in. "Don't even fuckin' think it Kensey."

"Ok Sweet Cheeks, but I thought you'd like to know what your share of this adventure is." I chuckled.

Before I could get it out he said, "How fuckin' much. I need a lot to make it up to Marcie."

"By my figuring your share is four million seventy one thousand two hundred fifty dollars and eight cents." I said as a matter of fact as I could.

Greasey stared at me. He worked his mouth like a guppy in a fish bowl. Finally he said, "Four million? You Sure?"

"Yep. All yours. Here's what we're going to do. We'll create an account that you can access. After you get home or wherever, access the account and transfer funds to any other account. Try and keep your transfers under ten thousand each so the government doesn't stick their nose into it. Ready?" I said talking as an instructor. Greasey just nodded.

It took a while to set up his account. He was still in shock. I had him assign a password and write it on paper. I assigned username . . . SweetCheeks.

"Done Sweet Cheeks. Go grab some rest." I didn't know if Greasey . . . Sweet Cheeks was in shock, dazed, or painkillers were taking effect. He left without so much as a whimper.

Next on my list was Fritz. Fritz did not have a clue on how to use a computer so I set up a debit transfer card for him. Again, I kept the single transfer a max of ten thousand. The card would be mailed to him at his address in Norfolk.

José was next and it took about twenty minutes to complete the setup. All he could talk about was the restaurant he was going to open in Chula Vista.

Sparks sent his pay to offshore accounts. I wasn't familiar with those procedures. I asked him if he would show me later. He agreed. That would give me something to do during the long transit back to Isla de Cedros.

Preacher was humble. "I was praying for this day since I first talked to you on the phone. What you got for The Lord and me?" he asked.

When I said a little over four million, he dropped into my chair a bit dazed. We set up his account. He was talking to himself with tears in his eyes when he left. "Yes sir. I can build several churches now!"

"Amen. You deserve it!" I said sincerely.

The Doc probably knocked Boats out and I'd seen Masters talking to Captain Shaw. I knocked on Boats' door and entered.

Masters was there with Boats shootin' the shit.

This was convenient "Glad you two are together. Save me a trip. It's payday. Boats and Bill, you each get four million seventy one thousand two hundred and fifty dollars and eight cents. I have to set up new offshore accounts for you two and transfer the money."

Masters stood up and removed an old beat-up black wheel book from his rear pants pocket. He thumbed through the pages and finally settled on one.

He handed the book to me and said, "Put the money into these two accounts. The first one is mine and the other one belongs to Boats'."

"You got it." I replied and started setting up the accounts. It took

238

about an hour to get it done to Masters' specifications. It was approaching 1900 and before I left, I reminded Boats and Masters that Captain Shaw had a special dinner for us tonight.

I still needed to talk to the Gonzales Brothers and pay them. I was thinking fifty thousand from each of us, the liberated green backs, funny money, and tube of ½ eagles would be about right. I'd already decided to give the tube of Maple Leafs to Captain Shaw. I thought I'd discuss it with Masters and see what he had to say about the subject.

Over the course of the afternoon, everyone except Boats, Masters, and the Gonzales Brothers stopped by sporting new bandages and sutures. Most finally had more than Tylenol to kill pain and it showed.

I freshened up, washed up, and stepped into the lounge a second or two before 1900. Dr. Madison, just Doc to us now, and the entire crew were there comparing wounds and damage. Greasey . . . Sweet Cheeks was unusually quiet and kind of off by himself.

Boats was looking and moving better and greeted me with, "Yo. Skipper!"

"Greasey glared at me and mumbled, "Don't say a fuckin' word Kensey!"

That was all it took. "Give us a vertical smile . . ." I answered back. I didn't expect it but he dropped his drawers and gave us the moon.

"Mein gott!" shot from Fritz.

Preacher clasped his hands together and exclaimed, "Sweet Jesus!"

"No. Sweet Cheeks!" I laughed. The entire crew turned that into a cheer.

Sweet Cheeks pulled his skivvies on buttoned up his pants turned with a smile on his face, shook his head and said, "Never trust a fuckin' taco-bender!" Then said, "Guess I'm stuck with it. Let's eat. Sweet Cheeks is starved!"

The next day at breakfast, my crew was acting rather like big shots. Well, they deserved it, as of now they were all multimillionaires. I just chuckled to myself. Captain Shaw told us at breakfast that we would be at Diego Garcia right after the noon meal. I wondered if Gman was there yet…

239

Chapter 38
Meeting with Gman

Three and a half days after our last encounter with hostile forces, we anchored in Diego Garcia's harbor. Captain Shaw wanted to wait until daylight before anchoring but the Brits insisted we anchor when we arrived at 0200. Captain Shaw requested fuel support and transportation for LCDR Madison. The harbormaster complied but requested no one else come ashore. The attack on a Somalia village was all over the internet and international news. It is likely the British weren't happy with a funny looking US flagged ship sitting in their harbor. The sooner *Scrap Dealer* was gone the more deniability they had. They certainly could put two and two together and probably wanted us gone before sunrise when satellites could see us.

The last message we'd received stated Gman was en route. That was two and a half days ago. I half expected him to be on the pilot boat; he wasn't. There wasn't a thing for me to do on *Scrap Dealer's* bridge. I told Captain Shaw I'd be in the lounge if any radio traffic came in for *Goat Locker*. Most of the crew was up. They were hoping to catch a hop back to the states. The perpetual Acey-Ducey game was in progress.

"What's up?" Boats asked the inevitable question. No self-respecting Chief Boatswains Mate could sleep during sea-detail even if it was someone else's ship.

"Liberty call is cancelled. The Brits don't want us invading their island. There's no word from Billings. We may have to leave before he gets here." That stirred everyone up. "We may as well hit the rack. There isn't much we can do. I'm going to check for radio traffic on *Goat Locker* then turn in myself"

Boats hobbled over to me on one crutch, "Skipper I have a bottle of *Laphroaig* single malt scotch stashed in Officer Country. Could you get that for me and drop it off in my stateroom? I'd like to surprise Gman if he ever shows up. If he doesn't we'll have a fine celebration when we return to the states!"

I went straight to comms, checked for HF traffic, picked up the *Laphroaig,* and then dropped it off with Boats. I was in my rack by 0250. Winston woke me at 0337. He said a Mr. Billings would be aboard in ten minutes and Captain Shaw would meet me at the accommodation ladder. A Navy Captain's gig hove to alongside. One passenger climbed the accommodation ladder. The Coxswain stayed with the gig. Gman didn't waste any time with idle chit-chat.

"Captain Shaw, the harbor pilot is aboard the gig. It would be advantageous if you could escort him to the bridge and prepare to depart within forty-five minutes. I can't tell you how much we value your help and this ship! We will keep an eye on you until you're near Guam. We will run interference if necessary. Right now, I need to talk to Kensey. I don't mean to be abrupt but time is of the essence." Captain Shaw thanked Gman, said he understood, and left us to prepare to weigh anchor.

"Damn! It's good to see you Kensey! *Goat Locker* looks beat up; any casualties? Doc fix you guys up?" Gman asked rapid-fire questions but continued before I could answer, "The wire services are full of what's being called 'The Raid'. They still don't have the whole picture but everyone is turning up the heat looking for a phantom, flying ship. The President had to bow and scrape some more to get you in here. You need to be gone ASAP!"

"How did they find out about the raid so fast? Who do they think did it? Do they still think *High and Mighty* was captured by Pirates?" We were both asking more questions than the other could answer. "Hold up Bill. Let's go to my stateroom. I have some information you want."

"Yeah. I can't believe you actually accomplished the mission . . . 'The Raid' probably would have been chalked up to a turf war except a wire service reporter doing a story on piracy chose the village you destroyed for his expose." This was interesting but we were at my stateroom and had other business to discuss.

Gman continued while I dialed the safe combination and removed the briefcase. "The locals really gave him an earful. Some said a low flying plane came out of the night and blew everything up. Others said a flying ship did it. The locals and evidently the wires aren't really sure what sunk three ships, destroyed the pier, reduced a yacht to splinters, set the jungle on fire, tore up the village, and shot up some troops that weren't

242

supposed to be there. Oh, and the Russians reported two spotter planes and three helos missing . . . You know anything about that?"

"We were busy!" I opened the briefcase and showed Gman the papers, CDs and thumb drives. "This is what it's all about."

Gman picked each item up and examined it then returned it to the case, closed the lid and simply said, "Seems like a whole lot of trouble for nothing much . . . Once the geeks get a hold of this we'll find out if it was worth the trouble."

"We know Al Qaida was there, but the Russians . . . How were they involved?" I understood why the Brits wanted us underway!

"Al Qaida, at least in that village, is no more. Reports say over one hundred died in the attack. The Russians, according to their embassy, were 'training' villager's counter-terrorism tactics. They were really sweating Don Carlos for information. The radio chatter about that stopped right after the attack. We assume he is dead and didn't talk. During the skirmish one of their halftracks and a hand full of men were killed. They are not happy!"

"Oops! It sounds like they were having gunnery practice at the wrong time . . . Any reports on the pirates or Don Carlos?" I asked.

"Like I said, Don Carlos is no more. DEA chatter says his third or fourth in command is attempting to put Humpty Dumpty back together again . . . He isn't having all that much luck! The pirates suffered about two hundred causalities. Their base of operation, mother ships, fuel and ordnance supplies, and most of their small boats were destroyed. The pirates moved completely out and the villager's are returning. I'll get with you in Seattle and fill you in on what transpires during your transit home. Right now, I'd like to know how everyone is. Doc said most of you guys were beat up. I won't have time to see everyone but I do want to see Boats and Masters. Anyone take a picture of Sweet Cheeks, cheeks? Doc says Mr. Sanchez is an artist!"

"No, no photos but next to Boats he probably took the most hits. Boats took a round through his left leg. Doc says he'll be ok but may walk with a slight limp from now on. We got bounced around pretty good and have a few broken fingers and ribs. Masters is sporting an eye patch, cracked ribs, and his left side looks like hamburger. His eyeball was scratched but will heal with no loss of vision. Preacher, Sparks, and the Gonzales Brothers all have nicks and cuts from shrapnel and small arms fire, and Jorge has some nasty burns on his backside. You already know about Sweet Cheeks so all in all we came out real well. I didn't lose anyone. That is truly a miracle." There was a rap on my door.

Boats, leaning on a crutch, opened it. Looked right at Gman and said, "Think fast motherfucker!" and lobbed a bloody pink apron at him!" If this hadn't of saved my ass from bleeding to death I'd make you eat it . . ."

The apron unrolled and a bottle of **Laphroaig** fell into Gman's lap. He started laughing and said, "God damn Boats you remembered . . . Thanks! And I can replace that apron if you'd like. Maybe one with a goat on it would be better . . ."

"No thanks but if you can get me some paint I would appreciate it."

"I can do that. While you are both here, there is still a bit of mystery surrounding Richard Kopf. What can you tell me about him?"

Boats got a devilish grin on his face. "He tried to come over on the high-line and I dumped him in the water. Last time I saw that needledick the barge crew was fishin' his ass out of the drink. Who was he?"

Gman hesitated and finally said, "Don't really know for sure. I think he was 'unofficially' working for CIA. I'm still trying to find him. Scuttlebutt around DEA is that a CIA field agent taking orders from a certain Senator is now head of the security detail on the Alaska pipeline."

Masters stepped into my stateroom; hand extended, and added, "Serves the dickhead right. Kensey you were too easy on him. I'd a shot the bastard!"

Gman pumped Masters' right hand in greeting. "You don't look all that bad . . . Glad all of you are here we don't have much time." We could feel **Scrap Dealer's** screw turning as she swung around the hook and put her bow out to sea before weighing anchor and getting underway. "The administration has a plan but right now they are in a pissing contest with CIA, DEA, and the Navy. I, we, want to refit **Goat Locker** at The Fortress and keep her available

244

for future operations. The administration wants her to disappear . . ." Gman reached into his inside jacket pocket and withdrew an envelope adorned with the seal of the President of the United States secured with a wax seal. "The Vice President handed this to me personally before I departed. It is one-hundred-percent legit. . ." Gman timidly handed me the document. "You are not to open this document until you receive the code word "NUTS" transmitted by two separate sources on the frequency you see on the envelope. This is an order directly from the President . . . ."

I looked at the envelope with dread and curiosity. Boats and Masters were silent. I placed the envelope in the safe shut the door and spun the dial." Nuts . . . I don't like this one bit. What is the pissing contest about Jim?"

"A lot of message traffic is flowing in and out of the State Department between Russia, Iran, Yemen, Columbia, Britain, Somalia, and the US. The Secretary of State is under a lot of pressure. CIA, and DEA are on pins-and-needles for keeping them out of the loop . . . mostly. The Navy is re-evaluating PHMs. Some with a lot of horsepower think scrapping them may have been a mistake. This should all blow over by the time you get back. That's why we're not flying you out of here. That brings me to another point. Bill would you be willing to fly everybody back to the States from Isla de Cedros? DEA has an airfield and hanger just outside Corpus Christie, Texas. We use it to fly informants and certain others in and out."

Masters nodded yes. "If you can file the flight plan I can arrange the flight. That will help a lot! I left without my passport and don't particularly want to sneak back across the border . . ." We could hear the clinking of the anchor chain being raised by the wildcat. This meeting was about over…

Gman handcuffed the briefcase to his wrist slipped the bottle of *Laphroaig* into his coat pocket started to shake hands but took a step back and saluted instead. "Kensey, you old farts did good! This isn't good bye . . . Aufwiedersehen!"

Chapter 39
Duty

The crew was restless two days out from Diego Garcia. Boats finally had a sling rigged and hobbled aboard *Goat Locker* for a look-see. He returned for lunch in a dark, depressed mood. "It's gonna take months to make my ship presentable. The Boatswain Locker is a disgrace! I should be thankful that round didn't go through one of Sweet Cheeks' spaces or worse yet one of Preachers . . . But, fuck! It pisses me off . . . All that paint and San Magoo . . . gone."

I was in the final stages of skunking Preacher at Acey-Ducey and wasn't paying all that much attention. Captain Shaw walked in and said, "Kensey I have two messages for you. They make little or no sense." He handed me two message forms with identical date-time groups but different senders. One was from POTUS.

NUTS

NUTS

I dropped both messages on the table and mumbled, "Shit . . ."

Preacher turned them around read one then the other."POTUS! What kind of congratulations is . . . NUTS?"

"It means I have a set of sealed orders in my safe from the President. Captain Shaw will you accompany me, and Bill you too?"

The safe opened on the first try. I couldn't even put this off a few seconds more. I retrieved the envelope, showed Captain Shaw and Masters both sides, flicked open my **Ka-bar** and opened it. My heart stopped, I couldn't speak. I handed the orders to Masters without a word. He was speechless. He passed them to Captain Shaw.

He just stared and then stammered."Immediately scuttle *PHM Goat Locker* . . . Is this a joke?"

"I'm afraid not Captain." Masters mumbled with moisture gathering in the corners of his eyes.

A drop of water streaked my cheek. "I'm not sure I can do this." I stammered. "This is bullshit . . . How can I tell the crew?"

"You have to. I sure as hell can't! I think this is one order we must obey . . ." Masters finally found his voice.

Captain Shaw said, "Gentlemen I'll be on the bridge. I know some ports in Borneo or Indonesia we can make it to if that's what you decide. And Skipper you said it . . . This is bullshit!" He did an abrupt about face and departed in haste.

"Bill . . ." I could barely speak. "Bill I don't want to do this." I couldn't concentrate.

"Skipper it's your call. The crew will support your decision . . . whatever it is" Masters was right.

"Inform Captain Shaw to make all preparations to float *Goat Locker*. If we don't do this we will end up just like those we just worked so hard to destroy . . . pirates." I slowly walked to the lounge. I dreaded what I had to do.

"Gentlemen . . ." My voice wavered and that snapped everyone's eyes on me." We received orders from the President of the United States . . ." I extended my hand with the orders and passed it to Boats. He didn't say a word. He blanched, dropped the orders on the Acey-Ducey board and sagged into his chair.

Bishop spun the orders around read them and forcefully pushed back from the table. "Bullshit! No fuckin' way! Scuttle *Goat Locker*! Who dreamed this up?"

Jorge and Manuel snatched the orders up, scanned them, and then dropped them back on the table. Fritz, Sparks, Preacher, and José joined the huddle, scanned the orders, and just stood there in utter shock.

Preacher broke the impasse. "Good Lord! Why?" The dam broke; everyone shouted, swore, and voiced disbelief all at once.

I picked up Boats' crutch, banged it down on the table for attention."Gentlemen . . . Our raid was too successful. We gained worldwide notoriety. Everyone wants us as a trophy. Remember the Pueblo?" I turned to wipe the unmanly tears away. I turned back, squared my shoulders, and continued." We have about an hour and a half to prepare *Goat Locker* for her final mission. Preacher I need you to set the scuttling charges, but anyone else not wanting to participate . . . I understand. I need help transferring weapons to *Scrap Dealer*." That was all I could say. I turned and left the lounge on my way to *Goat Locker*.

248

I climbed the ladder to *Goat Locker's* main deck for the last time. *Scrap Dealer's* crew already had most of the tarps removed and Captain Shaw and Masters were on the quarterdeck. The rest of the crew joined us shortly. It was a solemn gathering.

I needed to take charge of myself and this unpleasant evolution. "Captain Shaw we need to transfer weapons from our armory to yours. My gunners will be busy would your crew be willing to do that?" Captain Shaw nodded said aye-aye and descended the ladder to *Scrap Dealer*. I motioned for Masters to join me a little away from the others. "Secure the deck log. Put it with the CDs from *High and Mighty* and make sure *Goat Locker's* bell and chronometer are removed."

The next hour and a half was a flurry of activity. Each section went about preparing *Goat Locker* in silence and professional efficiency. Preacher was the last to leave. He bowed his head, said a prayer, descended the ladder, and then waded away. I was torn between staying aboard or departing. If she was dying I would remain, but *Goat Locker* was on her last mission. I descended the ladder, saluted smartly, and joined the crew on the staging platform. *Goat Locker* floated above the skids. *Scrap Dealer's* crew moved her away with a pusher-boat. When she was fifty yards off, the pusher crew returned. *Scrap Dealer* made a turn and slowly opened the distance. Ten agonizing minutes passed, then twenty . . . *Goat Locker* rocked in the waves three hundred yards away. She looked sad, forlorn.

Preacher handed me a detonator switch and said, "The honors are yours Skipper."

"This is no honor . . ." I replied. "It is a sad call to duty. Preacher, please say a few words."

"Lord . . . please tap Davy Jones on the shoulder and remind him *Goat Locker* enters his domain with grace and honor . . . Amen."

The shrill wailing of the Boatswain pipe sounded taps. With the dying note, I flipped the safety up and pressed the detonator switch. *Goat Locker* shuddered, shook, and started settling at the bow. She shuddered and achieved an even keel. She settled gracefully into the depths. When her mast slipped beneath the waves Boats piped all hands. We saluted as one. I dropped my salute, said farewell, pitched the detonator switch as far out to sea as I could and retired to my stateroom.

Chapter 40
Epilogue

Scrap Dealer set course for home. The State department requested we stop several places and take on fuel so the world could see the harmlessness of this unusual ship. We stopped in Singapore and again in Guam. I'm not sure anyone wanted to go ashore even if we could. I
didn't. . .

A few half-hearted Acey-Ducey games were attempted but mostly we stayed in our staterooms and kept to ourselves. Three days east of Hawaii was the first time we all gathered in the lounge. I promised Jorge and Manuel a bit of a payday and it was time. Each of us pledged fifty thousand dollars from our pay. In addition, I presented them with all the funny money, the greenbacks and tube of fifty, half-eagle, gold coins. The two Brothers spent several days thanking us and planning on what to do with the money. We suggested that they buy shares in *'Playboy'*.

I presented the tube of Maple Leafs to Captain Shaw and said I could not thank him enough for his support and hospitality. Sparks surprised us all and presented each of us with a ships clock mounted on a walnut base with the inscription *Goat Locker*. **One Hell of a Ship**. Masters presented Captain Shaw with *Goat Locker's* chronometer inscribed: **PHM Goat Locker Entrusted to Davy Jones**. Captain Shaw was embarrassed but accepted the chronometer with moist eyes.

I was presented with the ships bell. I couldn't find any words and just said, "Thanks. She was one hell of a ship . . ."

Things got back to normal a few days later. Masters and I stood bridge watches and all of us helped aboard *Scrap Dealer*. We were part of her crew.

Two days from Isla de Cedros Captain Shaw invited everyone to a coming-home party. Dinner was served by Winston with a fine wine and two bottles of San Magoo for me. I was astounded. Masters said he never got a chance to drink the two left in the icebox following 'The Raid' and saved them for me. I was pleased. They were good!

When the last crumbs of José's key-lime pie were whisked away, Captain Shaw stood and said, "Fill your glasses gentlemen." We did. "A toast: To the best crew of over-the-hill sailors I've had the pleasure to serve with." We drank to that. "Skipper Kensey tasked Rogers some time back with a job. He seems to have forgotten. It is my distinct honor to present these medallions to each of you."

Winston produced nine walnut boxes each containing a piece of shrapnel or flattened bullet surrounded by pure gold. Each was inscribed with a crewmember's name, nickname, and *Goat Locker* on one side and *Pirates Beware* on the other. *In God We Trust* was engraved around the outside edge and mine was adorned with **'Skipper'**. That was the second time Boats wished he'd kept his apron to dry the tears.

Scuttling *Goat Locker* put me in a purple funk. To keep from slipping into depression, I downloaded an electronic copy of *'The New York Times'*. I was surprised to read several articles in the paper about the Department of Justice crackdown on corrupt officials. Several border guards, four DEA agents, an FBI agent, and worst of all, two Senate Aides, and two White House advisors arrested. All charged with receiving bribes and selling information to drug cartels. Two state and one federal Senator suddenly gave up their seats and left the country for parts unknown. According to the paper, hundreds of low-level local and state officials have been or are going to be arrested for corruption. This was the biggest operation since 'ABSCAM'. Over the next several days, more and more corrupt individuals were arrested and charged. The smell went through the entire government. Gman really did his job. At least it took some of the sadness out of losing *Goat Locker*…

Several hours out of Isla de Cedros Captain Shaw knocked on my stateroom door and entered.

"We've kept monitoring your back-channel HF frequency. This just came in."

"What now?" Flashed through my mind. I wasn't sure I wanted to read any more messages.

Attention: Bob Kensey.

Goat Herder requests a meeting.
Safe Haven.
Will contact you before the Humpies run.
"That's curious. Guess we aren't throwaway items like our ship. Now what...?" I thought. I couldn't hide my bitterness and just said, "Thanks Captain."
The journey from the IO ended and we were ferried from ***Scrap Dealer*** into the harbor of The Fortress. Preacher stood on the dock, held up his hand, and recited the poem by A.E. Housman:
"Home is the sailor, home from sea:
Her far-borne canvas furled
The ship pours shining on the quay
The plunder of the world.
Home is the hunter from the hill:
Fast in the boundless snare
All flesh lies taken at his will
And every fowl of air.
'Tis evening on the moorland free,
The starlit wave is still:
Home is the sailor from the sea,
The hunter from the hill."

Chapter 41
Postscript

It was a joy to finally get home to Seattle. Frank took care of my apartment and filled the refrigerator with San Magoo and food. While sipping my beer I took out the laptop and looked up 'The Safe Haven'. I found out who owned the building and who held the mortgage. Armed with that information I took action. I bought the building, cleared the mortgage and gave the whole kit'n'kaboodle to Frank. Frank was the proudest and hardest working man in Seattle. This gift was heartfelt. It also insured 'The Haven' would stay in business and I would always have a ready supply of San Magoo and decent music. I commissioned a small addition to the building: the 'Radio Room'. This will be a small private lounge. Its centerpiece will be a Hallicrafters, SR-400A, Cyclone III transceiver I picked up from an old friend at Electronic Dimensions in Tacoma.

Preacher emailed nearly every week keeping me up on his project. His church rebuilding was in full swing. He was naming a chapel in his first new church 'The Robert Kensey Chapel.' I felt damn proud and thanked him. I promised Preacher I would visit my chapel and him in the near future. I also heard from Fritz. He called and informed me the 'Kensey and Schmidt Engine Machine Shop' was up and running. How do you say thanks to something like that?

Sweet Cheeks sent me a postcard from Spain. It was a goat wearing a pink blanket standing on a hill looking out to sea. The blanket had a hand drawn fouled anchor, and the goat's south-end was adorned with a pair of lips and a heart. Bishop included a note that said he and Marcie patched everything up and were on a world tour. The usual 'wish you were here' was written in a girlish hand as a postscript.

Sparks sent me an email and said he was traveling in Thailand and the Philippines. I wondered if he was looking for a wife.

Boats and Masters bought into the charter business as planned. Bill called the other day and asked if I could set aside a week sometime next spring. They commissioned a new flagship modeled after *Pure Joy* and expected to take delivery in April of next year. He and Boats wanted me to christen the *Bob Kensey* and take part in her maiden voyage.

Last weekend I received a FedEx package from José. It contained the architectural drawings for his new venture. It would be a destination restaurant located in Descanso nestled in the mountains above San Diego, California. He modeled it after the famous 'Goats on the Roof' restaurant near Nanaimo, British Columbia. The lounge is appropriately named *'The Goat Locker'*. The entire roof is a goat habitat. José's drawings show eight goats. Two stand out. One, named Boats, wears a blindingly pink blanket adorned with crossed anchors and the other wears a navy blue blanket trimmed in gold with USN on one side and Skipper on the other. The herd is one goat short. I will fix that. . .

It was late Saturday afternoon and I spent the morning fishing Deception Pass with an old retired Army buddy, Black Cloud. I put one King in the boat and he wrestled a sea lion for another. The sea lion won. Nine pounds of fillet were in the smoker. I stopped at 'The Haven' and was sipping a San Magoo while explaining to Frank why Black Cloud would carry his AR 30 lapua rifle on all future fishing trips when my cell phone rang. I checked the screen. The call was from Gman…

I could hear Jim on the other end take a breath, "Consider this 'contact'! See you soon."

"The game is afoot…"

About the Authors

Steven G Shandrow:

Born in Ilwaco, Washington, raised in Tacoma, Washington
Graduated Franklin Pierce High School
Joined the US Navy and spent twenty years wandering the world.
Retired from the Navy as a Chief Fire Control Technician.
Retired from civilian employment.
Married forty-two years, two sons, and five grandchildren.
Now resides in Buena Park, California
Playin' golf!

Gregory E. Riplinger
Born and raised in Lakewood, Washington
Graduated Lakes High School
Joined the US Navy and spent 22 years wandering the Western Pacific.
Retired from the Navy as a Senior Chief Fire Control Technician.
Retired from civilian employment.
Married forty-two years, two daughters, and two granddaughters.
Now resides in Tacoma, Washington.
Gone fishin'!